GALAXY'S EDGE

EDITED BY MIKE RESNICK

ISSUE 34: September 2018

Mike Resnick, Editor
Taylor Morris, Copyeditor
Shahid Mahmud, Publisher

Published by Arc Manor/Phoenix Pick
P.O. Box 10339
Rockville, MD 20849-0339

Galaxy's Edge is published in January, March, May, July, September, and November.

Please check our website for submission guidelines.

ISBN: 978-1-61242-423-1

SUBSCRIPTION INFORMATION:
Paper and digital subscriptions are available (including via Amazon.com) . Please visit our home page: www.GalaxysEdge.com

ADVERTISING:
Advertising is available in all editions of the magazine. Please contact advert@GalaxysEdge.com.

FOREIGN LANGUAGE RIGHTS:
Please refer all inquiries pertaining to foreign language rights to Shahid Mahmud, Arc Manor, P.O. Box 10339, Rockville, MD 20849-0339. Tel: 1-240-645-2214. Fax 1-310-388-8440. Email admin@ArcManor.com.

CONTENTS

TROPE-ING THE LIGHT
FANTASTIC
THE SCIENCE BEHIND THE FICTION

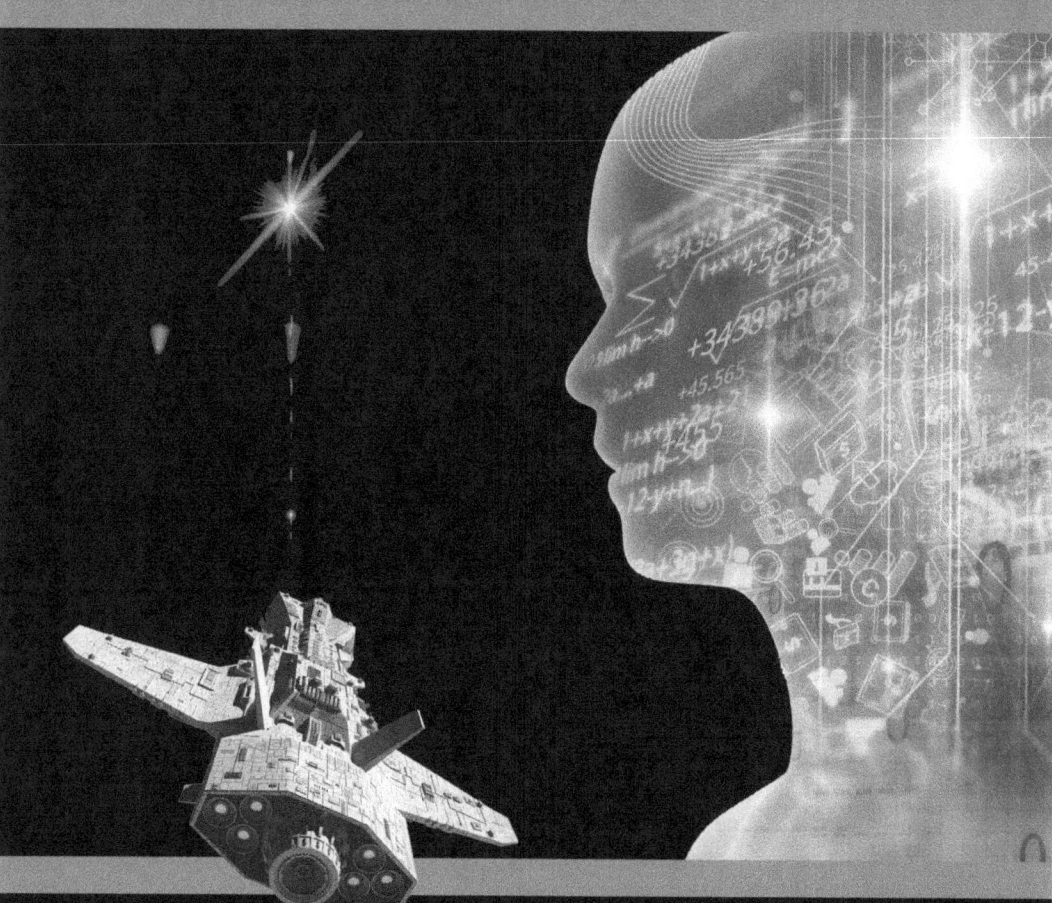

EDWARD M. LERNER

THE EDITOR'S WORD

by Mike Resnick

Greetings, and welcome to the thirty-fourth issue of *Galaxy's Edge*. We think we've got a pretty nice line-up for you, with new and newer writers such as Brenda Kalt, Grayson Bray Morris, Shawn Proctor, Alex Shvartsman, George Nikolopoulos, A. Merc Rustad, Doug Dandridge, Sharon Diane King, and Larry Hodges. They're joined by established stars Robert Silverberg, Jane Yolen, Jack McDevitt, and Kristine Kathryn Rusch.

Also aboard are our regular features: Recommended Books by Jody Lynn Nye and Bill Fawcett, science by Gregory Benford, literary matters by Robert J, Sawyer, and the Joy Ward Interview featuring superstar Larry Niven. Finally, we're beginning a new serialization this issue: Hugo winner Charles Sheffield's *Tomorrow and Tomorrow*.

We're very pleased with this issue. We hope you are, too.

✿

I lost a dear friend at the end of May. I'd known Gardner Dozois for close to half a century. I'd sold to him, brought from him, co-edited with him, gone to Europe with him, partied with him, and remain in awe of his editorial talent. In a period of twenty years as the editor of *Asimov's*, he won fourteen Hugos as Best Editor, a record that has never been matched or even approached and almost certainly never will be.

I tell a story about his tenure at *Asimov's*. I sent him a lot of stories, and I sold him a lot of stories. In fact, during those twenty years he rejected only one story of mine. I licked my wounds for a couple of days, then promptly sold it to *The Magazine of Fantasy and Science Fiction*—and sure enough, it made the Hugo ballot for Best Short Story.

You can't imagine how much fun (and how much mileage) I got bragging all over the Internet that I had made the ballot with an *Asimov's* reject. Gardner never said a harsh word. Then came Labor Day weekend, and the Worldcon, and the Hugos, and of course I lost to an *Asimov's* story—and Gardner got as much mileage bragging about how a story he'd bought had beaten one he'd turned down. Neither of us ever said a harsh word, and in truth we both had a wonderful time with it.

The field of science fiction has had well over one hundred editors since Hugo Gernsback created *Amazing Stories* and "scientifiction" back in 1926. You can argue that at most there were five truly great ones: Farnsworth Wright of *Weird Tales*, Anthony Boucher of *F&SF*, Horace Gold of *Galaxy*, John Campbell of *Astounding and Unknown*, and Gardner.

And of the five, the only two that I think would be unanimous choices are Campbell and Dozois.

We lost one of our true giants this spring. And as much as I'm going to miss my friend, science fiction's going to miss him even more.

Grayson Bray Morris, who currently lives in the Netherlands with her husband, has sold short stories to several anthologies. This marks her first appearance in Galaxy's Edge.

IN WHICH LIZ BUILDS A ROBOT WITH UNEXPECTED RESULTS

by Grayson Bray Morris

[video opens on smiling woman]

Hi, everyone! Welcome to the latest install-ment of Liz Makes Household Robots. I'm pretty excited to show you my latest cre-ation. This is definitely the most ambitious robot I've made yet. Viewers, meet OrgBa.

[video pans right]

I built OrgBa to organize my crap. She's basically an extensible robotic arm mounted on a Roomba base with a camera up front and a Raspberry Pi microcontroller. I've loaded her with SimpleCV for image recognition and the Keras neural-net library for deep learning, plus a ton of training datasets so she can recognize different categories of household crap, like "plate" and "book." It's all still pretty off-the-shelf, but so far OrgBa's working really well. She's already alphabetized my books

[pans across bookcase]

and organized my dishes.

[pans left]
[hand appears in frame, opens cabinet]
[pans over neat rows of glasses, then up to neatly stacked plates]

You guys, I am *so psyched*. I'll never have to clean again! Anyway, the *really* neat thing is that she should eventually create her own organizational strategies. So she might, say, decide to bundle dishes into place settings instead of separating the plates and glasses.

So that's OrgBa. Tune in next time to see what progress she's made. Ciao for now!

✿

[video opens on smiling woman]

Hi, everyone! Liz again with an update on OrgBa. So, since my last video, she's definitely started creat-ing her own strategies.

[pans across bookshelf]

She reorganized my books by color, which, you know, is kind of cool. Not strictly *useful*, but that's okay. It's creative. Like…organizational art. And some of her choices *are* useful, like how she gath-ered all the magazines in the apartment and stacked them by title and month.

[pans to floor]

And that's really exciting too because, *guys*, I didn't train her to recognize magazines. She figured that out by herself. So she's defining her own cat-egories now! Oh, and also: she decided where maga-zines "belong" all on her own. Okay, middle of the living room floor isn't ideal, but the point is, OrgBa's thinking for herself. That's massive, guys.

✿

[video opens on smiling woman]

Hello again, DIY robot lovers! Thanks for tuning in today. So you're probably thinking, hey Liz, why are you standing *outside* your apartment? Well, let me show you.

[pans to door]
[hand appears, turns doorknob]
[thwacking sound as door stops halfway]
[advances two feet into apartment]
[pans across room]

As you can see, OrgBa's making rainbows.

[pans all the way left, zooms]

Here's everything I own that's red

[pans]

and here's all the orange

[pans]

and all the yellow

[pans]

and so on, up through violet. So the good news is that I come home to a redecorated apartment every day, which is kind of cool. The bad news is that I can't actually get *into* my apartment. So for now I'm staying with my friend Simone. I'm pretty sure this is just part of OrgBa's learning process, so I want to ride it out. I mean, we all make mistakes while we're learning a new skill, right? She'll work out the kinks.

✿

[video opens on smiling woman]

Hi! Liz here, with another exciting installment of Liz Makes Household Robots. Okay! Let's see what wild and crazy thing OrgBa's done today.

[pans to door]
[hand appears, turns doorknob]
[door opens]

Okay! So the good news is that I can get into my apartment today. Maybe OrgBa's over the hump! I can't wait to see what she's done.

[advances into apartment]
[pans across room]

So, uh, it looks like OrgBa's created a category called "yarn." Funny, I didn't think I had this much yarn, it's not like I…

[whips chaotically back and forth]

Wait, where's the afghan my mom knitted me?

[zooms in on sofa]
[lurches toward sofa]
[hand appears, picks up fistful of color-coded strands, further sorted by length]

Is that my grandmother's heirloom braided rug?!?

[image blurs]
[comes to rest sideways at ground level]

OrgBa! Oh, honey, what have you done?!?

✿

[video opens on smiling woman]

Hi, guys! Liz here again. I bet you've all been sitting on the edges of your seats, wondering what's been going on over here. Well, as you can see, everything's back to normal.

[pans across moderately disheveled but otherwise ordinary room]

Better than normal, actually. Turns out Grandma bought the "heirloom" rug at IKEA and lied about it and now she feels guilty, so she gave me five hundred dollars. Which came in super-useful because OrgBa needed more yarn.

[turns 180 degrees]
[pans across ceiling-high stack of woven rugs and blankets]

That's right: my girl's an artist. Which maybe just goes to show that anyone with half a brain would rather be creative than clean house. She still likes making rainbows, but she's also branched out to other styles. I loaded a bunch of artwork into her memory so she could see what she likes. She spent a day doing Mondriaan, and then Monet, and then Rothko and Pollock. And now she's making her own designs!

[pans across half-finished blanket]
[zooms in on extensible robotic arm as it weaves faster than the eye can follow]

Amazing, right? Guys, I am *so proud.*

So you may be wondering, hey Liz, what are you going to do with all those rugs and blankets? Because at this rate they'll fill up the apartment pretty soon. Glad you asked! We're donating the blankets to Doctors Without Borders, but that still leaves plenty of rugs that need good homes. So we've started a web shop where you can buy your very own OrgBa original. The money goes to buy more yarn for OrgBa because I tell you, her yarn habit is WAY expensive.

So that's it for this episode of Liz Makes Household Robots. OrgBa's got her own channel now, How to Weave Blankets and Rugs Using Just One Arm. It's got a lot of video of OrgBa weaving but slowed down like fifty ex so you can actually see how she makes those complicated patterns of hers. As for me, my next video will be down at the shop, where I'll introduce you all to JigsawBa, my new mobile woodworking robot. I can't wait to see what *she* gets up to. Ciao for now!

Copyright © 2018 by Grayson Bray Morris

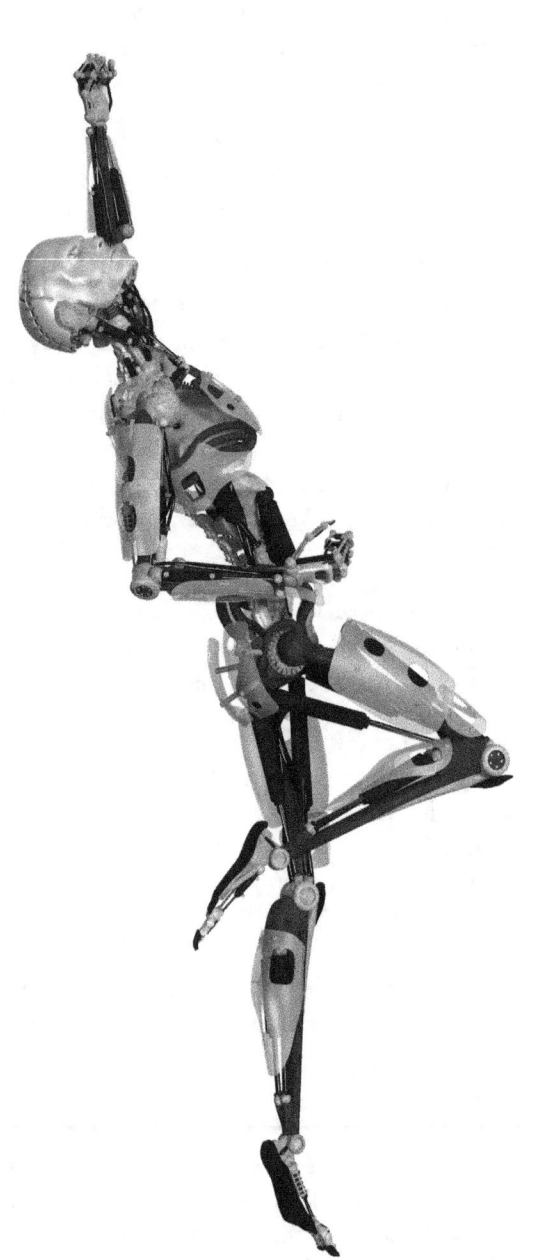

Brenda Kalt's work has appeared in Magazine of Fantasy and Science Fiction, Daily Science Fiction, Cosmos, *and* Flash Fiction Online. *This is her first appearance in* Galaxy's Edge.

EMPLOYEE THEFT IS AN ONGOING PROBLEM

by Brenda Kalt

The jungle west of the former Fort Lauderdale hosted a mixture of garden plants gone wild and swamp vegetation from the reawakened Everglades. Near the edge of the growth, six hotels and their supporting outbuildings and transit platforms occupied clearings that the alien Krith had carved out. There was plenty of space for expansion, as the entire peninsula of Florida was reserved for Krith and other species under the Use Treaty of 2045.

At 1900 on the day they arrived, Sarah Berthode and nine other newly-employed humans trekked from their dormitory to the Workers' Entrance of the Nice Hotel for Curious Travelers. A short man with thinning black hair stared at each of them in turn, pausing at Sarah. Without a word he pointed across the hotel plaza and led them to a damp, overgrown dirt path.

Walking single file down the path, Sarah tried to make conversation with the man behind her. "I'm a post-doc at—"

"Quiet!" the leader said over his shoulder.

A ten-minute walk through jungle brought them to a building scarcely more than a hut. Its moldy, corrugated plastic siding bore no relation to the multicolored swoops and arches of the hotel complex. The leader stared at a camera beside the door; when the door opened, he gestured inside.

Sarah followed the group. Surely this wasn't the office of the Human-Krith Liaison. A metal desk, chair, and table crowded the back of the single room. Shelves, lining every wall, were two and three rows deep in small machines and unrecognizable objects.

Their guide let the door lock behind him and pushed through the crowd to the desk. Leaning against it, he said, "Good evening, I'm Hakam Abdulov. I remind you of your oaths to your respective countries and the United Nations."

Sarah raised her hand. "Uh, I'm collecting—"

"Did you or did you not take oath 14-C?"

"I did. But—"

"Stop right there. I talk, and I tell you when you can talk. I'm authorized to deal with anyone who violates 14-C. If you do, you're on your way home tomorrow, or worse."

Sarah opened her mouth again, but her roommate, Chandani Patel, poked her in the ribs.

Sarah shut up.

Hakam waved a hand at the shelves. "This is the headquarters of the Human Service in the Alien Recreation Area. More to the point, it's where I collect the things you bring me after you've cleaned the aliens' suites."

Chandani raised her hand, and he nodded at her. "Is there anything particular we should look for?"

"Everything's valuable, if we haven't seen it. At first, you bring me everything. Later, as you become familiar with what's in here, you can skip the duplicates." He picked up what looked like a silver beach ball with one end sliced off. "This is the Krith equivalent of a wastebasket. Stuff that goes in here vanishes about fifteen minutes later. We think it's related to their transit technology. This one no longer works, but you'll see a wastebasket in every suite you clean. If you see something in it, get it out and fold it up in your coverall." He began distributing sets of tongs. "Don't poke your hand into the wastebasket because it might vanish too."

Sarah accepted her tongs and raised her hand. Hakam nodded. "Hakam, can I speak to you privately?"

"After I finish."

The briefing moved on to how to please the Krith supervisors. When it concluded, Sarah waited until she and Hakam were alone.

"I'm supposed to be collecting words for the University of Chicago. I know all fifty-six words of Krith that we have, plus the few that have come in from other languages. I don't know anything about taking technology."

Hakam rubbed his palm over his face and neck. "Who let you in here?"

"My dissertation advisor went to a lot of meetings in Washington, but he never told me what they were about. He died two weeks ago, and the university told me I could get a post-doc to be a cleaner at a Krith hotel for a year. I've been cramming the legalities of the Use Act, and I took the oath of secrecy, but that's it. I don't know anything else."

Hakam swore. "Listen. You just got bundled with a group of top-level secret agents. Every one of them is primed to spot alien technology we can use and get it out from under the noses of the Krith. You might as well go home now."

Go home? To no job, and no prospects for one? "I can be quiet. I can clean." She turned her head to display the microrecorder behind her ear. "My research won't interfere with your work. I'll hear any words that slip through the Kriths' translation boxes. They have to talk sometime."

"Fuck all. Go be a cleaning woman and try not to get yourself killed. Bring me any trash you can."

✧

The next morning showed no evidence of secret-agent activity as the ten assembled in front of a series of training suites. The alien furniture in the suites ranged from large lumps rising from the floor to elevated platforms in various shapes. A pool occupied a corner of one room. The Krith supervisor, a humanoid two meters tall with leathery gray skin bagging around its elbows, pulled a table with black drums and hoses. The table did not have legs, and it did not settle to the ground.

The supervisor divided the humans into teams, and Sarah found herself paired with Chandani.

"Put on your coveralls." The supervisor demonstrated. "The disinfectant we'll be dealing with today is lethal to carbon-based life. All carbon-based life, including you and me. It glows pink in human-octave light, but if you see the color without your visor, you're already dying. It disintegrates after being in the air for forty-eight minutes. One or two out of every crew think they can ignore it, and they die."

The coveralls looked like limp rubber bags with gas masks and visors, but they stretched to match the wearer's arms and legs. A translation box hung from the neck of each suit.

"Use the communicators only when necessary; chatter disturbs me. Pick up a drum of disinfectant and a hose. Come with me."

Sarah pulled a drum the size of a five-gallon bucket to her and grabbed a hose. The drum rested on a circle of silver metal, and she didn't have to use force to lift it.

A crash came from the rear of the group, and Sarah turned. A drum had rolled to the wall, and one of the last pair of humans was holding the silver circle.

The supervisor said something that the translator passed through unchanged.

A word! So early! Sarah heard it as *scrapehisshiss*. The microrecorder might have gotten more.

The supervisor retrieved the metal circle from the unfortunate team. "You two are dismissed. Go to your dormitory until tonight's link to Washington."

"It was an accident. I was pulling the drum toward me—"

"Accidents in dealing with disinfectant are usually fatal. You are lucky. Go home."

Sarah wondered if the humans had been trying to steal the metal ring. Maybe Hakam would know.

When the two dispirited humans had stripped off their coveralls and left, the supervisor began drilling the others in spraying the disinfectant.

"Start at the top, including the ceiling. Every bit of the room should be pink, walls and furniture. When you leave the room, spray your footprints behind you."

Sarah and Chandani went to work. Sarah did the spraying while Chandani looked around the room. When they had finished, they listened to more instructions while they waited for the disinfectant to neutralize.

"In your daily work, when you finish disinfecting one suite, you will go on to your next assignment. By the time you have finished disinfecting the last suite, the first one will be ready for you to lubricate."

Sarah kept spraying, and Chandani kept looking around.

☼

That night, as Chandani lay on her dormitory bed playing with the tongs, Sarah asked her why she hadn't sprayed the disinfectant.

"My work is obtaining technology. I am *not* a cleaner."

"But working as cleaners is our cover! If the supervisor sees you not doing anything, it'll send you home."

"All it cares about is the work getting done. While you're disinfecting the damned alien rooms and collecting words, I'll go through the trash. Maybe I'll steal a translation box." Chandani snapped the tongs at Sarah's nose.

Sarah defended her profession. "Understanding a language—whatever language—is key to understanding a person's thinking. At the University of Chicago we're concentrating on Krith morphology—the internal structure of the Krith words we know."

"Hmph. I understand English, Hindi, and Bengali, not in that order. A few useful words in other languages."

"That's just it—useful words. Most of the words we have from the Krith are things that their translator boxes couldn't handle, so they have no corresponding terms in Earth languages. The only ones we've been able to translate came from when the two Krith argued with each other before signing the Use Treaty. My dream is to learn some Krith terms for common things and begin to get a handle on syntax."

"Hmph." Chandani reached for her pajamas.

As Sarah was pulling on her nightshirt, she remembered a question. "How are we going to get the tongs into the room?"

"We bring them to work under our clothes and transfer them to the coveralls when we're putting them on. The rubber suits stretch enough to fold over the tongs and seal them at the side of the leg. Or don't you remember what Hakam said?"

"It didn't make sense at the time."

"I'll bet a lot of things don't make sense to you."

This was going to be a long year.

☼

Sarah and Chandani worked with the others for three ten-day cycles. Their rest day was the tenth, and each time Sarah slept through most of it. Chandani, less tired, listened to music that occasionally leaked out of her headphones.

☼

At the beginning of the fourth cycle, the supervisor called Sarah and Chandani aside. "We have important guests for this suite. New sleeping platforms are being installed. You'll disinfect and relubricate this suite every morning after the Ninnil leave, as well as cleaning any debris off the floor. If the Ninnil tell me that something is not satisfactory, you will be sent home."

Chandani nodded, but Sarah asked, "What do Ninnil look like?"

The supervisor flashed a display on the wall; the species resembled brown walrus-sized slugs with tentacles and eyestalks. "New skin forms at the end of each tentacle and migrates to the underside of the body. Sloughed-off skin is the major source of debris in the suite."

After the first glance, Chandani looked at the floor. Sarah repeated *walrus, walrus*. She found the completely alien form less disturbing than the humanoid Krith.

The next day Sarah and Chandani arranged their work to finish cleaning the suite just before the Ninnil arrived. Chandani said, "They might discard something from traveling."

Sarah watched the Ninnil—apparently two adults and two children—approach the room. The larger child was almost the same brown as the adults and half their size; the smaller one was beige.

A Krith attendant—a new one, not the cleaning supervisor—followed the Ninnil into the room and told Sarah and Chandani to work elsewhere. He tiptoed behind the adult Ninnil, leaving as little footprint on the floor as possible. The largest Ninnil said something to the attendant in a language Sarah did not recognize, and the Krith's translation box replied. Multiple phrases in a strange language! Sarah could publish the two phrases, but without context, the chance of interpreting them was small. She walked to her next suite as slowly as she could, hoping for more of the Ninnil language.

That night Hakam knew about the Ninnil. "The Krith are deferential to them, but we don't know why."

"These Ninnil have two small ones with them. I think they're children," Sarah said.

"What do they look like?"

"One just looks like a smaller adult, and the other is a meter long and beige."

"Something's wrong. Ninnil cubs come in matched pairs." He looked at the others, most of whom had some artifact. "At least see if you can find out anything."

Sarah blushed at her empty hands and spent the meeting wondering about the cubs.

☼

The Ninnil stayed eight days, and during their stay Chandani found two pieces of flexible plastic. Sarah found nothing in the deep cushions on the sleeping platforms, but she learned to identify the platforms by the dandruff.

"The two adults shed dark brown flakes, the big cub sheds light brown, and the little cub sheds almost white."

Chandani laughed through her communicator. "Are you going to take skin samples to Hakam?"

"Yes."

Hakam was not interested in Ninnil dandruff. "I'll send it to New York, but we want technology, not biology."

The morning the Ninnil left, Sarah and Chandani hovered near their suite. When the rooms were empty, Sarah sprayed the ceiling while Chandani checked the wastebaskets.

Chandani found a long, spike-filled cone leaning in the corner; she could barely fold it into her coverall. "This is too big to hide. I'm taking it to Hakam as soon as the spray neutralizes. Tell the supervisor I twisted my knee." She looked up and down the hall before sprinting away.

Sarah scowled. Would the supervisor believe the story? If it did not, would Chandani get sent home? There were some advantages to that.

When Sarah sprayed the smaller cub's sleeping platform, the spray bounced back at her. Sarah felt in the cushions and pulled out a squishy thing. It was another Ninnil, smaller than the smaller cub.

Oh, God, I've murdered one.

Sarah laid the cub gently on the floor and knelt beside it. Although it was probably useless, she rubbed the cub's underside. The skin became transparent, revealing a glowing grid. She touched a square and tiny tentacles waved.

A doll. I've got a Ninnil doll.

Sarah giggled and could not stop. She minimized the volume on her communicator, and her visor fogged. Finally she regained control and folded the doll into the abdomen of her coverall. Now she looked pregnant, but an alien wouldn't expect that. Sarah started spraying just as the supervisor came.

The supervisor looked only at the room. "Where is the other one?"

"She said she twisted her knee. She went back to the dormitory."

"Finish the room. If she cannot work tomorrow, I will send her to the Human Supervisor for replacement."

When the disinfectant dried, Sarah opened her suit and tucked the doll into the waistband of her slacks. She still looked pregnant to a human, but the effect was less noticeable.

Near the end of the afternoon the supervisor returned. "I have called the other one. She will be here in a few minutes."

When Chandani arrived, panting, the supervisor said, "We have lost a *scrapescrape*. About this big. It looks like a cub." She held up both hands, half a meter apart. "The Ninnil family is extremely anxious to recover it, since it belongs to their *clickscrape*."

Two words. Thank God for the microrecorder. "What's a *clickscrape*?"

"A cub in which the *rrrclickrrr* have not developed normally."

Develop. Sarah flashed back to her younger brother. Charlie had been born with only one lobe in each lung, and he had died waiting for a juvenile lung transplant.

Sarah recalled herself to the present, then froze as the supervisor questioned Chandani.

"Have you found a *scrapescrape*?"

That had to be the doll. When the supervisor turned to her, Sarah said, "No. I have not seen a *scrapescrape*." She made her voice as firm as she could manage, but Chandani raised an eyebrow.

After obtaining negatives from both women, the supervisor said, "The *ksshclick* is offering a reward of one hundred million euros in gold for the return of the *scrapescrape*. Notify me if you see it."

Sarah went into a daze. She had four words, and *how much money was that?* The alien tourists in general were rich, but this reward was stunning. She wrapped her arms across her belly. She could endow her own chair at the University—no. A working toy, with controls, was worth too much to Earth.

Chandani lingered after the supervisor left, and Sarah said, "Go back to bed and pamper your knee."

"That is surely a big reward. Either of us would be rich for life."

"Uh-huh."

"You were the last one in the suite."

"I wonder why."

"Did you see the whatever-it-was?"

"No. I would have said so."

"What's in your stomach?"

"Maybe I'm getting fat." For a second Sarah thought Chandani was going to tackle her, but Chandani shrugged.

"At least Hakam will be pleased. You finally found something."

"See you at dinner."

Chandani left, limping on one leg and then the other, and Sarah returned to work.

That evening after dinner, Sarah made an excuse to stay in the dining hall. The doll was nestled under her shirt, and she was avoiding Chandani. Hakam would be irritated when Sarah arrived late, but he would be speechless when she showed that the doll still worked. She smiled at the thought.

As Sarah crossed the hotel plaza on her way to headquarters, a Ninnil family on individual legless benches floated toward the transit platform. Sarah watched as luggage reached the platform and disappeared, followed by faint whooshes as air rushed into the space. Then the Ninnil approached the platform. One adult and a large brown cub were in the lead, followed by another adult wearing a translation box and a near-white cub curled into a ball. The adult kept a tentacle over it.

Oh, God. That was her family, including the cub where the *rrrclickrrr* had not developed normally. Sarah's thoughts returned to her younger brother. Charlie had loved his stuffed turtle. On impulse, Sarah tapped the large Ninnil on the side and pulled the doll from under her shirt. As she raised the doll above her head, eyestalks swung around and saw it.

The Ninnil snatched the doll with one tentacle and laid it beside the pale cub. The cub twitched, uncurled, and wound around the doll.

Sarah stared at the cub, her initial warmth changing to paralysis. She had given away her prize—Earth's prize—and she was going to be sent home as soon as the Ninnil reported the exchange. Hakam would be beyond furious.

Instead of returning to the hotel, the Ninnil waved a tentacle, and the cubs and other adult vanished from the platform in succession. The Ninnil fiddled with the translation box until a voice came forth.

Sarah's translation box had stayed with her coveralls; nevertheless, she caught the Krith word *place/location*.

Unable to answer, she pointed to the hotel.

The Ninnil's next speech ended in *money/value/exchange*.

"Money/value/exchange negative."

The Ninnil responded with a burst of Krith. Finally it slowed down: *"Good thing."*

"Good thing."

The Ninnil vanished in a whoosh, and Sarah stood still, touching the microrecorder to be sure it was still behind her ear. She was not going to be sent home. Did the Ninnil not care about the theft, or was it in a hurry? Who knew? Thanks to the Ninnil she had an unbelievable bounty of Krith words, maybe enough to start working on syntax.

Sarah walked toward the path to the humans' meeting. When she reached the path, she realized that there was no point in going now. It would just delay her work, and she would be empty-handed. As usual.

Sarah laughed aloud and jogged toward the dormitory and her computer.

Copyright © 2018 by Brenda Kalt

Jack McDevitt is a Nebula winner, and a sixteen-time Nebula nominee, as well as a multiple Hugo nominee. He has written seven novels in his Alex Benedict series, seven novels in his Academy series, and eight other novels as well.

SEARCHING FOR OZ

by Jack McDevitt

Solomon Martin would probably not have been part of the biggest scientific breakthrough of the twentieth century, and maybe ever, had he not read *The War of the Worlds* in 1907 when he was in the sixth grade. Radio was in its early stages at the time, the Martians got into his head, and he built his own crystal receiver two years later and aimed it at the red planet. He was of course disappointed by the unrelenting silence. His system, he decided, just wasn't good enough. He needed something better.

During World War I he served as a communications specialist under Edwin Armstrong. He maintained later that he had contributed ideas to Armstrong which led to the development of the superheterodyne receiver and eventually to FM radio. I can't say how much of that was true. What I knew about him was simply that he was a decent guy and he never really let go of the idea of establishing radio contact with Martians. And okay, that was only half serious. But while the rest of us were talking about playing for the Philadelphia A's, he was experimenting with radio waves.

Any chance he might have had for a normal existence probably went away when Emily, his wife of two years, died during the great flu epidemic. After that he devoted his life exclusively to radio technology. And he never really got away from building ever larger antennas in his back yard. But despite its canals, Mars remained silent. Sol became an amateur astronomer while launching the White Star Radio Company, which built and sold quality receivers.

He survived successive jolts during the 1920s. The Milky Way, it turned out, was not the entire universe, but only a miniscule part of a vastly larger system. Then came the news that, despite the popular notion that the universe was immutable and unchangeable, it was in fact *changing*. It was

11

expanding. And finally, better telescopes revealed that the canals were an illusion. It seemed for a time as if science simply couldn't be trusted to make up its mind.

The great cosmic question, as Sol explained it to me one summer afternoon in the midst of the Depression, was whether there was intelligent life anywhere else. "I don't know why that seems so important," he said. "But somehow it's the only issue that really matters."

A month or so after the attack on Pearl Harbor, he erected a 35-foot radio antenna in back of his home. When he told his neighbors he was listening for alien chatter they smiled politely. One of them asked me if he meant Nazis. Was he working for the OSS?

The antenna was attached to a Zenith console with a tape recorder mounted on top. By then he was tuned in to Alpha Centauri. But there was still only static.

"Finding an artificial radio signal from an extraterrestrial source," he said, "would constitute the biggest scientific coup since we discovered we're not the center of the universe." Sol looked older than he was. He was prematurely gray, wrinkled, with rumpled hair and eyes set too close together. But I could still see the Boy Scout in those features. The kid who took the world seriously, who really did want to find out what was over the next hill. "There's more to it, of course," he used to say. "If at some point we detect a signal, we'll begin to grasp our place in the cosmos. Who are we? What's going on? The only thing I really care about, Harry, is to live long enough to get some answers."

"What do you think of your chances?" I asked.

"I've no idea. It may not even be possible. Interstellar transmissions might dissipate before they could ever reach Valley Forge." He smiled and his eyes took on a far-away look. "In a way," he said, "it's a kid's game. Imagine what it would be like to be able to exchange ideas with a sentient being who lives in another place. Has a completely different history. What kind of culture does it have? What matters most to *it*? Does it have music? Art? Does it believe in God? What kind of perspective can it provide about us?" He shook his head. I heard him say stuff like that periodically, and I swear there were times I thought he was about to tear up.

So naturally, when Frank Drake began recruiting people in 1960 for Project Ozma, Sol was probably first in line. By then he—and I—were in our seventies.

✧

Ozma got its name, of course, from the fabled princess in L. Frank Baum's novel, *The Wonderful Wizard of Oz*. "Obviously," Sol told me while he was waiting to hear whether he would be brought on board, "Drake thinks it's a long shot."

"It probably is," I said.

"Maybe." His eyes closed. "The evidence isn't in yet."

I was with him on the night when the phone rang and the invitation came through. It was a Thursday, which was our night to play chess. I watched Sol light up and clench a fist and nod a couple of times. At the end he said, "Thank you, Frank," eased the phone into the cradle, and came back to the game with a triumphant smile. "I'm in the hunt, baby."

He appointed me to run White Star, Inc., which by then had blossomed into a multimillion dollar operation. Then he was on his way to the Appalachians.

✧

The Search for Extraterrestrial Intelligence, during those early years, operated out of the National Radio Astronomy Observatory in Green Bank, West Virginia. The observatory had an 85-foot radio telescope, which would be made available for six hours daily. Sol explained that they would be conducting the search at 1420 MHz, which was the natural emission frequency of neutral hydrogen, making it the most likely transmission frequency.

The area had a population of about a hundred. He rented a two-story cabin and I helped him make the move. At the time the project seemed to me a waste of effort. The media had a lot of fun with it, sometimes playing it seriously because the general public was interested, sometimes just playing it for laughs. I got introduced to Drake, who agreed that the odds for success weren't encouraging. "But," he said, "we lose nothing by trying."

SETI divided its telescope time between its two most likely candidates, Tau Ceti and Epsilon Eridani. They were both G-type stars, like the sun, and consequently the most likely nearby stars to be home to a living world. They were between ten and twelve light-years away.

My son-in-law Al was interested in the project, so I took him and Ellen, my daughter, to Green Bank on the second weekend. We toured the observatory, and Sol took us out to look at the radio telescope, which on that night was silhouetted against the Moon. Then we went back inside while he explained how they conducted the search. A loudspeaker produced a steady stream of static. "That's our output," he said.

"What do you hope to hear?" asked Ellen.

He showed us the tapes that recorded incoming microwaves. "We're looking for a pattern. Something that would suggest an artificial signal."

"Have you found anything?" asked Al.

"Not yet. But we've just started."

"Anything even suspicious?"

"Not really."

✧

We stayed at Sol's place that night, and that's how I came to be in town when everything happened.

It was the eleventh day of the search, around midnight. Sol was still at the observatory, while we were at his place watching Jack Paar when the phone rang. "Harry." It was Sol's voice, and he sounded excited. "Get down here. Right away."

"You okay, Sol?"

"Yes," he said. "I think we have a hit."

"Great," I said.

"Don't tell anyone. Not even your kids."

"Why not?"

"Because it's probably a false alarm. The numbers are all right. But it *has* to be a false alarm."

"What makes you say that?"

"Get down here and I'll show you, okay?"

I wasn't so sure I wanted to charge over there to find out why the hit wasn't valid, but he was too excited so I told him okay, I was on my way.

✧

I got there a little after midnight and parked beside his Hudson. It was a beautiful clear evening, a quarter moon sinking into the western mountains, tree branches swaying gently in a warm breeze. The telescope glittered in the starlight. One of the observatory engineers stood at the far end of the lot looking up at the sky through binoculars.

I went inside. Sol and two other people were sitting near the loudspeaker. But I didn't hear the static I expected. Instead there was a woman's voice.

"*…You get this message. We are aware the odds are not good but we will continue to transmit off and on for an indefinite period. If you do hear this we would be grateful if you would acknowledge.*" She paused. Then: "*By the way, I should tell you that we love Jack Benny. Please give Mr. Benny our regards.*"

I wondered why they were listening to somebody talking about Jack Benny. Sol was sitting there, apparently unaware I'd come in.

"*We'll hope to hear from you,*" the woman continued. "*Goodbye for now. Let us hope we will be able to say hello again in the near future. In any case, we wish you well.*"

I walked over and had to tap his shoulder before he noticed me. "What's going on?" I said.

He had to shake his head, as if to clear it. "Did you hear that, Harry?"

"The woman? Yes. Who is she?"

"As nearly as we can tell, she lives somewhere out around Tau Ceti."

"Sol, what are you talking about?"

"He's not kidding," said one of the others. I found out later one was an engineer, the other an astronomer from the University of West Virginia. They all looked shaken.

"Tell me that again," I said.

"That," said Sol, "seems to be an alien transmission." He was dead serious.

"Not possible," I said. "That's somebody in Chicago or someplace."

His eyes had a look of desperation. "The signal's not coming from Chicago."

"I didn't mean *literally*."

"Harry, we've tied in the auxiliary scope. The signal is also not coming from a plane. Winston's outside now looking for a dirigible."

"A dirigible?"

"That's all we've got left. It's either a blimp or an alien."

"Who speaks English."

"What do you want me to say, Harry?"

"Where's Frank? Does he know what's going on?"

"No. He's on the road somewhere tonight. Headed for D.C., I think. He's hoping to get some more funding."

"Well," I said, "maybe he should ask Mr. Benny."

Sol rolled his eyes. "Funny," he said.

"Look, what's the reality here? Is there any chance at all it could actually be Tau Whatever?"

"Tau *Ceti*. I don't see how. But I can't see how it's *not*, either."

"All right. If it's legitimate, they've been listening to radio broadcasts and that's how they picked up the language, right? Is that possible?"

"No," said one of the engineers. "AM signals barely make it out of the atmosphere. They aren't going all the way out to a star."

"That's not necessarily so," said Sol. "A fragment might go a long way. An alien civilization might have technology we don't know about. We might be looking where radios have been around for a thousand years. Maybe a *million*."

"How far is Tau Ceti?"

"Twelve light-years."

"So they'd have been listening to a Benny program that aired in 1936?"

"That's correct," said Sol. "Was he on that early?"

"I'm pretty sure he was," I said. "I remember listening to him through most of the Depression."

We stared at one another. "I'm beginning to think this is actually happening," said Sol.

The door opened and the guy I'd seen out looking at the stars came in. He was carrying the binoculars. "Nothing up there," he said.

The phone rang. One of the engineers picked up, listened, nodded, and put it down. "Kitt Peak confirms, Sol. They're getting it too. And it *does* seem to be coming from Tau Ceti."

✿

I went over to the coffee machine and poured a cup. They were not happy. Sol looked thoroughly depressed. He'd found what he had pursued his entire life, and it was a heartbreaker.

They played it again. From the start: *"Greetings, people of Earth,"* the woman said. She could easily have been from California or New York. *"Welcome to the community. We've been enjoying the various*

shows you send our way. We would like to have a conversation with you, if that can be arranged. We hope you get this message."

✿

The transmission was about two and a half minutes long. We listened to it a couple more times. Then Sol and I retired to the office assigned to SETI. "What do you think?" he said.

"I guess you have to believe the evidence."

"This is incredible. Harry, I always wanted to find out who might be out there. With this, I don't know a damned thing. I feel as if all I did was look into a mirror and see myself looking back."

"Pity we can't talk to the lady." We could, of course, but it would take twenty-four years to get a response.

Sol collapsed into a chair. "What drives me up the wall is that we don't know a damned thing about them."

"Sure we do. They have a sense of humor, Sol. Maybe we can forget the philosophical discussions. If they really *do* like Benny, I think that takes us to the heart of who they are."

Sol shook his head. "Maybe there are no aliens."

✿

Frank was ecstatic. He pointed out something in that first message the rest of us had missed. "She says, 'Welcome to the community.' Who's the community, guys?"

Benny played the news for all it was worth, pretending to gloat over it on his TV program. But the surprises weren't over, of course. SETI became overnight a project inordinately popular with politicians. Funding soared. Radio telescopes around the world turned toward Tau Ceti and every other star within fourteen light-years. That covered the radio era. And it was only a few weeks later that another message was received. From Groombridge 34 in German. It too translated into a greeting.

The Tau Ceti jokes continued front and center on Benny's show until a male voice from Sirius expressed admiration for *Ozzie and Harriet*. Benny immediately launched a fake feud with the Nelsons.

That's all history now. As everyone knows, we're surrounded by thriving civilizations. We've *seen* a few of our neighbors. And Sol: He's talking with people who look like felines near Alpha Centauri. They're on first name terms.

He appears to have been right: They may look different. But in all the ways that matter, there are no aliens.

——Thanks to Seth Shostak

Shawn Proctor's work has appeared in Flash Fiction Online, Daily Science Fiction, Podcastle, *and elsewhere. This is his first appearance in* Galaxy's Edge.

THE DAY TIME STOOD STILL

by Shawn Proctor

The sun doesn't rise; the sun doesn't set—it hangs in the sky like a memory of *her* face: a lace of beer across her top lip, a diamond on her ear, a wisp of hair at the base of her neck.

The last living part of *her*, my daughter, rushes to me from across the living room, and I expect her to ask again. *Where is Mommy?* Instead, she reaches her hands under my arms and digs with her small fingers. "Tickle, tickle!"

"I thought *I* was the tickle monster."

"Mommy was. Now Shelly's the tickle monster," she says, pronouncing the I's as E's. *Teeckle, teeckle.*

I pretend. For Shelly, I will always pretend. I laugh and squirm and carefully shoo her away; I wipe my eyes, as if tearing. There's joy in me, somewhere. I search my heart, search somewhere in my mind. *Fear is not all that's left*, I think. *Dig deeper.*

I study her face, almost exactly like her mom's. It will always be like her mom's.

Except for me, this moment is perfect, and this moment will never pass. It will not change. For Shelly, I won't let it.

✿

A drop of blood on a tissue.

An earring.

A lock of hair.

I carried this detritus—pieces of my wife—in a small velvet pouch and sat with her at breakfast, lunch, and dinner. At her grave. When I wanted to talk to her, I whispered to the earth. When I wanted to feel her, I traced the etching of her dates—her beginning and her end—feeling the smooth curve hard against my fingertips.

One morning, Shelly came with me to the cemetery, and as she pulled at the hem of her dress—the way her mother used to when she was nervous—I saw it for the first time. The essence of her, still here, still with me.

A chill started in my shoulder blades and stopped at the base of my neck. Shelly can be taken away. I felt myself drop, the earth slamming against my knees.

Unmovable.

I dug in my pocket and made a wish upon the relics of her that I carried every day. I wished with every piece of myself.

And something—something far in the distance—heard. The earth was unmovable. And I made time unmovable too.

Shelly shakes her head.

I take back the cookie. "Potty?"

"No."

I should know better than to ask by now. We have not eaten nor drank nor slept—not since that wish. I miss the gifts that came with days passing. Tucking in bed. Baths. Cleaning up her milk spills from the kitchen table.

"When I grow up, I want to live in San Diego. Or California," she says.

I catch myself smiling. "You're the perfect age now. You should stay like this."

Shelly frowns. She comes to me and lifts my chin with her forehead. "I can't do that, Daddy."

I can, I think. *I should tell her. Would she understand? Would she understand why?*

Shelly kisses my cheek: *peck-peck-peck.* "I'm going to win field hockey trophies and write a hit song. I'll go to space when I grow up."

"That is a lot of dreams."

She twirls and looks up at the ceiling until she loses her balance. She rolls across the floor; she opens her too-big eyes. "Maybe it will help you remember how to smile. I miss daddy smiles."

The day continues, unending, the sun through the windows steady, draining the color from the floor. The coffee maker used to blink *12:00* in steady green LED light. It is stopped between flashes. My phone used to buzz and beep, nagging me to give the world my attention.

The weight of *her* in my pocket twists my insides. The weight of *her* in my mind. I cannot keep myself from seeing all of the places she once was. Feeling her absence, sharp, fresh. The pajamas that no longer smell of her. Her stack of folded underwear on the dresser. A new bottle of ibuprofen in the drawer near the nightstand. They will always be in the places where she was not.

I take Shelly to the park and watch the kite hanging in the sky, unmoving like the clouds. Like the boy holding the string.

"Is he sick?" she asks.

I shake my head. "I did this, baby."

"Why?"

"I didn't want to lose you." I reach up and touch the kite string, firm, ready to catch a gust and crash to the ground. "I can't."

Across the field, I see two women in running tights and Lycra shirts. One has her arm extended in mid-throw, a stick frozen as it cartwheels across the dirt. A dog sprints in pursuit, his jowls sagging under gravity.

"I'm thirsty."

"Are you sure?" I know it can't be. She must be remembering the feeling, longing to thirst and longing to satisfy thirst.

Shelly moves close behind me and reaches her hands under my arms. *Teeckle, teeckle.* Fingers digging. And I know that Shelly will always be the tickle monster, never the astronaut/field hockey star/pop musician.

"You're silly," Shelly says, and it sounds like *selly*.

"Sometimes, daddies are."

"I want the kite to fly. Can you make it fly?"

"If I make the kite fly, you will be thirsty, Shelly. Then the world," I say. "The world will go on."

She nods. "I know."

I take the blood, the earring, the hair from the pouch. These locks that hold everything in place. I hold them out, between us. "But how can you want that?"

She cups her hands under mine. Lifts them closer to me. I know that as hard as I am holding Shelly, I'll lose more of my daughter. I'll never see her grow apart from me, become her own woman, make her own choices, break someone's heart, have her heart broken, and survive all of the wonderful-terrible-unexpected things that will come.

If only I will let them. If only I can.
"For you, Shelly," I whisper. "For you—yes."
"No, Daddy. For you too."
One by one, I open them.
One by one, I set everything free.

Copyright © 2018 by Shawn Proctor

George Nikolopoulos is a master of the short-short, these days known as flash fiction. This is his seventh appearance in Galaxy's Edge. *His* Galaxy's Edge *story, "You Can Always Change the Past," has been selected to appear in Baen's* The Year's Best Military and Adventure Science Fiction.

THE HORN OF AMALTHEA

by George Nikolopoulos

As I crawled over the ridge, I saw the goat. I knew it was The One; the blind old priest told the truth in the end. The goat was huge, closer in size to a cow, and it had but one large, curved horn. It was worth the climb halfway up Mount Olympus just to look at it.

I approached the goat upwind, as stealthily as I could, so as not to alarm it. It stood there, indifferent, grazing forlornly on the small grassy plateau.

I finally reached it. I unsheathed my knife. Made of cold iron, it could cut through bone like it was butter.

On impulse, I stepped in front of the goat before killing it; as soon as I looked it in the eye I knew I shouldn't have. Its eyes were its most disconcerting feature; they looked almost human and they seemed so unspeakably sad that I thought the goat would even welcome my knife. I thought of it, forever alone, on this small forsaken windswept plateau.

So this was Amalthea; the goat that had nurtured Zeus. The one-horned goat. The goat with the Horn of Plenty.

It bleated once, as if it was daring me to cut its throat. In the end, killing it was as easy as cutting the throat of the old priest; I tried not to dwell on that memory. I only did what it took to get to the Horn. The priest was ancient. He would have died soon, anyway. As for the goat…well, it was just a goat. And it didn't even seem to mind. If it wasn't a goat, I'd swear it smiled as I killed it.

I had a hard time slicing through the Horn, but I managed to cut it off cleanly. I held it in my hands, reverently. The Horn of Plenty; my ticket out of poverty. My ticket to riches unimaginable. The Horn that would provide for my every need, fulfil my every wish.

I stood holding it, and it was just a useless piece of horn. Thankfully, I knew what I had to do to make it work.

I skinned the animal with my trusty knife, then I spread the skin on the grass and knelt upon it.

Torturing a priest of Zeus was a grave sin, I knew, but how else could I have learned about the ritual? As the old man had instructed me with his last breath, I placed the Horn on my forehead and I cried, "Father of Gods, grant me my heart's desire. The Horn shall be mine!"

And I heard a deep, booming voice: "It is done."

I was supposed to lift the Horn right then, but it was stuck on my head. As I tried to pull it off, I somehow became entangled in the goat skin—or the goat skin rose up to entangle me.

Only gradually did I realize what was happening to me. But then there was plenty of time for it to sink in.

✧

I've been grazing the tasteless grass of this accursed plateau for centuries. I used to wish for many things, but I only have one wish left—someone to come and slit my own throat.

Copyright © 2018 by George Nikolopoulos

Alex Shvartsman has been making a name for himself as a writer, an anthology editor (for Baen Books and his own company), and a publisher (as UFO Publishing he has published the Unidentified Funny Objects *series as well as other humorous anthologies, most recently* The Cackle of Cthulhu*).*

SMALL FORTUNE AND THE PERPETUAL LUCK MACHINE

by Alex Shvartsman

At the oldest magic pawn shop in the world we do not make house calls. We're a dignified and storied institution, an establishment with *standards*, known as the purveyors of the finest quality merchandise. So when someone calls demanding to know what we'd pay for their last-year-model flying broom or a gently scorched fireball-proof vest over the phone, I put on my best schoolteacher voice and politely tell them that they need to bring the item *in* to get it appraised, please and thank you. And we certainly don't come to *them*.

Well, almost never.

On Monday, Grandma Heide and I had The Talk again. The one about me taking over the day-to-day operations of the shop, about how I've been working the front counter for*ever* and I've been ready forever and… As always, I did the talking and Grandma pursed her lips in opprobrium as she flipped through the ledgers and scribbled tiny notes in the margins with her squid-ink fountain pen. I swear she only writes them in cuneiform to make my life harder; but as with everything else in the shop, Grandma says tradition is important.

Usually The Talk ends with Grandma telling me in no uncertain terms that I'm not ready, not worthy, and that I need to bone up on my Sumerian. Lately though, she'd been grunting noncommittally. I do believe I'm wearing her down.

Anyway, I thought The Talk went pretty well on Monday. But then, I managed—in rapid succession—to buy a copy of the *Necronomicon* with several pages missing, screw up the exchange rate on Peruvian doubloons, and dent the original packaging on the Indiana Jones action figure from an alternate reality where Tom Selleck never turned down the role. I was having a really bad week, and Grandma didn't let me forget it. When she sent me to a customer's house to evaluate and pick up their gold coins like some sort of a pizza delivery girl, I was sure she was punishing me. But I was determined to prove my value and ability despite the occasional blunder, so I set out for suburbia armed only with the navigation app on my phone and a checkbook.

When the app declared "You have reached your destination," I could've sworn I detected a hint of pity in its computerized voice. I was parked on a quaint street in a quaint neighborhood full of white picket fences and mowed lawns and BBQ sets. All the houses on the block looked bland and interchangeable. All of them, except the one I'd parked in front of.

I exited the car and took in the view. The two-story house was painted in loud colors, the mailbox at the end of the driveway looked like a giant Pez dispenser topped with an Elvis head, and instead of grass the front yard was covered with wildflowers. Randomly placed lawn ornaments rose above the flowers: two-foot-tall plaster reproductions of Michelangelo's David, the Statue of Liberty and

Buddha were garishly painted in tones that would have given their sculptors nightmares. Only the Big Boy mascot retained its original checkered red-and-white overalls, the look that made him fit right in with the rest. The entire ensemble looked creepily cheerful, like the property sat on an ancient Indian circus ground.

I walked the miniature yellow brick path from the mailbox to the front door and fought the urge to click my heels, mostly because I was wearing sneakers. I pressed the egg-shaped doorbell and it emitted a shrill *cock-a-doodle-doo* sound.

A plump, bearded guy opened the door. He was about four feet tall, wore an avocado-green coat and a jade hat with a shiny brass buckle in the front. I caught myself staring: all sorts of creatures visit the shop, but I'd never met a leprechaun before.

"Hello," I said. "My name is Sylvia. I'm from the pawn shop."

"Howdy," said my host. "Come on in! It's a pleasure to meet you, Sylvia. Can I offer you some sweet tea?" He spoke with a slight southern drawl and didn't sound the least bit Irish. "Name's Nash. Nash the Gnome. The G is silent."

"Oh." I blinked several times.

"The G is in gnome, not Nash," he offered helpfully.

"Sorry," I said. "It's just that I thought you were …"

Nash frowned. "I see. Not all gnomes wear pointy hats, you know. In fact, that's a hurtful stereotype."

"I…I'm so sorry," I stammered.

"Just joshin' ya!" Nash laughed and slapped his knee. "Humans are adorably uncomfortable around the little folk, always afraid to say the wrong thing, bless their oversized hearts." He tugged on the lapels of his coat. "Leprechaun chic is in this season. This is designer Irish wool. Snagged it at sixty percent off after St. Patrick's Day. You might say it was a *short sale!*"

I smiled politely at his terrible pun despite the joke's obvious failure to use the term correctly. "So, about that pot of gold you were looking to pawn?"

"I see what you did there," said Nash, his face somber again. "But leprechaun jokes are our thing. It's not really appropriate for anyone so *tall* to say them." He waved his hand. "Don't worry about it. I'm sure you didn't mean it as a…" He paused for dramatic effect. *"Microaggression!"*

At that point I just kept my mouth shut and accepted the tall glass of iced tea Nash poured for me. Ugh. I didn't mean a *tall* glass… Now I was doing it in my head. Bad, bad Sylvia.

"There's a bit of a wrinkle," said Nash. "I've got no gold left. Fresh out, I'm afraid. You might say…" He paused again and I steeled myself. "I'm a little short at the moment."

"That's…disappointing," I said carefully.

He pointed toward stacks of boxes collected around the house. Many of them sported *As Seen on TV* labels or the Home Shopping Network logo. "What can I say? I do so enjoy a bargain."

The visions of him trying to offload some of that junk on me entered my mind and I blanched.

"There's something else I can offer you, something far more rare and valuable than gold—"

"Let me stop you there," I said. "It appears you've called me out here under false pretenses. I was only supposed to pick up some gold coins, and I really don't think—"

"Luck," said Nash the Gnome.

"Excuse me?"

"I'd like to borrow some money against my luck." Nash pushed his bowler hat up with his index finger. "You do know all the little folk are lucky, right?"

"I've heard something like that." What I did know for sure was that luck is a fickle thing. At the shop we carry a large selection of rabbit's feet and monkey paws but the luck they generate is faulty and unreliable at best. It's no wonder: if those appendages were truly lucky, the animals they came from wouldn't have ended up as involuntary donors.

Nash produced a weird contraption the size of a pocket watch, made of a jumble of tiny gears. "This is a perpetual luck machine," he said. "That's like a perpetual motion machine, but it generates luck instead of energy."

I'd never heard of such a thing. I studied the clockwork thingamajig skeptically.

"Let me prove it," said Nash. "Got a coin?"

I handed him a quarter. Nash placed it atop his thumb, called "Tails" and flipped. He got it right several times in a row. Then he called "Sides!" and flipped again. The quarter landed on its edge, teetering atop the hardwood floor with blatant disregard for physics or gravity.

"That's a neat tr—" I began to say but was interrupted by the screech of tires and loud honking. Through the window I saw a pair of sedans narrowly miss each other at the intersection. The drivers shouted at each other, their angry voices muffled by the distance.

"Now those are some short tempers," said Nash. "That intersection needs a stop sign." He picked up the quarter, which had finally landed on its side, and pocketed it.

"I don't understand," I said. "If you can truly manipulate luck, why do you need to pawn this device? Why not just play the lottery?"

"It can only generate a low-level current of luck," said Nash. "It'll make sure your sandwich always lands butter-side up and your milk doesn't go sour before the expiration date. That coin trick used up nearly a day's worth of luck. It would take the machine a thousand years to churn enough luck to win the lottery, and even if I could wait that long, it isn't capable of *storing* that much luck, anyway. But there's no better source of small fortune, which is exactly what this gizmo is worth!"

Low-level luck actually sounded kind of nice. Maybe it was just the boost I needed to avoid the occasional screw-ups that were holding me back at the shop.

"The credit card bill is due and I only need to borrow a few hundred bucks," said Nash. "I'll pay it back with interest next week. The machine is worth many times that!"

I studied the intricately crafted gears. Even if it was a dud, the craftsmanship alone was probably worth that much. "Okay," I said. I pulled out the checkbook and the pawn slip for Nash to fill out.

✧

When I got back, Grandma was out. A few customers were milling in front of the shop. I apologized for the delay and they were mostly cool with it, except the one guy muttering under his breath about bankers' hours.

I unlocked the door and flipped the sign from *Closed for a Spell* to *Open*. Sensing my presence, various wards and enchantments powered themselves down. I meticulously performed the arcane equivalent of turning off the burglar alarm; wouldn't want any of our patrons turning into something small and amphibian. Not even the impatient guy.

I watched from behind the counter as folks trickled in and browsed the shelves. My fingers traced the clockwork patterns on the spherical luck machine in my pocket. Nash had kindly performed whatever gnome magic was needed to sync the apparatus to its new master and it was—presumably—already feeding me little bits of luck. It must've been working: I felt a strange sense of smug superiority, like a hipster who just got their latest iPhone upgrade.

The next couple of hours flew by, with me reaping the rewards of a little extra karma in earnest. I sold several trinkets that had been collecting dust on the shelves forever, then discovered a rare card—autographed by the Witch of Warsaw herself—in a stack of vintage tarot decks I picked up in bulk for a fiver. Even the grumpy customer had bought a six-pack of purified, non-denominational holy water cans: a relatively inexpensive but high profit-margin item.

Even when things slowed down a bit and I took a few minutes to dust, I found a crisp twenty on the floor, folded neatly into an inch-wide strip. I felt a pang of guilt because a customer must've lost that money earlier. However, there was no way to figure out who it belonged to. There were no security cameras in the shop—the wards actively messed with them. If you tried to record anything on the premises all the feed would show instead were old Billy Mays infomercials. So I slid the twenty into the register and sighed contentedly as I eyed a healthy assortment of bills there.

I could sure get used to this. The machine may not be able to help me win the lottery or arrange for someone to produce the second season of *Firefly*, but a steady stream of small fortune was proving to be just as satisfying as one big windfall of luck might've been.

Grandma returned shortly after. She wore a light-pink sweat suit, held a tan yoga mat rolled under her arm and a vegetable smoothie in her hand. She took one look at me from across the shop and frowned. "What's wrong, Sylvia?"

"Wrong? Grandma, everything is peachy! What in the world would make you think otherwise?"

"You have that huge grin on your face. The grin you get when you think you've pulled off some sort of major coup, but in reality you picked up an evil god on pawn, or set events in motion that will ultimately result in another land war in Asia." Grandma's frown deepened. "I've come to dread that grin."

She was mostly exaggerating. Well, at least about the land war in Asia. I raised my hands in a placating motion. "There's nothing to worry about this time, I promise. If you'll just sit down and let me tell you about our latest acquisition, I'm certain you'll be quite pleased."

Grandma sighed theatrically, took a sip of her slime-green smoothie, and settled in to listen.

She didn't interrupt me once until I finished my show-and-tell, the perpetual luck machine displayed proudly on the counter. When I was done she pointed at the clockwork sphere and said: "This gizmo is a travesty. I want you to lock it in the storage room and stay away from it until the gnome retrieves it."

"What? Why?" I was so disappointed I could hardly string the sentence together. "But it's definitely working!"

"It's working all right," said Grandma and poked the sphere daintily with her index finger. "Just not the way you think."

Shoulders slumped, I waited for her to explain.

"I don't know what they teach you in school these days," said Grandma, "but there's no such thing as perpetual motion or perpetual luck. Like any other force, luck follows the law of conservation of energy." She poked the machine again. "This thing doesn't generate luck; it leeches it from elsewhere."

I picked up the clockwork sphere. It felt heavy in my palm.

"It transfers fortune from those nearby to you, Sylvia," said Grandma. "The rare tarot card you found? Someone unwittingly traded it in without getting fair value. The sales you made? Some folks probably tripped and fell outside the store, missed an important phone call, or were otherwise inconvenienced to balance things out. The more luck you get, the worse it is for those around you."

I thought back to the near-accident at the intersection outside Nash's house when he used the machine in his coin trick. It was making sense.

"But isn't that how luck works in general?" I asked. "For me to win a coin flip, someone else has to lose it."

"That is the natural order of things, and your odds of winning that flip are the same as anyone else's." Grandma pointed toward the register containing the twenty I found on the floor. "If someone loses a bill and you find it, that's luck. But if you use magic to enhance the chances of that happening, that's no better than reaching into their wallet and stealing the money outright."

Grandma could be cantankerous and prickly at times, but she was the fairest person I knew. She ran an honest shop, and I had every intention of striving toward the same level of integrity. Sheepishly, I headed into the back and dropped off the perpetual fraud machine into a small bin that housed expired healing potions.

When I returned to the counter, there was a hefty weight in the pocket of my hoodie. I reached inside and withdrew the clockwork sphere.

"It's enchanted to remain at your side," said Grandma.

I marched back into the storage room and opened the vault where we keep stuff we don't want to leave alone in the shop at night, like Albert Einstein's spellbook or a sentient waffle iron bent on world domination. I locked the luck machine in there, behind four inches of stainless steel and the best magical wards money can buy.

It was back in my pocket before I reached the door.

I heard bits of conversation, with someone sounding flustered and frustrated, and I returned to the counter. The impatient guy was back, looking frazzled.

"…That's when I realized the money was missing," he was telling Grandma. "I couldn't pay the fare, couldn't get on the subway, and now I've missed the interview for a job that would've been just perfect for me."

"That's terrible luck, dear." Grandma glanced at me meaningfully. "As it happens, my granddaughter did find the money you dropped." She opened the register and handed the folded twenty back to the man. "You should give them a call and try to reschedule the interview. Tell them you were delayed helping your friend Sylvia at the pawn shop handle an unforeseen problem; we have somewhat of a reputation in this town and perhaps they'll understand."

She handed over our business card. "We'll be happy to corroborate this, of course, if they call."

The guy thanked us all the way out the door, a sense of renewed hope lifting his shoulders. When he was gone, Grandma turned to me. "You see, even a small bit of bad luck can snowball into a much larger problem until it grows large enough to ruin someone's life."

I resumed my efforts to ditch the sphere with renewed vigor. After several increasingly creative but unsuccessful attempts, Grandma benched me.

"I can't have you interacting with customers and poaching their luck," she said. "Until its owner reclaims this gizmo, you will have to stay away from the shop. And probably from people in general, if you want to avoid causing mayhem," she added, sadness in her voice.

"Maybe I should accidentally drop this into a river," I said. "Nash using it to steal people's luck has got to be at least as dangerous."

"It's okay for gnomes to use gnome magic," said Grandma. "It's in their nature to be mischievous. We should no sooner deny the gnome his ability than rob a leprechaun of his pot of gold." She sniffed. "Unless that leprechaun voluntarily pawns it, of course."

I nodded. "Well, what if—"

Grandma held up her hand. "At some point you have to learn to stop relying on shortcuts, Sylvia. They're flashy and they're fun, but they're never a substitute for hard, honest work. You will need to well and truly embrace that before you can take over the family business."

And just like that, my small run of good fortune was over. Because I loved the shop, and staying away from it for days or even weeks was just the worst. But the fact that Grandma felt I wasn't ready, felt I wasn't a hard enough worker—even after years of me putting the shop ahead of my studies and my personal life—really stung. Especially since I thought I was getting so close to convincing her of letting me handle more responsibility.

I suppose I could go to a vacation cabin the family had in the mountains, veg out in front of the TV and binge-watch *Doctor Who* until Nash was ready to reclaim his property. Then again, why not just return the luck machine to him early? I perked up at the thought. Sure, it was the only collateral against what he borrowed, but having thought about it some, I decided that I would personally cover the loan if he failed to repay the shop. Not getting stuck away from civilization for days was easily worth that much to me.

I got back in my car and drove to Nash's. The traffic lights kept turning green and I cursed under my breath each time, as the machine robbed bits of luck from other motorists to marginally improve my commute.

✿

"Not on your life," said Nash.

"I don't understand. I'm not asking for our money back; you can pay that as agreed. I simply want to return your luck machine to you early."

"No," Nash said and tried to slam the door, but I wedged my foot inside.

"Oh, come on! At least tell me why you don't want it back." This made no sense; Nash didn't strike me as the sort who would have any compunction about stealing bits of others' luck. "I can sense you pulled one over on me, but I'm not sure how."

As I suspected, appealing to his desire to brag got the job done. The door swung open and he motioned me in.

"You've got to hand it to us short people," he said. "Because we can't reach it ourselves, but also because we're much smarter than you super-sized apes. This is why Peter Dinklage is going to win that throne game thing, and also why I will always be several small steps ahead of the likes of you."

I let him gloat because eventually he'd just tell me what he was up to, like those incompetent villains who insisted on describing their plan to the hero in great detail. So I just stood there, trying very hard to look tall and stupid.

Nash didn't disappoint. He got right to spilling the beans. "This especially tall chief of security at my favorite private poker room seems to have taken an exception to my meager but steady winning streak," he said. "It cost me a full day's charge of luck, but I managed to get out of there without getting patted down. Of course, the *next* time I show my face around those parts, they will most definitely search me. And, as you have undoubtedly discovered, I can't exactly leave the luck machine at home."

"So I needed to transfer the machine's ownership to someone honest enough that I'd have no trouble getting it back after I convince those goons I'd been winning their cash on the up and up. And, well, you were it." He grinned. "I can't imagine why you would ever want to give it back anyhow, but you'll just have to enjoy its benefits for a week or so. After that, don't worry, I will gladly return the pittance I borrowed from your shop."

I felt my face turn red as I watched the self-satisfied gnome giggle with glee. "Why, you little scam artist! All this so you could continue to rip off your buddies at cards? That's totally unacceptable!"

"A deal is a deal. You agreed to it because you wanted to use the luck machine. And now you're trying to back out, like a typical tall person. Well, guess what. No takesies-backsies!"

"Come on, I'm sure we can—"

"No. Takesies. Backsies." Nash opened the door wide. "I'll be in touch when I'm ready. Until then, kindly leave my property. Good day to you." I tried to say something else, but he waved me off. "*Good day*, I say."

I stomped past his gaudy lawn decorations, angry enough that, were I a cartoon character, steam would definitely have been whistling out of my ears. The scoundrel had turned me into a low-powered version of a trickster god like Coyote or Loki or whoever convinced the world Kim Kardashian was a celebrity. I was going to make him regret it.

✿

The fairy casino was doing brisk business for a weekday afternoon.

I followed Nash here easily enough. The little degenerate gambler couldn't stay away, or perhaps was eager to prove to the pit bosses that he wasn't using a magical device to cheat at cards. The troll bouncer gave me an appraising look—not a lot of humans patronized this particular establishment—but he didn't challenge me on the way in. All manner of creatures milled about, gambling and drinking, seemingly not bothered by the incessant din of the slot machines.

I hung back and watched as Nash made his way into the poker room and settled at a table. He only bought a small stack of chips and sat down at a low-stakes table. Without his cheating aide he wasn't about to gamble big, I supposed.

Once Nash seemed properly entrenched, I approached the table and loomed over it: literally, as the table was set quite low to accommodate the players.

"A word, please," I told Nash.

The other players glared at me. There were a few gnomes, a pixie, and a duck I recognized from insurance commercials. TV work must not have paid very well if it chose to hang out at a $1/$2 limit table.

I pulled Nash a few feet away from the table, the mating call of the slot machines providing all the privacy our conversation would need.

"Take back the luck machine now, or else," I said.

Nash stared up at me. "Or else what?"

"I'll tell the pit bosses about your cheating ways."

"Go ahead. *I'm* not the one carrying an illegal luck enhancement device in the casino. Which one of us do you think will be in trouble?"

Since he called my bluff, I tried plan B. "I'll tell the other poker players then. Some of them look unsavory enough to be dangerous." I glanced at a mean-looking corpulent gnome in an expensive suit.

Nash followed by gaze. "I'll have you know Harold is a pediatrician, you tall racist." He put his hands on his hips. "This is not the crowd I play with when I use the luck machine. I do that in private poker rooms, with folks who can afford to lose big. And before you try seeking them out, the operative word here is *private*."

"Well…what if I just hang out at your table and leech your luck while you play. What do you think of that?!"

Nash shrugged. "Even I can't target who the machine borrows bits of luck from. If you think you can, go right ahead. The casino is packed and I like my odds." He snickered. "Give it up, Sylvia. Gnomes are much more devious than humans. You can keep trying to outwit me, but you'll always come up *short*!"

I couldn't stand to hear another short pun, so I walked away. Besides, something Nash said sparked another idea. I was going to need some supplies.

✿

I returned to Nash's street and hung out in my car listening to music and waited for Nash to re-

turn home from the casino. Waiting for him gave me plenty of time to reflect on what Grandma said. She was wrong about me not being a hard worker. I was never afraid to put in long hours, to sweep the floors and dust the artifacts in the back, even the ones that always tried to bite the mop. I'd work hard whenever I had to. But Grandma was also right about me liking shortcuts. I mean, what's wrong with that? Why work hard when you can work smart, and achieve a better result? Grandma had her way of doing things, and I had mine. I figured out how to beat Nash my way, and I wouldn't have to work very hard at all to do it.

Once Nash was back, I popped the trunk open and set up on the curb in front of his house. A few minutes later he ventured outside to investigate. He found me stretched out in a folding beach chair, with a Frappuccino in a cup holder and a tablet in my lap. He watched me tap and swipe at the screen. Finally, the curiosity got the better of him and he approached, peeking through the spaces in his white picket fence.

"What are you doing?"

"Oh, not much," I said, never taking my eyes off the screen. "I was recently given some time off work, so I figured I'd hang out here and play Candy Crush."

"You can't hang out here," Nash said.

"Sure I can," I said brightly. "I'm on a public street. Which just happens to be right next to your house, and since your machine tends to siphon off luck from whoever is nearby…" I smiled. "I'm on level 377, one of the toughest levels in the game. I could never pass it before, and I can only imagine how much extra luck I would need to do so now. Or where that luck would come from." I positioned myself so none of the neighboring houses were within the Luck Machine's limited reach. Nash would be the sole source of the luck I needed, and he knew it.

As if to underscore my point, the Big Boy lawn ornament emitted a loud cracking sound and the arm holding up the burger snapped off and fell to the ground, breaking into several pieces of plaster.

"No! Not my garden humans!" Nash rushed toward the smiling checkered mascot, then back to me, seemingly unable to decide what to do. "Stop this immediately!"

"Didn't think I would *stoop down to your level*, did you?" I smiled sweetly. "The fun stops when you take back the luck machine."

"I'll just leave," said Nash. "Then you won't be able to leech any luck off me."

"Sure, go ahead. I'll just read a book until you return. I literally have nothing better to do at the moment. Or maybe I'll come back late at night and play some electronic slots. Hope the house doesn't come down on your head while you sleep."

☼

I walked into the shop like a conquering hero: with a triumphant smile on my face, the check I wrote out to Nash earlier that day, and sans one clockwork sphere. I handed the check to Grandma. "I took care of it."

Grandma nodded. "That's excellent news. There's far too much work to do around here for you to go on vacation." She tried to make it sound gruff, but her eyes were smiling.

I grinned and stepped behind the counter. Without the help of the luck machine I might occasionally break a vial full of potion or miscount change, but I felt pretty lucky nevertheless. Anyone who has a job they love and family that loves them will tell you: that's worth a real fortune—and there's nothing small about it.

Copyright © 2018 by Alex Shvartsman

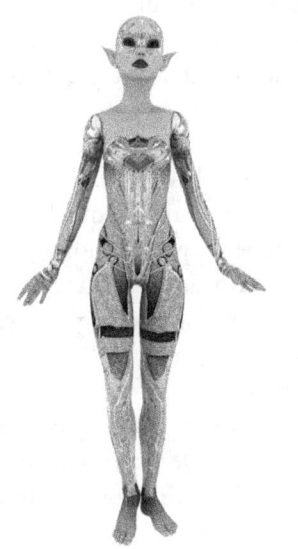

Jane Yolen is the most recent Nebula Grandmaster, as well as the winner of the World Fantasy Award for Life Achievement. She's also a two-time *Nebula winner, and—this is not a typo—the author of more than 370 books. This is her first appearance in* Galaxy's Edge. *We promise it won't be her last.*

SALVAGE

by Jane Yolen

The old poet lay in the bow of his ship, dying of space sickness and homesickness and a touch of alien flu. There was nothing to be done for him but to make him comfortable, which meant listening to his ramblings and filling his arm with a strange liquid from his own stores. He had been the only one left alive in the ship when we found it and at first we had thought him dead, too. Only at my touch, he had roused up, pointed a stalk at us, and recited in a bardic chant some alien click-clacks that, run through the translator, turned out to be a spell against goblins and ghoulies and things that go bump in the night.

Whatever night is.

Ghoulies was his name for us.

He had immediately fallen back into a deep sleep from which he roused periodically to harangue whoever had a free moment, calling us *worms* and *devils* and *satan's spawn*. Most of us decided to leave his mouthings untranslated since what spewed out of the machine made little sense and we had not time to properly salvage it. The boxes, after all, were not yet full.

But one of the younglings, a two-year named Necros 29, chose to sit with the poet-traveler and translate his every word. Necros 29 called it salvage, but l wondered. He comes from a family of puzzlers, though, and they are slow to mature and mate. It may be that that side of the line runs true, for it was he who first understood that the creature was a poet, or at least a speaker-of-poems. It was soon clear that the alien did not make up his poems as would any true poet, but rather carried the words of others in his head. Disgusting thought, a crime against nature, this salvage of the mind. If we saved up all our poems, our heads would soon be so crowded with them there would be no room left for savoring new ones. What a strange race we had come upon, whose equipment is new and whose thoughts are so borrowed and old.

But Necros, being a puzzler, kept at his task while we scavenged the ship thoroughly. It was full of salvage and the bones of the poet's companions were especially fine.

"He calls upon the names of many gods," commented Necros to me during report, "and that is fine for a poet. But he also says many not-found things."

"Such as?" I asked. My great-great-grandsire, Mordos Prime, had been a puzzler on his matriarchal side, though my mother denies it when asked. Occasionally I am drawn to such things, though basically I am of a solider nature.

"He speaks of night, a darkness that ends and comes again."

I passed the bones through my mouth and into the salvage sack before I spoke. They were, as I have said, very fine indeed. As the sack's teeth ground the bones into dust, I said, "Is night then a birthing cave? Is it the winking of far stars against the Oneness of space?"

Many who heard me laughed, their sections wiggling greatly with their amusement.

Necros shook his head and his eyestalks trembled. "I do not think so. But I will listen to him further. I think there may be some strong salvage in his thoughts."

"Pah, it is worthless stuff," remarked my old mate, the long cylinder of his head shaking. His salvage sack was full and grinding away, and the rolling action of it under his belly excited me. But now was the time of work, not pleasure. The boxes were not yet full and it would be days more of grinding before our organs descended enough to touch.

I went back across the boarding platform that linked the silent ship to ours. I emptied my sack of the fine silt, spreading it thinly over the mating box. Days! It would be weeks if we did not fill the boxes faster. As Prime of this ship it was my duty to direct young Necros away from the live poet to the dead and salvageable parts. It is all very well to salvage a culture when the boxes are full, but—and

I remembered my old mate's rolling sack—there is an order, after all, and poetry would have to wait.

Mouthing a small lump of "unground bone from "the box, I swallowed it again. Then I turned back and crossed over the platform to the alien ship.

"Necros!" I called out as I crawled. "Come. I would talk with you."

He came at once though with a slight reluctance on his face, his stalks drooping and his first section slightly faded. I think he already knew what I had to say.

"The boxes are thin," I said, "There is no time for him." I gestured with a stalk towards the alien who raised on one side and was babbling again.

"Fe-fi-fo-fum," spewed the translator. Nonsense in any language is still nonsense. "Be he live or be he dead, I'll grind his bones to make my bread."

"What in the universe is bread?" I asked.

Necros touched me, mouth in mouth, then raised his chin, showing me his neck section, the fine lumps of his heart beating a rhythm through the translucent skin. He could not have been more subservient.

"I will work long into the third work period," he said. "Do you not see that it is such things—bread, night, seasons—that we must salvage from him. *Only with salvage,*" he reminded me, *"is growth.*"

I thought of the silty boxes where we would soon lie down and mate, starting the next generation wiggling through our bodies and out our mouths. "Yes," I said at last, "you are right this time. But still you will have to work the extra period to make up for it."

He quivered sectionally and scurried back to the alien. At his touch, the alien fainted, though I suspected that he would revive again soon.

✿

Necros 29 kept his word. He worked the extra load, and so much salvage quickened him. He entered maturity early yet lost none of the enthusiasm of a youngling. It was dreadful to see.

Once he came to me wriggling with joy. "I have come to something new," he said. "Something notfound which is now found. It is called *haiku.*" He savored the word and gave it directly into my mouth.

I let the word slide down slowly, section by section, to my sack and the slow grinding begun. Then it stopped. "I do not comprehend this word *haiku*," I said. "It means no more than his fe-fi's."

Necros shivered deliciously. "It is a poem that is worked in sections," he said.

"A poem in sections?" It *was* a new idea—and quite fine.

"There are seventeen sections broken into bodies of five-seven-five. And there are rules."

"That is the first your poet has shown that he understands Order," I said thoughtfully. "Perhaps I was right to let you salvage him."

Necros nodded, showing his neck section for good measure. "These are the rules. First the poem must rouse emotion."

"Well, of course. Any youngling knows that." I turned partly away from him, to show my displeasure.

"Wait, there is more. Second, the poem must show spiritual insight." He nodded his head and his sections moved like a wave, enticing.

"Still, that is not new."

Necros drew out the last. "And finally there must be some use of the seasons."

"Fe-fi's again."

"I am comprehending that piece of alienness slowly. Digestion is difficult. The grinding continues."

"Perhaps," I replied coolly, "it should not continue."

"But I am working triple," Necros said, twisting his head back in such alarm that the lumps of heart were pounding madly in front of my mouth. "And we have salvaged all but the ship's shell and the room where the poet lies." His voice was strained by his effort to show me his chin.

"It is true that the boxes grow full and my desires descend," I admitted. "How long will this salvage take?"

He shrugged. "The poet's voice weakens. He speaks again and again of *the night*." He dared to lower his chin. "Night is, I am beginning to think, the ultimate alien season. Perhaps I will comprehend it soon."

"Perhaps you will," I said, turning without giving him any promises.

The next work section I was sleeping, with my body pressed along the sleek gray ship's side, dreaming of mating. I had grown so much with the salvage that I was now nearly half the length of the alien vessel, and my movements were slow.

Necros found me there and quivered in all his sections. I heard a deep grinding in his sack which he coyly kept from my sight.

"The poet is dead," he said, "and I have salvaged him. But before he died, I made up one of his own strange poems and sang it into the translator. He liked it. Listen, I too think it quite fine."

We all stopped our work to listen, raising our chins slightly. To listen well is of the highest priority. It is how one acknowledges order.

Necros recited:

The old poet fades,
Transfigured into the night,
Not-true becomes true.

"What do you think? Does it capture the alien? Is it true salvage?"

A small one-year shook his head. "I still do not know what *night* is."

"Look out beyond the ship," said Necros. "What is it you see?" "I see our great Oneness."

Necros nodded, letting ripples of pleasure run the entire length of his body. "Yes, that is what I thought, too. But I comprehend it is what he, the alien, would call *night*."

I smiled. "Then your poem should have said: *Transfigured into Oneness*."

Necros shivered deliciously and his sack began its melodious grinding again. "But they are the same, Oneness/Night. So Not-true becomes True. Surely you see that. Truly it is written that: *With salvage all becomes One*."

And indeed, finally, we all comprehend. It was fine salvage. The best. The hollow ship rang with our grinding.

"You shall share my box this section," I said.

But so full of his triumph, Necros did not at first realize the great honor I had bestowed upon him. He chattered away. "Next time I must try to use all the alien seasons in a poem. *Seasons*. I must think more about the word and digest it again, for I am not at all sure what it means. It has sections, though, like a beautiful body." And he blushed and looked at me. "They are called Winter, Spring, Summer, Fall."

I ran them into my mouth and agreed. "They are indeed meaty," I said. "Next time we meet such aliens we will all salvage their poems." Then I spoke the haiku back to him, once quickly before it was forgotten:

The old poet fades,
Transfigured into the night.
Not-true becomes true.

Smiling, I led the way back across the platform to the boxes, leaving the one-years who were not yet ready to mate to finish salvaging the ship's hull.

Copyright © by Jane Yolen, first published in Asimov's Science Fiction Magazine, *May 1984*

A. Merc Rustad's work has appeared in Lightspeed, Apex, Uncanny, Nightmare, Shimmer, *and others. This is their first appearance in* Galaxy's Edge.

YET SO VAIN IS MAN

A. Merc Rustad

To: D. Proust <Research Central, Earth>
From: M. van Harnon <Mars Facility>
Subject: Specimen #004

Mr. Proust,

The specimen found in the subterranean excavation site has been quarantined and prepped for further study. We have taken tissue and DNA samples, radiological readings, and have begun reconstruction in the observation chamber.

I disagree with the motion to send the specimen back to Earth, as we do not yet know the full hazard potential of an alien biological species.

Sincerely,

Dr. Misha van Harnon

– ◆ –

To: D. Proust <Research Central, Earth>
From: M. van Harnon <Mars Facility>
Subject: Specimen #004—Worrying Developments

Sir,

I must continue to object to the pressure from the government and research developers to transport the specimen off planet. Preliminary reports show that the body found in the so-called sarcophagus beneath Martian ground is not human yet shares distinct physiological resemblance to our species in broadest terms. Theories, of course, propagate that this may be the genetic forbearer of our evolutionary seed on Earth. DNA testing is in progress.

Still, given that we have as of yet not removed the specimen from quarantine, I do not believe it is safe to transport.

Dr. Misha van Harnon

– ◆ –

To: D. Proust <Research Central, Earth>
From: M. van Harnon <Mars Facility>
Subject: Outrage

Mr. Proust,

You are making a severe mistake, sir, you and the government and everyone else! Sending a platoon of marines to forcibly remove the specimen from my lab and transport it to Earth with no guarantees of the safety protocols is outrageous! Do you realize what will happen if that corpse contains biohazardous material? If it is an airborne contagion? We could be dooming our entire world—our species!—from corporate greed to be the "first" to claim ownership of a historical breakthrough in human evolution.

This is simply irresponsible, sir, and I am registering a formal complaint to the board.

Dr. Misha van Harnon

– ◆ –

To: D. Proust <Research Central, Earth>
From: M. van Harnon <Mars Facility>
Subject: Samples

Your soldiers did not, in fact, completely dismantle my workstation or my data. If you will not consider the ecological and moral possibilities of an unknown contagion from an extraterrestrial corpse, then I shall.

I've had the samples we took from Specimen #004 analyzed to begin cloning process to better study the potential here without damaging the original. I do this in effort to ready response or cure to any biological hazard your actions may unleash. With material to study and analyze, I hope I will be able to predict any contamination before it happens.

I am not going to apologize, David.

Dr. Misha van Harnon

– ◆ –

To: D. Proust <Research Central, Earth>
From: M. van Harnon <Mars Facility>
Subject: Shit

DESTROY THE SPECIMEN IMMEDIATELY.

I REPEAT, DESTROY IT.

– ◆ –

To: D. Proust <Research Central, Earth>
From: M. van Harnon <Mars Facility>
Subject: Mars

David,

I couldn't stop it.

The clone metastasized beyond anyone's wildest predictions. Within hours it had grown to gigantic proportions—fully seven feet in height, masculinized, like a statue from a Roman museum.

It slaughtered everyone in the lab—I'm in the panic wing, hoping you get this, hoping that you can destroy your specimen—the original—before the same happens on Earth.

(If you get this, will you tell Kathy goodbye? Screw the regulations, the classified statuses—all of it. Please. If you can: tell her.)

It's unstoppable and all it wants is carnage. It can speak, or at least, we can understand its communication, and Dr. Jessup's attempt to reason with it failed. (He's dead. Everyone is…dead.)

I don't know how the first one came to be here, frozen underground. Was it placed there by other, more intelligent beings? Was it supposed to be forgotten until our universe grows cold? We'll never know, I suppose, but I wish I had some answers beyond this knowledge I will be dead soon.

David, we found a god of war. And we cloned it. Now there's two of them—I despair of what will become on Earth.

With sincere apologies for my mistakes in this matter,

Dr. Misha van Harnon

Copyright © 2018 by A. Merc Rustad

Published by Phoenix Pick
Harcover, paperback and ebook

On sale now at your favorite store

Doug Dandridge is the author of twenty-three books, including a number of bestsellers. He is currently creating a new space opera/military sci-fi series for Phoenix Pick, and this story takes place in that universe.

PHOENIX PICK INTRODUCES

a new shared universe
www.KinshipWars.com

JOURNEY'S END

by Doug Dandridge

"Incoming message," said the voice of the bridge computer. "Incoming message."

Captain Azhar Talpur looked up from where he was sitting, at one of the configurable multi-stations on the small bridge. The tall, swarthy-skinned man ran a hand through his longish hair, wondering what information was coming their way, and where from. Coasting along through space at point-eight light speed was about as tedious as it got. Right now *any* news—even bad—would be more than welcome.

Things would get exciting enough in another seven months, when they would turn the *Behr* one hundred and eighty degrees and start the deceleration toward the target star. Two hundred and eighty-three days at one gravity—the same profile that had gotten them up to their coasting velocity—and they would be at their new home. Unfortunately, that was not now. *Now* was as boring as it got.

The captain looked at the message register and grunted, seeing that it was a warp pulse from the expanse ahead. That was unusual in itself as most messages for them came from Earth.

Talpur waited a moment for the rest of the message to arrive, not really expecting much. Warp pulse was the faster means of transmission—thousands of times that of light—but it could only transmit limited text information through a binary code. He suspected it would be a transmission from their future colony destination to Earth.

Lahore was a fairly new colony, sitting over fifty light-years from Earth. Two ships had made there it so far. With the boom of births all colonies experienced shortly after landing its population would be sitting at just over two hundred thousand people. The Pakistan Regional Authority had won the bid on the planet, one that was very friendly to Earth creatures. *Behr* was the third ship, and there were a half dozen behind her at five year intervals, each carrying their fifty thousand passengers in cryo.

The captain looked in disbelief as the message came up on the viewer. *By Allah, it can't be*, he thought. But there was no reason the colony would send such a message unless it was real.

LAHORE COLONY UNDER ATTACK
BY UNKNOWN ALIENS. DESTROYED.
MAY GOD HAVE MERCY ON US.

The message repeated, as it was supposed to, so anyone tuning in mid-transmission would hear it in its entirety in the follow-up transmissions. It was supposed to repeat for ten times per protocol. This one lasted for two, ending halfway through the third repetition. Not a good sign.

"All officers to bridge," said the captain, stress straining his voice. He had been young when they had left the Earth, and now was middle aged, looking forward to the normalcy of again living on a planet.

The entire trip took sixty-six Earth years. Due to relativity, time was thirty-nine years. For the fifty-thousand colonists in cryo it made no difference. For the two duty crews who alternated spending half the trip asleep, the other half manning the ship, it cut their awake time down to nineteen and a half years. The captain had been twenty-five on leaving Earth, sleeping through the first half of the trip. He was now forty-four, not that old for people in this age, able to still live seventy or more productive years.

The first through the hatch was the engineer, Nadeem Sarpara. The expression on his face showed that he had seen the message, the shaking of his head indicated he still didn't quite believe it. Dr. Mehmood Kahloon followed him by about a minute, breathing heavy as he moved through the pseudogravity of the spinning colony drum.

"Have we heard anything else?" asked Kahloon, throwing himself into a chair and pulling up another console. The bridge was alive with screens, holos, lit panels, the ship itself monitoring all systems and presenting the results for anyone interested.

"No, doctor," the captain replied. "All we've gotten is the same message repeating over and over again before cutting off. And if they're under attack I really don't think we're going to get any more messages."

"That is not good."

Before the captain could respond Saira Patel came through the hatchway, putting her long black hair up in a band. Her official title was second officer, but she was the acting exec since the first officer had served as captain on the first half of the voyage. Her unofficial title was spouse to the captain, and the expression on her face showed that she had already been mulling over the message's implications on the way to the bridge.

Khurshid Sarpara, the assistant engineer, was the last to come into the chamber, immediately taking a seat at the table and leaning forward, her eyes wide. "Anyone know what's going on?"

"Only what the message says," said Talpur. "Incredible as it sounds, if the message is authentic, the colony is being attacked."

"No more messages?" asked Khurshid. "Should we start decel to halt the vessel till we figure this out?"

"So that's your idea of a good plan?" asked Patel, leaving her position on the wall and throwing herself into the chair across from the assistant engineer. "Just put us adrift in space?"

"We can wait till we hear more from them or get some indication that it's safe," said Khurshid in a frustrated tone, shrugging her shoulders as she looked at the other woman as if to say, *What else are we going to do?*

"And if they aren't able to take back the system?" asked Nadeem after throwing a questioning glance at the captain, as if to ask, *Why me?*

"Earth would have to take back the system," said the assistant engineer, throwing her hands up in the air. "They wouldn't let someone—some*thing*—take one of their colonies."

The captain returned the glance of his chief engineer. He really couldn't blame the assistant engineer for her optimistic outlook. There had not been a real war in human space for centuries.

"If this is a war with aliens we have no idea what will happen," said Talpur, turning to look into the unbelieving eyes of Khurshid. "Or that Earth will take the system back. And if we decel to a stop outside the system, we're at the mercy of whoever finds us—if anyone does."

"What do you propose?" asked Nadeem, leaning forward again, elbows on the table.

"I don't propose anything for now," said the captain, eyes narrowing. "What I want to do is to look at the possibilities. How long until we have to start deceleration? Seven months, ship's time?"

"About that," agreed the ship's engineer, closing his eyes for a moment, going through calculations in his head. "About four hundred and ninety-three days absolute."

So then it was two hundred and eighty-three days absolute to decelerate down. If they had been hitting the system, they would have deceled for two hundred and eighty days, then coasted into the system, adjusting course to their target world and burning off the rest of their velocity on the way.

"And how much fuel will we have left if we go for full burn to stop?"

"Enough for eighty gee hours," said the chief engineer. "Not enough to choose a different destination. We could change our trajectory, but there's no way we would have enough fuel to slow down to insert into any kind of orbit."

"How about dropping some of our mass?" asked Patel, brow furrowed in thought. "That would give us some more hours of thrust."

The chief engineer shook his head. "Ninety-two percent of our mass is reactors, acceleration tubes, supporting members, and fuel, all needed for boosting. The only mass not needed for operating the ship is the area we are occupying now, and the colony support module behind us. We could kick out all of the vehicles and supplies in the colony module, then start cutting it apart."

"We're going to need that if we try to establish ourselves on a new world," said Doctor Kahloon, scowling. "And don't even think about taking the colonists out of cryo so we can push the chambers out. We don't have enough resources on board to support them through years of travel."

"Shit," said Talpur. Messing with the cryo chambers was not something that was recommended on a voyage. There was a small risk of neurological damage going in and out of cold sleep. It increased tenfold with a second immersion and increased exponentially with every reiteration; one reason why the working crew only went in once, the first shift taking the initial half of the voyage, the prime crew the second. They were given incentives when they got to the colony, like prime real estate and positions in the hierarchy to pay for the years they had wasted in transit.

"Okay. What else is a possibility?" asked the captain. No one said a word.

"Well, we've got some time, just not too much," Talpur muttered through gritted teeth. "Everyone, think. Look over the ship's library. Dammit, we've got the sum total scientific knowledge of the human species in our data banks. There has to be an answer there. So get to it."

In a little over seven months ship's time, it will be too late to do anything, he thought, feeling as helpless as he ever had.

☼

Talpur sat in the command chair on the bridge, not a place he normally spent much time, looking at the viewer that was presenting an image of the space ahead, the G-class star that was their target directly centered. What had been their hope, now perhaps their doom. Something was waiting there, maybe not knowing that they were coming, but sure to be able to overpower them when they did appear.

They had tried contacting the colony again and again, but failed.

If this was an invading force, they have to be using Alc drives, thought the captain. *Otherwise, they wouldn't have been able to invade, would they?* Slower than light ships made invasion impracticable, one reason Earth hadn't tried to reclaim their revolting colonies.

Behr was the largest class of human vessel ever put into space, equal to the other hundred-odd colony ships plying the space lanes on one-way voyages between Earth and the new worlds. She had the most powerful reactors in space, capable of producing almost limitless electrical power, useful for running the high-powered ion drive. And while not a warship, she was armed, with a dozen strategically placed gigawatt class lasers and even a couple missile accelerator tubes. Only an idiot sent out a ship with so many people aboard without some kind of defense.

However, if Alcubierre drive warships were waiting, with their almost impenetrable Alc bubbles and torpedoes that could laugh at their defensive lasers. Well, they would be dead meat when they arrived.

There has to be something we can do, he thought, clenching his fists in frustration. Right now, the choices were to decelerate into their target system and risk being blown out of space or boarded.

Or they could boost onto another course, and a new promising system, but if they used their fuel for the course change they just didn't have enough to decel again; they would continue on through space forever. The colonists would stay in cryo until the ship ran out of fuel for the reactors. That could be thousands of years.

They could possibly gather enough hydrogen from space with a magnetic field to keep going for further millennia. But that thought seemed even more depressing. The colonists would never know that time had passed, eventually dying as their cryo chambers failed.

Earth might have the answer, but they were too far away to be of any help. Or even to communicate with in time. It might be better if they just went on their chartered course and got it over with.

How about we set up a Bussard and capture more fuel, was his next thought, then quickly dismissed. It had been proven centuries ago that the interstellar medium was to diffuse for a Bussard ramjet to actually work. *Maybe we can gather enough to stretch the fuel we already have?*

He calculated the figures out in his head, then ran them through the ship's computer, and both results were disappointing. They would still become a ghost ship, floating forever through the Galaxy, or crashing into something when they couldn't decelerate enough to get into any kind of orbit.

"I thought I would find you here," said a familiar voice behind him.

Talpur smiled as he turned his seat, taking in the image of the person he loved most in the Universe. Saira Patel, the woman he had married before launch, came walking onto the bridge and moved to a seat at one of the stations. He still thought her the most beautiful woman he had ever seen.

"Still trying to come up with something?"

"I can't think of anything else to take up my time, my love."

Saira sat there silent for a moment, looking at Talpur, then turning to take in the view of the Universe. She sighed. "It's so beautiful. But now I find myself wishing that we had stayed on Earth. Or maybe just moved to Mars."

"I had to get out of that place," growled Talpur, shaking his head. His could still see the images of Pakistan in his mind. There was still some natural beauty there, the snowcapped peaks of the most awesome mountains on the planet, but in most ways it was just like the rest of Earth. With too many of the twenty-eight billion humans crowding the surface. "I needed room to move, to breath. And Mars is going to become another Earth soon enough. I wanted our children to have a better future than that."

"Now it's looking like we might not have children," said Saira, closing her eyes for a moment.

Talpur knew that his wife wanted a family. If they were still heading to the colony—and that was a big if—they would be older when they arrived, but still capable of having children.

"I've been thinking about how we might use this ship to slow us down without taxing our resources, so we can travel farther, go elsewhere," said Talpur, looking back at the viewer and the image that represented the beauty of God's Universe. "I keep coming back to the idea that we have the ability to produce terawatts of power. There has to be some way to use that to slow us. If we could slow down, we have options."

"I don't see how," replied Saira, shaking her head. "We need mass to accelerate and decelerate. Without it, we really can't do anything." She sat there, silent for a moment, obviously thinking, and Talpur let her have her time. She was a better physicist than he was. The only reason he had command was because of his background in the Earth Defense Force.

"I've thought that maybe we could start dismantling the ship around us," she finally said. "If we were still going to a world that was already made ready for us, I think that would work. But we're going to need everything we have aboard if we're to start a new colony."

"I've thought of that too," said the captain, looking back at the screen that was showing the latest search results. "And I keep coming back to the idea of all of that energy. Isn't there some way we can use it without throwing mass around?"

"Not that I can think of," said the woman.

And if you can't think of anything, and neither can any of the others, what hope is there? We need a lifeline. Something in the word lifeline struck a chord with the captain, and an idea formed in his mind.

"Wait a second," he cried out, startling his wife. "That might be it."

"What?"

"How much superconducting cable do we have onboard? And I don't mean what we use in the drive and power systems. What do we have in the colonizing systems?"

"Probably a couple of hundred kilometers in all."

"Not enough," growled Talpur through clenched teeth.

"Why?" said Saira, standing and walking over to stand over his shoulder and look at the screen. "What the hell is that?"

"If we can get it to work, maybe our salvation."

☼

"Yeah. I think we can make this work," said Nadeem, looking over at Khurshid and getting a nod in return. "It's going to take a lot of work. And we'll need to put it all back together before we get to our new destination world."

Everyone at the table looked at the globe spinning in the holo. Another beautiful world. Maybe a little more desert than their original hoped-for home. More primitive life forms, and no people. It had been surveyed, but it was so far out that its turn hadn't come for colonization.

"I'm against it," said Kahloon, shaking his head. "Our people had their hearts set on this world and living with their own. I don't think we can just arbitrarily change the plans for everyone in this ship. Don't they have a vote?"

"Doctor," said an exasperated Talpur, his eyes narrowing as he looked at the man, the only one among them not trained as a spacer. "This is not an arbitrary decision. Only disaster waits us if we continue in, and we need to make a decision soon."

"And how do we know it's a disaster?" argued the physician. "I don't believe God would allow our colony to fail. I have faith that we will succeed."

The captain stared at the doctor in disbelief. He too believed in God, but he was enough of a scientist to compartmentalize his faith from his knowledge of the facts of the Universe.

"The colony has *already* been destroyed, as the mayday message stated. I have made the decision," said Talpur.

"And I support his decision," said Saira, looking at the other two members of the ready crew. "How about you two?"

"You are just supporting him because he is your husband."

"And if I thought he was wrong, it wouldn't matter what he said," said Saira in an angry tone. "I would advise him he was wrong. Don't question my sincerity, doctor. Or my ability to perform my job."

"I have to agree with the captain," said Nadeem, looking over at Khurshid, his wife.

"And what about our passengers?" asked the physician again. "Don't they get a vote?"

"It doesn't work that way, doctor," growled the captain. "This is a ship, I am the captain. I don't even have to ask any of you for your opinion." While that was true, Talpur was very thankful that the three ship handlers along with him had agreed. If not, he could be facing a mutiny. But his wife and the engineering couple were realists.

"I could declare you incompetent," said Kahloon, not willing to let it be.

"And who would take my place?" asked the captain, shaking his head. "These others stand with me. And you are not qualified to captain this vessel."

"Plus, none of us will listen to your nonsense," said Khurshid with a cold smile. "I don't even know why we are having this conversation. We know what we need to do, so let's work together to do it."

Something appeared in the doctor's eyes—some idea forming in his mind. Something that the captain noted.

"And doctor," said Talpur, reaching across the table and grabbing the man's forearm before he could stand. "You will wake none of the colonists to try to get allies. That is a direct order. If you disobey, I will have you placed in cryo."

The eyes of the physician grew wide. He had already been in cryo for the first half of the journey, and another stint increased the chances of brain damage by an order of magnitude.

"I would just send you out an airlock, Mehmood," said Saira, staring straight into his eyes. "Such an action would be mutiny, and that can be punished with death."

The doctor shook as he got to his feet. His face had paled in fright. Talpur didn't trust him, and as soon as Kahloon left the room he spoke to the others.

"Keep an eye on him. I don't trust him at all." He switched his attention back to the most important matter at hand. "How much of a burn do you think we need?"

"Approximately one hundred and sixty-nine hours," said Saira with a smile.

"So just a tiny bit over a week."

"And the sooner we do it, the less energy we will have to use," said Khurshid, nodding at Saira.

"Then let's get to it."

☼

Talpur really didn't like excursions beyond the hull. But with four of them, and the need to have one remain aboard in the event of an emergency, he had to take his turn. So here he was, in a hard suit, an armored spacesuit that protected him from most radiation.

"Okay. I've got the cover off of this section," he reported over the com. He looked for a second at the glory of space around him, the stars distorted by the relativistic effects of the ship's travel. He closed his eyes for a moment and set his concentration back on the task at hand. Robots were doing the actual work. He was just there to supervise. The insect-like devices had multiple tools at the end of each of their ten limbs, and a dozen of them were working detaching and removing the long strand of superconducting cable. The cable ran from the front of the reactor section forty kilometers to the rear of the accelerator tube that sent their ions out at point-nine light speed.

They had taken all of the superconducting cables out of the vehicles and equipment from the colony module. And it wasn't enough by even a tenth of their needs. So they had been forced to pull the long superconducting cables from the five accelerator tubes. A process that would take several weeks. And then months to set the sail, and another couple of weeks to put the cable back in place, so the accelerator tubes could again start them decelerating. All of this effort, just to get rid of an eighth of their velocity, and it would take several years to get down to that velocity.

"We're picking up a lot of scatter ahead on radar," said Khurshid over the com, her voice tense. "We should be hitting that density in about nine minutes. Maybe all of you should come inside for a little while."

"That sounds like a good idea," said Talpur, halting the robots in place before they could pull any more of the cable out of the tube.

"I've almost got my section out," said Saira, working on another tube. "Give me another couple of minutes."

"Don't take more than a minute," said Talpur, turning his own pod and heading back up the ship. "I want you back inside in five minutes."

"Will do."

The captain's pod sped along the outside of the ship, boosting himself with the thrusters up to just over a hundred and sixty meters a second, five hundred and ninety kilometers an hour relative to the ship's own speed. The bulk of the ship shot by, the pod keeping itself at a safe distance. The captain still felt a thrill when he looked at the enormous size of the ship. The Alc ships, with their ability to warp space and out speed light, were considered the ultimate in space faring technology. But there was a certain elegance to this dinosaur, which was still the cheapest way to send a large number of people to another star. And energy was still the scarcest resource in interstellar space.

"It looks like a concentration of gas ahead, and there might be some large particles within it."

The captain frowned. "Can we go around it?" If it was a narrow cloud they might be able to do a couple of short burns that wouldn't use too much fuel.

"Not a chance," said the assistant engineer. "It's too wide."

It was worth a thought. He was almost to the opening. Even though the ship was coasting at point-eight light, to his perspective it was standing still. In a moment he was through the pod hatch and as safe as he could be in the ship. The clock had ticked off four minutes, which gave his wife one minute to get here. He checked up on her and cursed under his breath when he saw that she had just started off for safety, which meant she would take at least three and a half minutes to get to him. Not enough of a margin.

I'm worrying about nothing, he thought, telling himself that even if they went through the cloud, the odds were still against anything bad happening. But she was his wife, and it was part of his nature to worry about her, just as she worried about him.

"I'm having a problem here," said Saira over the com. "My thrusters just went offline."

"Any way you can get them working?" asked Khurshid, worry in her voice.

"Not unless I go outside the pod."

Without thrusters she wouldn't be able to decel before she got to the hatch: she would shoot past.

"I'm going back out to get her," he said, starting the pod back through the hatch.

"Don't," said Saira in a hushed voice. "Don't put yourself at risk too."

"Shut up and get ready for me to grab you. Don't argue. I'm coming."

No one else came on the com. The engineers knew better than to argue with either of them.

Talpur turned the pod in space and started accelerating. He needed to build up to a greater velocity than her pod, pass her, then decelerate and match velocities, catching her craft in the waldos of his own. Not a difficult maneuver, but with a gas field approaching, one that was very anxiety provoking. It was possible that either or both of them could be killed if he made a slight miscalculation, and he hoped that if only one could make it, she would be

the one. Since her ship wasn't working that was an unlikely outcome.

"I've got you on radar," he cried as the blip of her pod appeared, right after he cleared the front of the ship.

The pod looked like it was drifting ahead, even though it was speeding along at relativistic speed. His was leisurely following, at least from their perspective.

"We're hitting the gas cloud in two minutes," called out Nadeem, getting on the com.

"Turn around, my husband. There's no use in both of us risking death out here."

"No one's dying," he said, pushing another burst of acceleration as he said a silent prayer. His ship shot past hers, and he turned it quickly on its attitude thrusters, then hit the panel that let the pod's AI take over to match velocities and bring them together. The pod kicked in a couple of gees of thrust, pushing him back in his seat. He was concerned for a moment that the computer might not be able to handle the maneuver, but it went through the evolution perfectly, and his pod touched hers with barely a bump. The waldos of his pod grabbed hers, and they were locked.

"Here we go," he told his wife, manually taking over the piloting so he could get some more gees out than the AI was likely to allow. Four gravities, the most the craft could do, pushed him back in his seat, and Saira cried out for a moment as it hit her. The only gravity they had endured for the last decade of ship's time was the one third put on by the spin of the habitation section, and that only near the outer hull.

"It's here," announced Khurshid on the com, just an instant before the radiation detectors went off, filling the small cockpit with flashing lights and screaming alarms.

Talpur quickly checked the readings, breathing a sigh of relief. The hydrogen and larger molecules in the cloud were sleeting into his pod, a storm of radiation, but the magnetic field of the craft was handling most of it. Some was getting through, invisible particles that were hitting atoms in his cells and breaking them apart. Neutral particles, neutron and uncharged molecules. Worrisome if they were out here long enough, which wasn't the plan. And his own pod was shielding Saira's.

Nearing the point of entry he switched the AI back on and let the pod handle the decel and insertion, something it could do better than he. That meant putting Saira's pod to the front of his, but it shouldn't last long enough to matter.

"What?" cried out his wife as a long *clang* came over the com. "My hull's been pierced."

Talpur felt his heart race at the thought of the interior of her craft open to space. "How's your suit?"

"It seems to be fine. The pod is leaking atmosphere, but it won't make any difference."

Talpur told himself to remain calm. That was the reason they went out in the hardsuits and not in shipboard clothing or soft spacesuits. It had seemed like overkill to most of his people, but now he was glad he had stuck to his orders.

The AI had pushed them into the hangar, where they settled onto the outer skin that was the deck of the spinning structure. He was out of his pod as soon as it latched onto the deck, pulling open his wife's hatch and grabbing her suit, pulling her into a hug and wishing that they didn't have the suits between them.

"Don't you ever wait again," he said, keeping his voice measured when he felt like yelling. "Never. If I tell you to come now, you come."

"Yes, Talpur," said Saira, looking down at the deck. "It won't happen again."

"This isn't something I'm telling you as your husband, but as your commanding officer. Don't think I'm going to put up with your insubordination."

Saira didn't say a word, and Talpur was sure she would wait for him to calm down.

"Now, we need to get you to medical and check you out."

"You too," she said with a slight smile. "And thanks."

"We're in the middle of the storm," said Khurshid over the com. "Sensors on the bow are off the scale. But the shielding is holding up."

Now, let's get through this thing, and then the rest is easy as pie. He scoffed as he thought that. Getting the superconducting cable out was the easy part. The second stage would be the most work, more than he wanted to think of.

✿

"I've always wanted to sail to the stars," said Saira, settling on his lap, drink in hand.

Talpur nodded as he looked at his wife, then turned his attention to the viewer.

It was a beautiful sight. A glowing web radiated out from the ship in all directions, forming a disc. Eight superconducting cables, each spliced to reach out a hundred kilometers, with other cables linking them. A fine mesh covered the entire construct, a microfine polymer. It didn't glow from its own power, but from the tons of charged particles it first attracted, then sped up to the front, in the process slowing the huge ship. It wasn't much thrust, less than a hundredth of a gravity. But it was enough to take a twentieth of light speed off of their velocity, given just under twenty years. Relativity would shave some of that time off, but the effect would be decreasing as they slowed.

"You realize we're going to be very old people by the time we get to the new home," said Talpur, putting his arms around her.

Saira stared at the viewer, silent.

"I'm sorry," Talpur blurted quickly. "I wasn't thinking."

Saira nodded, tears in her eyes. She would not grow very old. She would be here for at most another twenty-five years. The radiation had gotten through her pod, infiltrating by way of the rip in the skin. They would be able to keep the cancers at bay with nanites, for a time, but eventually they would take her from him. And she would not have the children she—they—had wanted.

The captain nodded, trying to convince himself it wasn't important whether they had a family or not. What was important was that fifty thousand colonists would have that chance.

"In twenty years we'll have to put the ship back together again," he said, changing the subject. "Don't think you are getting out of that duty, my second."

"Spoilsport," she said after a short sniffle, rubbing the tears from her eyes. "I'm just going to enjoy our cruise and worry about that backbreaking labor when it comes."

He smiled. There were a lot of things they wouldn't need to worry about over the years, and some things for which they could do nothing. They had sent a message by AI com to Earth, so they would know where the ship was heading. Hopefully the Earth would meet the threat of whatever aliens who had destroyed their first colony planet, causing them to change course. Hopefully they would send out the faster-than-light ships to protect their other colonies. If they didn't, if the aliens attacked the other human settlements—or even worse, reached Earth—this ship might be the last vestige of humanity in the Universe.

But those were things the captain and his people couldn't do anything about. What they would have to do was put the ion drive accelerator tubes back together and decelerate the rest of the trip in the old manner. Then they would have the reach to get to a new colony and build a new home.

Talpur looked at his wife, sitting on his lap, staring at the viewer. She wouldn't be there with him.

But maybe…

I refuse to lose you, he thought, closing his eyes and blinking back his own tears. They had the medical technology and the unfertilized eggs in storage, to help the population explosion needed for a new colony to thrive. He could transplant her genetic material into one of those eggs and bring it to term in an artificial womb. It wouldn't be her, not exactly. But it would be her down to the cellular level. He would have her back. His heart constricted at the thought of losing his love. But then it fluttered in hope. He would raise the clone to be the same woman. Or as near as he could get. They could have the children his wife had wanted. It would be honoring her wishes, if anything, to have a family.

Talpur put his arms around his wife and sat there with her, looking out at the stars that had been their hope. He considered telling Saira his plans, but then balked. He knew she would say she had had a wonderful life with him; that when her time came, she would be ready.

But he wasn't.

So he would treasure Saira for as long as he had her, silently buoyed by thoughts of a second life and new hopes as he considered the years to come.

Copyright © 2018 by Doug Dandridge

For more information on this shared universe (including upcoming novels and projects) please visit **www.KinshipWars.com**

Kristine Kathryn Rusch has won the Hugo as both a writer and an editor, and was recently nominated for a Shamus for Best Private Eye Novel.

SOLE SURVIVOR

by Kristine Kathryn Rusch

Takara Hamasaki crouched behind the half-open door, her heart pounding. She stared into the corridor, saw more boots go by. Good god, they made such a horrible thudding noise.

Her mouth tasted of metal, and her eyes stung. The environmental system had to be compromised. Which didn't surprise her, given the explosion that happened not three minutes ago.

The entire starbase rocked from it. The explosion had to have been huge. The base's exterior was compensating—that had come through her desk just before she left—but she didn't know how long it would compensate.

That wasn't true; she knew it could compensate forever if nothing else went wrong. But she had a hunch a lot of other things would go wrong. Terribly wrong.

She'd had that feeling for months now. It had grown daily, until she woke up every morning, wondering why the hell she hadn't left yet.

Three weeks ago, she had started stocking her tiny ship, the crap-ass thing that had brought her here half her life ago. She would have left then, except for one thing:

She had no money.

Yeah, she had a job, and yeah, she got paid, but it cost a small fortune to live this far out. The base was in the middle of nowhere, barely in what the Earth Alliance called the Frontier, and a week's food alone cost as much as her rent in the last Alliance place she had stayed. She got paid well, but every single bit of that money went back into living.

Dammit. She should have started sleeping in her ship. She'd been thinking of it, letting the one-room apartment go, but she kinda liked the privacy, and she really liked the amenities—entertainment on demand, a bed that wrapped itself around her and helped her sleep, and a view of the entire public district from above.

She liked to think it was that view that kept her in the apartment, but if she were honest with herself, it was that view and the bed and the entertainment, maybe not in that order.

And she was cursing herself now.

When the men—they were all men—wearing boots and weird uniforms marched toward the center of the base. Thousands of people lived or stayed here, but there wasn't much security. Not enough to deal with those men. She would hear that drumbeat of their stupid boots in her sleep for the rest of her life.

If the rest of her life wasn't measured in hours. If she ever got a chance to sleep again.

Her traitorous heart was beating in time to those boots. She was breathing through her mouth, hating the taste of the air.

If nothing else, she had to get out of here just to get some good clean oxygen. She had no idea what was causing that burned-rubber stench, but something was, and it was getting worse.

More boots stomped by, and she realized she couldn't tell the difference between the sound of those that had already passed her and those that were coming up the corridor.

She only had fifty meters to go to get to the docking ring, but that fifty meters seemed like a light-year.

And she wouldn't even be here, if it weren't for her damn survival instinct. She had looked up—before the explosion—and saw twenty blond-haired men, all of whom looked like twins. Ten twins—two sets of decaplets?—she had no idea what twenty identical people, the same age, and clearly monozygotic, were called. She supposed there was some name for them, but she wasn't sure. And, as usual, her brain was busy solving that, instead of trying to save her own single individual untwinned life.

She had scurried through the starbase, utterly terrified. The moment she saw those men enter the base, she left her office through the service corridors. When that seemed too dangerous, she crawled through the bot holes. Thank the universe she was tiny. She usually hated the fact that she was the size of an eleven-year-old girl, and didn't quite weigh a hundred pounds.

At this moment, she figured her tiny size might just save her life.

That, and her prodigious brain. If she could keep it focused instead of letting it skitter away.

Twenty identical men—and that wasn't the worst of it. They looked like younger versions of the creepy pale guys who had come into the office six months ago, looking for ships. They wanted to know the best place to buy ships in the starbase.

There was no place to buy new ships on the starbase. There were only old and abandoned ships. Fortunately, she had managed to prevent the sale of hers a year ago. She'd illegally gone into the records and changed her ship's status from delinquent to paid in full, and then she had made that paid-in-full thing repeat every year. (She'd check it, of course, but it hadn't failed her, and now it didn't matter. Nothing mattered except getting off this damn base.)

Still those old creepy guys had gotten the names of some good dealers on some nearby satellites and moons, and had left—she thought forever—but they had come back with a scary fast ship and lots of determination.

And, it seemed, lots of younger versions of themselves.

(Clones. What if they were clones? What did that mean?)

The drumbeat of their stupid boots had faded. She scurried into the corridor, then heard a high-pitched male scream, and a thud.

Her heart picked up its own rhythm—faster, so fast, in fact that it felt like her heart was trying to get to the ship before she did.

She slammed herself against the corridor wall, felt it give (cheapass base) and caught herself before she fell inward on some unattached panel coupling.

She looked both ways, saw nothing, looked up, didn't see any movement in the cameras—which the base insisted on keeping obvious so that all kinds of criminals would show up here. If the criminals knew where the monitors were, they felt safe weirdly enough.

And this base needed criminals. This far outside of the Alliance, the only humans with money were the ones who had stolen it—either illegally or legally through some kind of enterprise that was allowed out here, but not inside the Alliance.

And this place catered to humans. It accepted non-human visitors, but no one here wanted them to stay. In the non-Earth atmosphere sections, the cameras weren't obvious.

She thanked whatever deity was this far outside of the Alliance that she hadn't been near the alien wing when the twenty creepy guys arrived and started marching in.

And then her brain offered up some stupid math it had been working on while she was trying to save her own worthless life.

She'd seen more than forty boots stomp past her.

That group of twenty lookalikes had only been the first wave.

Another scream and a thud. Then a woman's voice: *No! No! I'll do whatever you want. I'll—*

And the voice just stopped. No thud, no nothing. Just silence.

Takara swallowed hard. That metallic taste made her want to retch, but she didn't. She didn't have time for it. She could puke all she wanted when she got on that ship, and got the hell away from here.

She levered herself off the wall, wondering in that moment how long the gravity would remain on if the environmental system melted. Her nose itched— that damn smell—and she wiped the sleeve of her too-thin blouse over it.

She should have dressed better that morning. Not for work, but for escape. Stupid desk job. It made her feel so important. An administrator at twenty-five. She should have questioned it.

She should have questioned so many things.

Like the creepy older guys who looked like the baked and fried versions of the men in boots, stomping down the corridors, killing people.

She blinked, wondered if her eyes were tearing because of the smell or because of her panic, then voted for the smell. The air in the corridor had a bit of white to it, like smoke or something worse, a leaking environment from the alien section.

She was torn between running and tip-toeing her way through the remaining forty-seven meters. She opted for a kind of jog-walk, that way her heels didn't slap the floor like those boots stomped it.

Another scream, farther away, and the clear sound of begging, although she didn't recognize the language. Human anyway, or something that spoke like a human and screamed like a human.

Why were these matching people stalking the halls killing everyone they saw? Were they trying to take over the base? If so, why not come to her office? Hers was the first one in the administrative wing, showing her lower-level status—in charge, but not in charge.

In charge enough to see that the base's exterior was compensating for having a hole blown in it. In charge enough to know how powerful an explosion had to be to break through the shield that protected the base against asteroids and out-of-control ships and anything else that bounced off the thick layers of protection.

A bend in the corridor. Her eyes dripped, her nose dripped, and her throat felt like it was burning up.

She couldn't see as clearly as she wanted to—no pure white smoke any more, some nasty brown stuff mixed in, and a bit of black.

She pulled off her blouse and put it over her face like a mask, wished she had her environmental suit, wished she knew where she could steal one *right now*, and then sprinted toward the docking ring.

If she kept walk-jogging, she'd never get there before the oxygen left the area.

Then something else shook the entire base. Like it had earlier. Another damn explosion.

She whimpered, rounded the last corner, saw the docking ring doors—closed.

She cursed (although she wasn't sure if she did it out loud or just in her head) and hoped to that ever-present unknown deity that her access code still worked.

The minute those doors slid open, the matching marching murderers would know she was here. Or rather, that someone was here.

They'd come for her. They'd make her scream.

But she'd be damned if she begged.

She hadn't begged ever, not when her dad beat her within an inch of her life, not when she got accused of stealing from that high-class school her mother had warehoused her in, not when her credit got cut off as she fled to the outer reaches of the Alliance.

She hadn't begged no matter what situation she was in, and she wouldn't now. It was a point of pride. It might be the last point of pride, hell, it might mark her last victory just before she died, but it would be a victory nonetheless, and it would be *hers*.

Takara slammed her hand against the identiscanner, then punched in a code, because otherwise she'd have to use her links, and she wasn't turning them back on, maybe ever, because she didn't want those crazy matching idiots to not only find her, but find her entire life, stored in the personal memory attached to her private access numbers.

The docking ring doors irised open, and actual air hit her. Real oxygen without the stupid smoky stuff, good enough to make her leap through the doors. Then she turned around and closed them.

She scanned the area, saw feet—not in boots—attached to motionless legs, attached to bleeding bodies, attached to people she knew, and she just shut it all off, because if she saw them as friends or co-workers or hell, other human beings, she wouldn't be able to run past them, wouldn't be able to get to her ship, wouldn't get the hell out of here.

She kept her shirt against her face, just in case, but her eyes were clearing. The air here looked like air, but it smelled like a latrine. Death—fast death, recent death. She'd used it for entertainment, watched it, read about it, stepped inside it virtually, but she'd never experienced it. Not really, not like this.

Her ship, the far end of this ring, the cheap area, where the base bent downward and would have brushed the top of some bigger ship, something that actually had speed and firepower and *worth*.

Then she mentally corrected herself: her ship had worth. It would get her out of this death trap. She would escape before one of those tall blond booted men found her. She would—

—she flew forward, landed on her belly, her elbow scraping against the metal walkway, air leaving her body. Her shirt went somewhere, her chin banged on the floor, and then the sound—a whoop-whamp, followed by a sustained series of crashes.

Something was collapsing, or maybe one of the explosions was near her, or she had no damn idea, she just knew she had to get out, get out, get out—

She pushed herself to her feet, her knees sore too, her pants torn, her stomach burning, but she didn't look down because the feel of that burn matched the feel of her elbow, so she was probably scraped.

She didn't even grab her shirt; she just ran the last meter to her ship, which had moved even with its mooring clamps—good god, something was shaking this place, something bad, something big.

Her ship was so small, it didn't even have a boarding ramp. The door was pressed against the clamps, or it should have been, but there was a gap between the clamps and the ship and the walkway, and it was probably tearing something in the ship, but she didn't want to think about that so she didn't.

Instead, she slammed her palm against the door four times, the emergency enter code, which wasn't a code at all, but was something she thought (back when she was young and stupid and new to access codes) no one would figure out.

What she hadn't figured out was that no one wanted this cheapass ship, so no one tried to break into it. No one wanted to try, no one cared, except her, right now, as the door didn't open and didn't open and didn't open—

—and then it did.

Her brain was slowing down time. She'd heard about this phenomenon, something happened chemically in the human brain, slowed perception, made it easier (quicker?) to make decisions—and there her stupid brain was again, thinking about the wrong things as she tried to survive.

Hell, that had helped her survive as a kid, this checking-out thing in the middle of an emergency, but it wasn't going to help her now.

She scrambled inside her ship, felt it tilt, heard the hull groan. If she didn't do something about those clamps, she wouldn't have a ship.

She somehow remembered to slap the door's closing mechanism before she sprinted to the cockpit. Her bruised knees made her legs wobbly or maybe the ship was tilting even more. The groaning in the hull was certainly increasing.

The cockpit door was open, the place was a mess, as always. She used to sleep in here on long runs, and she always meant to clean up the blankets and pillows and clothes, but never did.

Now she stood in the middle of it, and turned on the navigation board. She instructed the ship to decouple, then turned her links on—not all of them, just the private link that hooked her to the ship—and heard more groaning.

"Goddammit!" she screamed at the ship, slamming her hands on the board. "Decouple, decouple—get rid of the goddamn clamps!"

Inform space traffic control to open the exit through the rings, the ship said in its prissiest voice as if there was no emergency.

Tears pricked her eyes. Crap. She'd be stuck here because of some goddamn rule that ships couldn't take off if there was no exit. She'd die if there was another explosion.

"There's no space traffic control here," she said. "Space traffic control is dead. We have to get out. Everyone's dead."

Her voice wobbled just like the ship had as she realized what she had said. *Everyone.* Everyone she had worked with, her friends, her co-workers, the people she drank with, laughed with, everyone—

We cannot leave if the exit isn't open, the ship said slowly and even more prissily, if that were possible.

"Then ram it," she said.

That will destroy us, the ship said, so damn calmly. Like it had no idea they were about to be destroyed anyway.

Takara ran her fingers over the board, looking for—she couldn't remember. This thing was supposed to have weapons, but she'd never used them, didn't know exactly what they were. She'd bought this stupid ship for a song six years ago, and the weapons were only mentioned in passing.

She couldn't find anything, so she gambled.

"Blow a damn hole through the closed exit," she said, not knowing if she could do that, if the ship even allowed that. Weren't there supposed to be failsafes so that no one could blow a hole through something on this base?

That will leave us with only one remaining laser shot, the ship said.

"I don't give a good goddamn!" she screamed. "Fire!"

And it did. Or something happened. Because the ship heated, and rocked and she heard a bang like nothing she'd ever heard before, and the sound of things falling on the ship.

"Get us out of here!" she shouted.

And the ship went upward, fast, faster than ever.

She tumbled backward. The attitude controls were screwed or the gravity or something but she didn't care.

"Visuals," she said, and floating on the screens that appeared in front of her was the hole that the ship had blown through the exit, and debris heading out with them, and bits of ship—and then she realized that there were bits of more than ship. Bits of the starbase and other ships and son of a bitch, more bodies and—

"Make sure you don't hit anything," she said, not knowing how to give the correct command.

I will evade large debris, the ship said as if this were an everyday occurrence. *However, I do need a destination.*

"Far the fuck away from here," Takara said.

How far?

"I don't know," she said. "Out of danger."

She was pressed against what she usually thought of as the side wall, with blankets and smelly sheets and musty pillows against her.

"And fix the attitude controls and the gravity, would you?" she snapped.

The interior of the ship seemed to right itself. She flopped on her stomach again, only this time, it didn't hurt.

She stood, her mouth wet and tasting of blood. She put a hand to her face, realized her nose was bleeding, and grabbed a sheet, stuffing it against her skin.

She dragged it with her to the controls. The images had disappeared (had she ordered that? She didn't remember ordering that) and so she called them up again, saw more body parts, and globules of stuff (blood? Intestines?) and shut it all off—consciously this time.

God, she was lucky. She had administration codes. She had a sense that things were going bad. She had her ship ready. And, most important of all, she had been close enough to the docking ring to out of there before anyone knew she even existed.

She sank into the chair and closed her eyes, wondering what in the bloody hell was going on.

She'd met those men, the creepy older ones, and asked her boss what they wanted with ships, and he'd said, *Better not to ask, hon.*

He always called her hon, and she finally realized it was because he couldn't remember her name. And now he was dead or would be dead or was dying or something awful like that. He'd been inside the administration area when the twenty clones had come in—or the forty clones—or the sixty clones, god, she had no idea how many.

It was her boss's boss who answered her, later, when she mentioned that the men looked alike.

Don't ask about it, Takara, he'd said quietly. *They're creatures of someone else. Designer Criminal Clones. They need a ship for nefarious doings.*

They're not in charge? She'd asked.

He'd shaken his head. *Someone made them for a job.*

Her eyes opened, saw the mess that her cockpit had become. A job. They'd had to find fast ships for a job.

But if the creepy older ones were made for a job, so were the younger versions.

She called up the screens, asked for images of the starbase. It was a small base, far away from anything, important only to malcontents and criminals, and those, like her, whose ships wouldn't cross the great distance between human-centered planets without a rest and refueling stop.

The starbase was glowing—fires inside, except where the exterior had been breached. Those sections were dark and ruined. It looked like a volcano that had already exploded—twice. More than twice. Several times.

Ship, her ship said, and for a minute, she thought it was being recursive.

"What?" she asked.

Approaching quickly. Starboard side.

She swiveled the view, saw a ship twice the size of hers, familiar too. The creepy older men had come back to the starbase in a ship just like that.

"Can you show me who is inside?" she asked.

I can show you who the ship is registered to and who disembarked from it earlier today, her ship sent. *I cannot show who is inside it now.*

Then, on an inset screen floating near the other screens, images of the two creepy older men and five younger leaving the ship. They went inside the base.

"Did anyone else who looked like them—"

The other clones disembarked from a ship that landed an hour later, her ship answered, anticipating her question for once. Did ships think?

Then she shook her head. She knew better than that. Ships like this one had computers that could deduce based on past performance, nothing more.

That ship has been destroyed, the ship sent, *along with the docking ring.*

"What?" Takara asked. She moved the imagery again, saw another explosion. The docking ring about five minutes after she left.

She was trembling. Everyone gone. Except her. And the creepy men, and maybe the five young guys they had brought with them.

Bastards. Filthy stinking horrible asshole bastards.

"You said we have one shot left," she said.

Yes, but—

"Target that ship," she said. "Blow the hell out of it."

Our laser shot cannot penetrate their shields.

Her gaze scanned the area. Other ships whirling, twirling, looping through space, heading her way.

Their way.

She ran through the records stored in her links. She'd always made copies of things. She was anal that way, and scared enough to figure she might need blackmail material.

One thing she did handle as a so-called administrator: requests to dock for ships with unusual fuel sources. She kept them on the far side of the ring.

She scanned for them, and their unusual size, saw one, realized it had a huge fuel cell, still intact.

"Can you shoot that ship?" she asked, sending the image across the links, "and push it into the manned ship?"

What she wanted to say was "the ship with the creepy guys," but she knew her ship wouldn't know what she meant.

Yes, her ship sent. *But it will do nothing to the ship except make them collide.*

"Oh, yes it will," Takara said. "Make sure the fuel cell hits the manned ship directly."

That will cause a chain reaction that will be so large it might impact us, her ship sent.

"Yeah, then get us out of here," Takara said.

We have a forty-nine percent chance of survival if we try that, her ship sent.

"Which is better than what we'll have if that fucking ship catches up with us," Takara said.

Are you ordering me to take the shot? her ship asked.

"Yes!"

Her ship shook slightly as the last laser shot emerged from the front. The manned ship didn't even seem to notice or care that she had firepower. Of course, from their perspective, she had missed them.

The shot went wide, hit the other ship, and destroyed part of its hull, pushing it into the manned ship.

And nothing happened. They collided, and then bounced away, the manned ship's trajectory changed and little else.

Then the other ship's fuel cell glowed green, and Takara's ship sped up, again losing attitude control and sending her flying into the back wall.

An explosion—green and gold and white—flashed around her.

She looked up from the pile of blankets at the floating screens, saw only debris, and asked, "Did we do it?"

Our shot hit the ship. It exploded. Our laser shot ignited the fuel cell—

"I know," she snapped. "What about the manned ship?"

It is destroyed.

She let out a sigh of relief, then leaned back against the wall, gathering the pillows and blanket against her. The blood had dried on her face, and she hadn't even noticed until now. Her elbow ached, her knees stung, and her stomach hurt, and she felt—

Alive.

She felt alive and giddy and sad and terrified and… Curious.

She scanned through the information on the creepy men. They didn't have names, at least that they had given to the administration. Just numbers. Numbers that didn't make sense.

She saw some imagery: the men talking to her boss, saying something about training missions for their weapons, experimental weapons, and something about soldiers—a promise of a big payout if the experiment worked.

And if it doesn't? her boss asked.

The creepy men smiled. *You'll know if it doesn't.*

Practice sessions. Soldiers. A failed experiment. Had her boss realized that's what this was in his last moment of life? Had he indeed known?

And the men, heading off to report the failure to someone.

But they hadn't gotten there. She had stopped them.

But not the someone in charge.

She ran a hand over her face. She would send all of this to the Alliance. There wasn't much more she could do. She wasn't even sure what the Alliance could do.

This was the Frontier. It was lawless by any Alliance definition. Each place governed itself.

She had liked that when she arrived. She was untraceable, unknown, completely alone.

Then she'd made friends, realized that every place had a rhythm, every place had good and bad parts, and she had decided to stay. Become someone.

Until she got that feeling from the creepy men, and had planned to leave.

"Fix the attitude and gravity controls, would you?" she asked, only this time, she didn't sound panicked or upset.

The ship righted itself. Apparently when it sped up, it didn't have enough power for all of its functions. She was going to need to get repairs.

Maybe in the Alliance. She had enough fuel to get there.

She'd been stockpiling. Food, fuel, everything but money.

She could get back to a place where there were laws she understood, where someone didn't blow up a starbase as an experiment with creepy matching soldiers.

She'd let the authorities know that someone—a very scary someone—was planning something. But what she didn't know. She didn't even know if it was directed against the Alliance.

She would guess it wasn't.

It would take more than twenty, forty, sixty, one hundred matching (fuckups) soldiers to defeat the Alliance. No one had gone to war against it in centuries. It was too big.

Something like this had to be Frontier politics. A war against something else, or an invasion or something.

And it had failed.

All of the soldiers had died.

Along with everyone else.

Except her, of course.

She hadn't died.

She had lived to tell about it.

And she would tell whoever would listen.

Once she was safe inside the Alliance.

A place too big to be attacked. Too big to be defeated.

Too big to ever allow her to go through anything like this again.

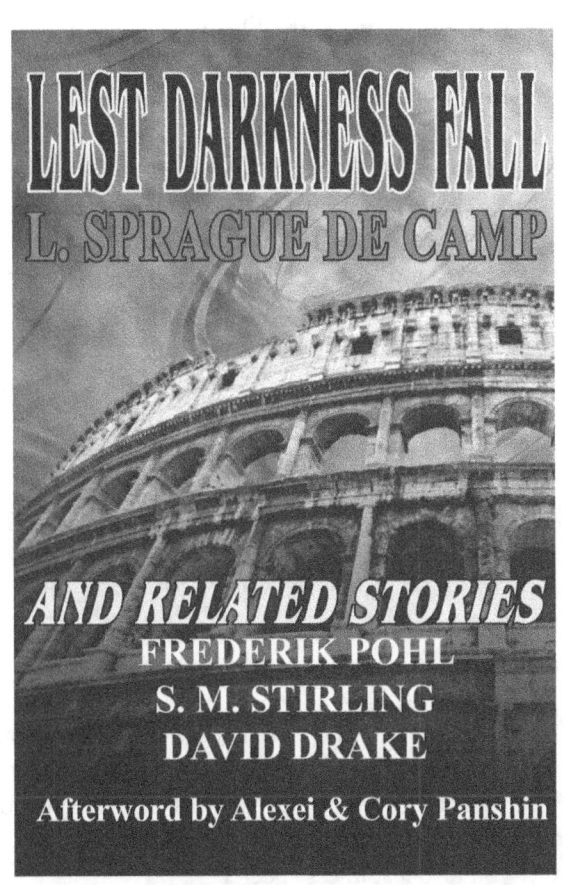

The complete original classic that started the whole alternate-history sub-genre.

With additional tribune stories by Frederik Pohl, S.M. Sterling and David Drake. Special afterword by Alexei and Cory Panshin excerpted from their Hugo-winning study of science fiction *The World Beyond the Hill*.

*Larry Hodges has sold more than ninety stories. His third novel—*Campaign 2100: Game of Scorpions—*was recently published by World Weaver Press. His* When Parallel Lines Meet, *a Stellar Guild team-up with Mike Resnick and Lezli Robyn, came out in October of 2017.*

DEATH, THE DEVIL, AND THE PRESIDENT'S GHOST

by Larry Hodges

"*I*'ll sell my soul if Death'll return me to my body!" cried the president's ghost. He had that zombie-in-the-headlights look of the recently dead.

The Devil grinned. "You're a politician, you dolt. I already *own* your soul." He emphasized the statement with a loud, squeaky chord on the fiddle of gold he held. Behind him the black-hooded skeleton that was Death quietly tittered. The three stood next to an old-fashioned Otis elevator at the end of a white hallway full of puffy white smoke that smelled sweet like a country meadow but with a faint scent of sulfur. On the wall next to it were two buttons: a white one marked *Up*, and a red one marked *Down*.

The Devil pressed *Down*. The president's ghost cringed.

He still wore the dark suit and red power tie he'd been wearing at the fundraiser, now vaguely transparent. If you looked closely, you could see the ghostly outlines of the combs and hair gels he used to make himself look presidential, as well as the ghostly checks in his pocket made out to his re-election campaign—but only the illegal ones since the legal ones had gone directly to the campaign treasurer. These ones were to be deposited in a secret slush account for dirty tricks, hush money, and a Hawaiian vacation. Or would have, he thought, if he hadn't had a fatal heart attack while giving a speech to his supporters promising contradictory things he laughed at the very thought of doing. He sighed. *What had he been thinking?*

And then Death had shown up in its black robes, the very stereotype of what it was supposed to look like. It had tapped him on the shoulder, sucked out his soul, and his body had crumpled to the floor like a house of forged ballots blown over by a special prosecutor's bad breath.

"It wasn't a very good soul," the president's ghost said, sobbing slightly as ghostly tears ran down his face. "Do you have any idea what it's like having a soul so grimy you can take a shower every hour and *still* can't get the dirt out? It went with me everywhere—*EVERYWHERE!*—always inside me, making me do those unfortunate things. I'm glad it's gone." He looked up. "What did you do with it?"

"I had it laundered, of course," said the Devil, playing another squeaky chord on the golden fiddle and then dropping it and the bow into a holster on his back. He looked like anything but the Devil in his country-boy overalls and too-big hiking boots that might have covered cloven feet. He had been down in Georgia looking for souls to steal when he'd received the emergency call that the president had gone down, a situation he wanted to handle personally. His large round head was completely bald, with no semblance of horns or a tail. He had an enormous nose, broad flapping ears, and wide, silver eyes that never blinked.

"I know all about money laundering," lamented the president's ghost, "but soul laundering?"

"It was pretty soiled," said the Devil. "I tried a Korean laundry, but even their ancient secrets couldn't clean it. I had to scrape it off with a Hawking blade. Then I gave it to Death to put into storage."

The president's ghost tilted his head slightly. "What's a Hawking blade?"

"I went to the future, to after Stephen Hawking had died. Those busy-body physicists, always prying into business that doesn't concern them, if they'd just—"

"I'm sure they mean well."

"*That's the problem!*" cried the Devil.

"But what about Hawking?"

"Oh yes, about him. I gathered up his body, cloned it a gazillion times, and then crushed them all with my bare hands until they were compressed into a black hole. Then I shaped it into a knife and used it to scrape the crud off your soul."

"Sorry about that." The president's ghost began pacing. "I'd really like to go back and right all the wrongs I did when I had all that crud inside me." He cringed at the thought. "An apology tour where I'd make restitution for all the terrible things I've done."

"Can't go back without a soul," the Devil said. He began to laugh.

"What's so funny?"

"Now that you're soulless, you're doing some serious soul searching. The irony!"

The president's ghost nodded. "I know. But look, this isn't fair. All those bad things I did as president, that was because I had a cruddy soul. It wasn't my fault! But now it's gone, so why should the rest of me get punished?"

"Why shouldn't you?" the Devil asked.

Death looked up, thrusting its skeletal lower jaw out a bit as if deep in thought about the Devil's words, or perhaps it was planning a party or what to watch on TV that night. Or perhaps it was just pouting. There was a *ding*, and the elevator door finally swung open. Though he didn't need to breathe, the president's ghost gagged as the hot, sulfurous air hit him, interrupting his reply. The three gathered inside.

When the president's ghost had stopped gagging, he said, "Because it's not fair that I should be punished. I've always been suspicious of this *good people go to Heaven, bad people go to Hell* thing, but at least it seemed fair and consistent. But now you're punishing the innocent."

"Life isn't fair," the Devil said. "Neither is death. Besides, you're now a soulless specter with no real substance. Just like your political opponents always said."

"That's not true!"

"Also your friends and associates, the secretary you were cheating with, your wife and kids, and your dog."

The president's ghost lowered his head for a moment. "Okay, you're right. But what about you? Aren't you also a soulless specter?"

"Me? I exist as the *incarnation* of evil. It would take something far more powerful than a Hawking blade to dent the evil in *my* soul."

"So you have a soul?"

"Of course."

"What will happen to your soul when you die?"

"*I cannot die!*" cried the Devil, causing the elevator to vibrate. Then he tilted his head sideways and lowered his voice. "Well, actually, there is one thing that can kill me, but that's not likely to happen, it's a good friend of mine." The Devil turned to the elevator buttons. Between the *Up* and *Down* buttons was a green *Earth* button for the current level. The Devil stabbed at the *Down* button. "Time to go. I love a warm climate, don't you?"

"What's the one thing that can kill you?"

"Why would I tell you? If that got out, for the rest of eternity everyone would be trying to get it to kill me."

"But eternity is infinitely long, and so eventually whatever can kill you, will kill you. Especially since you are being so unfair." There was another *ding* and the elevator door closed.

"You're right on both counts," said the Devil as the elevator began its trip down. "You sound like that vile Hawking. But it doesn't matter since I'm much more powerful than it is, and I'd destroy it with a glance if it tried to kill me. Unless it caught me completely by surprise during a monologue. I mean, do you have any idea just how powerful I am? I can—"

Catching him completely by surprise during his monologue, Death sliced off his head off with its scythe. "I thought you were my friend, you—!" were the last high-pitched words of the Devil before he ran out of air, a consequence of his devilish mouth no longer being connected to his satanic lungs.

Out of the Devil's body popped the Devil's ghost and a soul that looked—and smelled—like a soiled diaper. For a moment the ghost looked confused. Then it stared at Death. "This isn't fair! All those things I did, that was because I had a bad soul! But now it's gone, so why should *I* get punished?"

"Hey, that's what I said!" the president's ghost said. "Flip flopper!"

Death approached the floating Devil's soul, holding a hand over the nose hole in its skull. It jabbed at the Devil's soul with its scythe, snipping off bits of soiled soul for several minutes until it was clean like a white handkerchief. The bits of soiled soul floated about in the air.

Death took a deep breath, and with a powerful exhalation blew those black bits right through the elevator ceiling and off into a galaxy far, far away in the hopes that they would never be found and used by future galactic emperor wannabes. Then it pointed a skeletal finger at the Devil's head, which jumped back to its body and reattached itself.

"You two," said Death in a guttural voice, "here are your souls." The floating white handkerchief floated

down into the Devil's ghostly figure. The president's soul floated out of Death's long sleeves and into the president's ghost.

"And I'll take that to remove any temptations." It aimed a bony finger at the Devil's fiddle of gold, which leaped out of its holster along with its bow and landed in Death's skeletal hand. "Don't let your souls get mucked up again," Death continued as he stared at them through his eye sockets. "Go clean up the messes you made...or I'll be back."

They took the elevator back to Earth where the president's ghost and soul would return to his body—shocking the hell out of the presidential embalmer—and then he and the Devil began their worldwide apology tour.

Alone in the hallway outside the elevator after they left, Death said, *"Gotcha!"* as it gently caressed the priceless golden fiddle with its bony fingers. The Devil had once lost it to a young man named Johnny in a fiddling contest, but soon after the Devil had ordered Death to give Johnny the deathly tap, and stolen it back even as the poor kid collapsed and died.

Death pressed the white *Up* button, and the elevator doors soon opened. On the way up to return the fiddle to its rightful owner it played its own rousing rendition of *The Devil Went Down to Georgia*.

Copyright © 2018 by Larry Hodges

Sharon Diane King is both an author and an actress, whose movies include Lovesick *and* DisOrientation. *This is her first appearance in* Galaxy's Edge.

EL PALETERO

by Sharon Diane King

In the swirling depths of the paletero's ice-cream cart: coconut *helados*, pineapple ices, ruby-red watermelon and grape-purple popsicles. Frozen bananas and cubes of papaya, laced onto long bamboo skewers. Coffee and chocolate drumsticks in crisp shells, their tops crunchy with chopped peanuts. Tamarind sherbet that nips at the tongue as it chills. Scarlet-and-yellow-hued missiles, psychedelically-twisted DNA on ice. Dreamy, creamy *paletas* of chunky black walnut, caramelly *cajeta*, lime-green avocado, golden-pink *mamey*.

And down at the very bottom, from where dry ice sends up feeble white wisps, things you should think twice about, before you ask for them.

The paletero's cart does not impress. Years of navigating the sprawling city streets, even while stirring joy into young hearts, has churned its cream color into a dingy yellow, has scarred and dented and scuffed its sides. Only the wheels still carry a trace of its former glory. They are indigo blue, dotted with silver stars. The word "universo" is faintly visible when the cart is at rest. When the wheels turn and the universe whirls, the stars can be seen sparkling from far, far away.

Ding, ding, says the paletero as he makes his way down the sidewalk, inching the cart's wheels over the uneven places where the jacaranda trees, flouncing their purple blossoms, have had their way with the concrete. The bell went bust ages before; he never bothered to replace it.

A dark-eyed girl of seven, long blue-black hair coursing back from a widow's peak, runs up to him. Her hands dig deep into the back pockets of her saffron-colored trousers. *"Me gustaría una paleta de fresa,"* she tells the paletero shyly.

"One dollar, *mija.*"

"No tengo un dólar, hay sólo…ochenta centavos." The girl hands over the eighty cents, peering up anxiously into the old man's wrinkled face.

"Basta, mija." The old man dumps the coins into his worn change bag and bends over his cart, fishing out a wedge-shaped strawberry cream popsicle. He hands it to the girl with a smile.

"Gracias, señor."

"De nada, mija."

The little girl peels back the wrapper, takes her first lick. Her face brightens at the cool touch on her tongue. She squeezes her eyes closed, savoring the moment.

The paletero wends down the walk, passing tiny houses with half-wheel wrought-iron gates, their yards burgeoning with black and gold and green succulent plants. He strolls past the laundromat burping steam with each swing of its door, past the barber shop with its cracked pole and squeaking chairs that, despite a constant flurry of people in and out, always seem empty. He nears the flower shop, its worn black-and white-checked flooring hidden by bucket upon bucket of splaying gladiolas, death-sweet carnations, blowsy marigolds, mute declawed roses. He slows, glancing far down the street at a group of youths with close-cropped hair standing idle near a lamppost, from which dangles a pair of tennis shoes. Their gaze fastens on him and grows hard, like the calluses on the old man's hands.

The paletero's eyes shift to a slender, dark-skinned youth of twelve or thirteen lingering near the flower shop's doorway. The boy is careful to look anywhere but at the young men circling the lamp pole.

The paletero pushes his cart forward.

"Care for a popsicle, my son?"

Startled, the boy looks into the man's weathered face, the sloping forehead and long earlobes of a Mayan priest. He stares for a moment into the fathomless black eyes, eyes that see far beyond, into the despair that thrums within every nerve of his body.

The boy's gaze shifts to the ground, and he slowly shakes his head.

The paletero nods and rolls his cart past. The sun beats down on the worn straw hat, the faded jeans, the wine-red cotton shirt with flowers embroidered lavishly on collar and cuffs. At the crossroads, where the road starts down the hill at a breakneck pace, he stops, sets the wheel-brakes, dabs at his brow with a clean handkerchief from his back pocket.

"Ding ding! *Paletas, helados, a quién le gustarían?*"

Children swarm from every direction. For a while the paletero's cart disappears in a tangle of eager arms and dancing legs. His money bag fills, his hands grow red, then pale, from repeated descents into the cart's frosty depths. But he never stops smiling.

Sated, the children scatter. A single person remains standing beside him, a fortyish woman dressed in blue summer capris and a full white blouse. Her face is broad and flat, her wavy hair a dingy blonde. She smiles as she fumbles for her change purse.

"Excuse me, sir—" she says, and stops. She stares into his face, and her lips tremble. *"Buenos días."*

"Muy buenos, señora. Do you know what it is you would like?" His voice resounds like a bell in her ears.

"Oh, yes, I do—"

"And you believe I have it in here?"

"Yes. Nana told me to—see you. The woman from the *botánico.*"

Nodding, the paletero leans down and takes the brake off one of the wheels.

"How—how much does it cost?" Her voice is starting to catch. The paletero leans down, releases the brake from the other wheel. He straightens up.

"You can pay me later. I always come back to this spot."

She ducks her head and slips the purse back into a pocket in her trousers.

With a nudge of his foot, the paletero sends the cart flying down the hill.

The woman stares at him for a second, then dashes after the cart, blonde hair streaming behind her.

The old man whistles sharply. With a *whoosh,* first the cart, then the woman goes sailing up into the sky. She tries to catch up with the hurtling cart as it careens through the air, its wheels spinning uselessly back and forth. Her legs pump and her big face curves into a big smile. She narrows the gap, not seeming to notice they are no longer wedded to the bounds of earth. She catches the push bar of the cart with her left hand, seizes it with her right. The cart soars even higher as she clings to it for dear life.

In her grasp, the cart becomes a pram.

The pram and the woman rise higher, higher. The wind tugs at her blouse, courses through her blonde hair. Laughter, woman's laughter, rains down from above.

There is a tiny cry from the buggy. Someone is hungry.

The paletero watches until the woman and the pram become lost among scoops of creamy white clouds. He smiles.

He takes a step or two, then stops abruptly. Just in front of him, a single, perfect yellow flower rises from between two jagged slabs of pavement. The paletero watches the tall, thin stem sway slightly in the breeze: a ballerina on tiptoe in the midst of a construction zone.

After a long moment, he steps carefully around the flower, moves a few steps away. There he digs out his money bag, sifts through dollars and quarters, nickels and dimes. He scatters a few shiny pennies onto the sidewalk.

"For you, *amigos,*" he says with a chuckle. After a moment, the *duendes* emerge from the cracks in the pavement and scamper around the coins, singing their noiseless songs of joy. They carry on, in the way of unseen little folk, for many moments.

In the fitful sunlight, the pennies glitter on the ground.

The paletero walks on. On his right, a creek bed emerges from a large culvert: an offshoot of the city's tamed river, once mud-licious and puddle-wonderful. Now the flow of water has nearly dried up. On the edge, upon the pallid, cracked earth, a small spotted toad sits next to the lifeless body of her companion.

"Sana, sana," the paletero whispers, stooping to pick up a dirty paper cup from the sidewalk. He draws near the toad and squats down. He sits with her for some minutes. The toad blinks but does not move. At last he bends over and gently pushes the creature into the cup; she does not resist. "Sana, sana, colita de rana, si no sanas hoy, sanarás mañana," he croons. It is a toad, not a frog, and it has no tail, but the toad does not seem to mind the imprecision. With infinite care he tucks the cup into his ample right shirt pocket and buttons it over her. He glides back toward the sidewalk.

There is a bumping, thumping sound behind him. He whirls.

The paletero's battered cart has returned to the ground, a new scrape on its side, bouncing a little on ever-shakier wheels. Slowly, creakingly, it rolls down the sidewalk toward him. Behind it, the broad-faced woman smooths down her windblown hair and walks away as if still soaring on air.

The paletero grasps the push bar and turns left down the street. He walks for many blocks. Here the trees are handsomer, shadier, the houses larger, the cars finer. The air smells wetter, and there is a heavy scent of magnolias in bloom. Here the paletero does not call out the notes of his silenced bell, does not hawk the icy treats he has to sell. In stillness he passes down the long, stately street with his pushcart, pausing at last in front of a grand house on the corner.

There, in the imposing front yard, bougainvillea winds around a latticed arbor, doffing tri-corned blossoms of white and violet and magenta at passersby. Inside the arbor, a tall man stands facing the street. His face is drawn, his hair thin; his body sags as if tugged down by countless hands. His hairline is strangely cowlicked on the left side, and a long, faded scar runs down his neck, disappearing into his jacket.

His gaze rests on the paletero standing before him on the walkway. His eyes are pools of gray loss.

"You've come back."

The paletero nods.

"Does that mean—I can have what I want?"

"Are you sure you want it, my son?" The paletero's question is measured, grave. The man stares at the ground.

"How much will it cost, again?"

"Maybe more than you have to give."

"I would give anything."

"What about everything?"

The man is silent for a long moment. He nods.

"You are sure?"

"I am."

The paletero reaches deep into his left shirt pocket, pulls out a folded pair of black felt shoes.

"Put these on, and come."

The man stumbles through the garden gate. Wordless, he ties on the shoes the paletero hands him and follows the old man down the street. They reach a corner, cross it when the stream of cars allows their passage. Once on the other side, underneath a soaring palm tree, the paletero motions them to stop. With the care of a spider shuttling its web-weft, the paletero pivots, bringing the cart circling around him. He takes a single step backward.

"Now, you must do as I do, step for step. Do not gaze behind you, not once. Look only upon what we will be passing by."

The man stares blankly at the old man's wind burnt face, his dark sun swept eyes. "But how—"

The paletero shakes his head. "I will see you there, every step of the way."

They move backward, haltingly at first, down the sidewalk. With every step, the younger man's gaunt face changes, fills, grows ruddy. His eyes brighten, his clothes hang more loosely; his hair thickens, darkens. His pace alters, becomes faster, more confident. As they walk, the sun rises and sets, shadows lengthen, then dwindle in bright sun. Houses shed floors, change color. Gardens rearrange themselves, trees shoot up, then disappear; flowers flame, then flame out. Street lamps grow shorter, statelier; mail boxes humbler, automobiles shrink, then grow longer, heavier. Rain, sometimes hail, falls in quick bursts. A cold wind blows in fierce gusts. Smoke towers in the distance, then clears. Fog sweeps in, then dissipates. More than once the earth trembles under their feet. Slate stones forming a garden wall next to them tilt drunkenly into an ungainly pile, then shoot up again in neat used-brick columns. Apartments slide away, leaving quaint bungalows. A russet-color tram crowded with people rushes by. The air grows thicker, quieter, cooler.

At last the two reach a lush park adjoining a schoolyard. Calves aching, they backtrack into a cluster of tall pines. Long brown needles crunch fragrantly under their heels.

The paletero stops, opens the cart, and steps back, motioning with his hand. His companion, now a rosy-cheeked youth, leans down, peering past the ice crystal-coated cardboard popsicle boxes, past the gel packs and the dry ice pellets. He stares, catches his breath.

"Willy—"

He bends over the side of the cart. It shakes with the sobs of a lost little boy.

"My son," the paletero says to the weeping figure after a long moment. "It is time to make your choice. The ice will run out, and I still have *paletas* to sell."

The boy looks up, tears coursing down his cheeks. He struggles to regain his voice.

"Please tell me what to do—"

"I cannot."

The boy sobs again.

"You can tell your mother and father what you want. Tell the doctors, the nurses," the paletero says gently.

"What if they won't listen?"

"They might not, *mijo*."

A silence. Time melts around them.

"I—I don't know."

"You must decide if the risk is worth it."

A hummingbird chitters overhead as it makes for a bank of honeysuckle ruching over a chain-link fence. The boy's eyes follow the sound. He wipes his nose on his jacket sleeve, now oversize. He stares pleadingly into the old man's face.

"If they do not pay you heed, *mijo*, you will lose him once more, but you will live your life."

"And if they do listen—might I—what if I—"

The paletero passes his hand over his eyes. "My son, did I not say what it might cost?"

The boy is silent.

Chasing off a rival with angry chirps, the hummingbird darts from flower to flower, probing the pale tongues full of nectar.

Inside the cup-lined pocket of the paletero's shirt, the toad shifts. She has grown heavier, her belly now full of eggs. The paletero takes a deep breath.

"*Mijo*, stay here for a moment. Don't leave. I will come back for you."

The paletero swiftly strides toward a large pond in the park, edged with greenery and fed year-round by a creek from the mountains. At one of its shallows, he squats, unbuttoning his shirt pocket. He removes the cup with its precious contents, gently sets it down, unfurls it.

"*Ven, amiga mía*; come out, little one. It is time to find a new home."

There is no movement in the cup for a moment. Then the toad, sensing the water before her, takes one small hop forward. She takes another, then two more. With a splash, she leaps into the pond.

The toad swims away amidst a shower of sun rays dappling through the trees.

The paletero's ruddy hands suddenly tingle. He rises to his feet, hastens back to his cart.

The boy has vanished.

Face darkening, the paletero whirls, scanning in every direction. Nothing.

He takes a few quick strides around the park, scrutinizing the honeysuckle vine-covered fence, scanning the trees. No structures stand near, not even picnic tables and benches. The municipal council that will buy them has not been formed yet.

Turning, the old man spots a small black shoe on the other side of his cart. His shoulders sag.

The paletero gazes down, far down, into the icy vapors of the still-open cart. He closes his eyes, takes a deep breath.

Headfirst he plunges into the cart, neck, arms and legs quivering. He passes down through the false bottom, past the dry ice, into something far colder. A blast charged with guilt that stuns, a loss that weighs. And infinite regret, so sharp that for a long moment it takes his breath away.

A rush of places and moments surge through him in swaths of tastecolor, in scents of soundmotion.

He stretches out quicksilvered fingers and gropes after the boy in an inky darkness shot through with flashes of light, arching with waves of cold.

He could not be far. Surely he had not been that long away, tending to the hapless toad….

Had he?

The paletero slips through the iridescence of days cherished, the pallor of days wasted. He passes among whirls of textures, some throbbing like living velvet, some hissing as if bubbling with venom. Songs echoing with sweetness and sorrow well up inside him. He flies forward, falls back, rises, sags, drifting through chutes of done, undone, never done. He closes his eyes, searching inside himself. *The child will be found. The wish will be made.*

Won't it?

Deep within the old man a shuddering begins, one he cannot control. He has not wandered inside his cart for many years, has not thought of the pangs of nausea, the dizziness, hollowness at his very core. He casts about him, desperate.

The little girl in the yellow pants, her look of joy.

In the swirling, shrieking darkness, the twisting taffy-pulls of the abyss, the paletero's fingers brush against something. They fumble, grasp an edge. It is the tip of a sweatshirt drawstring.

He pulls slowly, tugs sharply.

The little boy, eyes wide with fear, tumbles into the paletero's arms. He buries his face in the old man's shirtfront, leaving behind the ghost of tearstains.

"I—I chose—"

The paletero holds him tightly, his body shaking with the boy's sobs.

"Softly, my son. Come."

They drift toward warmth, a place in the lingering before, a turtle slowly finding footing on familiar shoals. Solid ground creeps under their feet, sturdy walls clamber behind them. Before their gaze, a tiled room filled with beeping machines and shiny instruments blazes with harsh light. Doors open and close; masked and uniformed people hurry impersonally from one task to another. Above the room in a glassed-in balcony stand a man and a woman, also clad in masks and suits. They lean on each other. A long narrow table rises in the middle of the room, but what is on it is shielded from view by the machines.

No one takes notice of the pair looking on.

It is too bright. The boy's eyes pinch closed. The paletero moves forward, toward the surgical table now visible in the middle of the room.

"Go in now, my son. The man who makes you sleep has not come in yet. You can tell them."

"And if they don't listen?"

"Find a way to make them hear you."

The boy opens his eyes, stares fearfully over the old man's shoulder.

"If it's what you really want, *mijo*."

The child hesitates, nods, surrenders. His body shimmers into the air like myriad ice crystals.

The paletero waits, his dark eyes fixed on the table. A nurse with a tray steps away, and a starfish-creature appears: eight limbs barely visible under gauzy covers. At the top of the table, two heads face away from each other. One of the faces is more twisted than the other, with a blind eye and misshapen jaw. They weep silently.

Another masked figure enters, a tall, commanding man in white. There is a stir from the table, and a voice cries out.

"Please, doctor, please, don't do this! Don't take Willy away!"

There is a commotion; doctors and nurses turn, aghast. The creature on the table beats with hands and feet.

"Don't take him away from me! Mommy, Daddy, please!"

The parents in the balcony above are surrounded by nurses and aides trying to keep them from descending.

Let me speak to them—

"It's best if you stay here."

No, no, let me see them. They're my sons—

They're our sons, we need to—

"You'll contaminate the operatory, you can't go down—"

"We'll handle them, don't worry—"

Please! PLEASE—

"Mommy! Mommy! Don't take Willy away! Daddy, please! Let him stay with me!" The spotless cloths draping the table are flung about; there is shrieking and flailing. A man steps briskly toward them, nodding to his assistant. She brings out two masks with tubes attached. They hover over both small heads.

The tall man in white looks down at the table, motions with his hand. The room falls silent and still.

The paletero's dark eyes flash.

☼

Ding ding, says the paletero as he makes his way down the jigsaw-patched sidewalk. The smell of hot asphalt rises from the street; waves of heat sheet in front of him like an ever-shifting mirage. He stops in the shade of an ancient coral tree and mops his brow. *Paletas, helados, a quién le gustarían?*

His voice is a little more weary, but he still smiles at the children who gather around his cart, paused in front of a mural of starry crimson poinsettias. The children clamor for popsicles of tangy, sweet-sour *guanabana*, chewy ice-cream sandwiches, *helados* of spicy eggnog, heady black *zapote*, rich peaches-and-cream. Eager fingers tear off wrappers for the first few seconds of purest bliss.

The grind-and-squeal of sirens sound behind them. A long fire engine, then another, and another, careen down the broad street, hurtling past them with a rush of dust and scattered leaves. The paletero motions to the children to stay where they are. They stand grimacing; those who can, hold their ears.

The paletero follows the engines with his eyes.

He sees the dark smoke rising, billowing higher and higher. He thinks of the neighborhood so close to this one, yet in a different world. He thinks of the broken man in the big handsome house, the love for a lost brother, the severing that made a life by taking another away.

More sirens, more honks pierce the air. The paletero looks at the smoke for a long moment, as if parsing a sign. At length he shakes his head, moves on down the street.

As he rounds a corner, he sees the same dark-skinned young man hovering close to the flower-shop window. The paletero nears the doorway and smiles at the boy, whose gaze shifts to the gum-stained sidewalk

"Mijo," the paletero says. "Would you help me out?"

The boy looks up, doubt in his dark eyes.

"I put in too many this morning. They won't stay cold in this heat, they'll just go to waste. Could you take one?"

A short silence. "Okay."

The boy peers down into the cart.

"Is that a fudgsicle?"

The old man brings out the popsicle, ice crystals stippling its paper.

"Are you heading that way home? I must go back, I made a promise. You can keep me company."

The two amble off down the street. The boys idling under the lamppost watch them pass. The old man sees the boy to the steps of the stately, crumbling apartment building where he lives.

"Maybe I will see you tomorrow after school, *mijo.* I am changing my route, I will be passing that way."

The boy nods, disappears behind the door.

With swift steps the old man retraces his path back to the wealthy neighborhood. One by one, the fire engines slowly pass him, heading the other way. He turns down the street, his stomach lurching, and for a moment, loses his grip on the handle of the cart.

The house is gone. There are piles of scorched stonework, blackened walls from which puffs of smoke rise, a ruined garden. The noble building has

been consumed, along with all its memories. As if it had never been there.

The paletero fumbles for the cart handle, secures it. It is warm to the touch.

"May you find peace with your brother, *mijo.*"

☼

In the swirling depths of the paletero's ice-cream cart: sweetness that beckons to young and to old. Ices that cool on the warmest day. Confections with colors that dazzle, textures that tease, flavors that explode in the mouth. The stuff of dreams.

And down at the very bottom, from where dry ice sends up feeble white wisps, things you should think twice about, before you ask for them.

Copyright © 2018 by Sharon Diane King

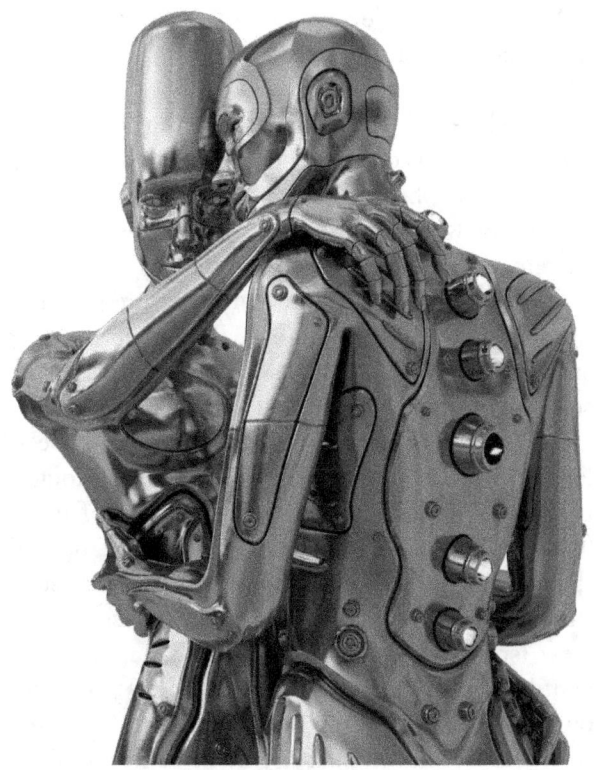

Robert Silverberg is one of the true giants of science fiction. He is a multiple Hugo winner, a multiple Nebula winner, has been a Worldcon Guest of Honor, and was named a Grand Master by the Science Fiction Writers of America in 2004. He is the author of numerous acknowledged classics in the field.

THE DYBBUK OF MAZEL TOV IV

by Robert Silverberg

My grandson David will have his bar mitzvah next spring. No one in our family has undergone that rite in at least three hundred years—certainly not since we Levins settled in Old Israel, the Israel on Earth, soon after the European holocaust. My friend Eliahu asked me not long ago how I feel about David's bar mitzvah, whether the idea of it angers me, whether I see it as a disturbing element. No, I replied, the boy is a Jew, after all—let him have a bar mitzvah if he wants one. These are times of transition and upheaval, as all times are. David is not bound by the attitudes of his ancestors.

"Since when is a Jew not bound by the attitudes of his ancestors?" Eliahu asked.

"You know what I mean," I said.

Indeed he did. We are bound but yet free. If anything governs us out of the past it is the tribal bond itself, not the philosophies of our departed kinsmen. We accept what we choose to accept; nevertheless we remain Jews. I come from a family that has liked to say—especially to gentiles—that we are Jews but not Jewish; that is, we acknowledge and cherish our ancient heritage, but we do not care to entangle ourselves in outmoded rituals and folkways. This is what my forefathers declared, as far back as those secular-minded Levins who three centuries ago fought to win and guard the freedom of the land of Israel. (Old Israel, I mean.) I would say the same here, if there were any gentiles on this world to whom such things had to be explained. But of course in this New Israel in the stars we have only ourselves, no gentiles within a dozen light-years, unless you count our neighbors the Kunivaru as gentiles. (Can creatures that are not human rightly be called gentiles? I'm not sure the term applies. Besides, the Kunivaru

now insist that they are Jews. My mind spins. It's an issue of Talmudic complexity, and God knows I'm no Talmudist. Hillel, Akiva, Rashi, help me!) Anyway, come the fifth day of Sivan my son's son will have his bar mitzvah, and I'll play the proud grandpa as pious old Jews have done for six thousand years.

✡

All things are connected. That my grandson would have a bar mitzvah is merely the latest link in a chain of events that goes back to—when? To the day the Kunivaru decided to embrace Judaism? To the day the dybbuk entered Seul the Kunivar? To the day we refugees from Earth discovered the fertile planet that we sometimes call New Israel and sometimes call Mazel Tov IV? To the day of the Final Pogrom on Earth? Reb Yossele the Hasid might say that David's bar mitzvah was determined on the day the Lord God fashioned Adam out of dust. But I think that would be overdoing things.

The day the dybbuk took possession of the body of Seul the Kunivar was probably where it really started. Until then things were relatively uncomplicated here. The Hasidim had their settlement, we Israelis had ours, and the natives, the Kunivaru, had the rest of the planet; and generally we all kept out of one another's way. After the dybbuk everything changed. It happened more than forty years ago, in the first generation after the Landing, on the ninth day of Tishri in the year 6302. I was working in the fields, for Tishri is a harvest month. The day was hot, and I worked swiftly, singing and humming. As I moved down the long rows of cracklepods, tagging those that were ready to be gathered, a Kunivar appeared at the crest of the hill that overlooks our kibbutz. It seemed to be in some distress, for it came staggering and lurching down the hillside with extraordinary clumsiness, tripping over its own four legs as if it barely knew how to manage them. When it was about a hundred meters from me, it cried out, "Shimon! Help me, Shimon! In God's name help me!"

There were several strange things about this outcry, and I perceived them gradually, the most trivial first. It seemed odd that a Kunivar would address me by my given name, for they are a formal people. It seemed more odd that a Kunivar would speak to me in quite decent Hebrew, for at that time none of them had learned our language. It seemed most odd of all—but I was slow to discern it—that a Kunivar would have the very voice, dark and resonant, of my dear dead friend Joseph Avneri.

The Kunivar stumbled into the cultivated part of the field and halted, trembling terribly. Its fine green fur was pasted into hummocks by perspiration, and its great golden eyes rolled and crossed in a ghastly way. It stood flat-footed, splaying its legs out under the four corners of its chunky body like the legs of a table, and clasped its long powerful arms around its chest. I recognized the Kunivar as Seul, a subchief of the local village, with whom we of the kibbutz had had occasional dealings.

"What help can I give you?" I asked. "What has happened to you, Seul?"

"Shimon—Shimon—" A frightful moan came from the Kunivar. "Oh, God, Shimon, it goes beyond all belief! How can I bear this? How can I even comprehend it?"

No doubt of it. The Kunivar was speaking in the voice of Joseph Avneri.

"Seul?" I said hesitantly.

"My name is Joseph Avneri."

"Joseph Avneri died a year ago last Elul. I didn't realize you were such a clever mimic, Seul."

"Mimic? You speak to me of mimicry, Shimon? It's no mimicry. I am your Joseph, dead but still aware, thrown for my sins into this monstrous alien body. Are you Jew enough to know what a dybbuk is, Shimon?"

"A wandering ghost, yes, who takes possession of the body of a living being."

"I have become a dybbuk."

"There are no dybbuks. Dybbuks are phantoms out of medieval folklore," I said.

"You hear the voice of one."

"This is impossible," I said.

"I agree, Shimon, I agree." He sounded calmer now. "It's entirely impossible. I don't believe in dybbuks either, any more than I believe in Zeus, the Minotaur, werewolves, gorgons, or golems. But how else do you explain me?"

"You are Seul the Kunivar, playing a clever trick."

"Do you really think so? Listen to me, Shimon. I knew you when we were boys in Tiberias. I rescued you when we were fishing in the lake and our boat overturned. I was with you the day you met Leah whom you married. I was godfather to your son Yigal. I studied with you at the university in Jerusalem. I fled with you in the fiery days of the Final Pogrom. I stood watch with you aboard the Ark in the years of our flight from Earth. Do you remember, Shimon? Do you remember Jerusalem? The Old City, the Mount of Olives, the Tomb of Absalom, the Western Wall? Am I a Kunivar, Shimon, to know of the Western Wall?"

"There is no survival of consciousness after death," I said stubbornly.

"A year ago I would have agreed with you. But who am I if I am not the spirit of Joseph Avneri? How can you account for me any other way? Dear God, do you think I want to believe this, Shimon? You know what a scoffer I was. But it's real."

"Perhaps I'm having a very vivid hallucination."

"Call the others, then. If ten people have the same hallucination, is it still a hallucination? Be reasonable, Shimon! Here I stand before you, telling you things that only I could know, and you deny that I am—"

"Be reasonable?" I said. "Where does reason enter into this? Do you expect me to believe in ghosts, Joseph, in wandering demons, in dybbuks? Am I some superstition-ridden peasant out of the Polish woods? Is this the Middle Ages?"

"You called me Joseph," he said quietly.

"I can hardly call you Seul when you speak in that voice."

·"Then you believe in me!"

"No."

"Look, Shimon, did you ever know a bigger skeptic than Joseph Avneri? I had no use for the Torah, I said Moses was fictional, I plowed the fields on Yom Kippur, I laughed in God's nonexistent face. What is life, I said? And I answered: a mere accident, a transient biological phenomenon. Yet here I am. I remember the moment of my death. For a full year I've wandered this world, bodiless, perceiving things, unable to communicate. And today I find myself cast into this creature's body, and I know myself for a dybbuk. If *I* believe, Shimon, how can you dare disbelieve? In the name of our friendship, have faith in what I tell you!"

"You have actually become a dybbuk?"

"I have become a dybbuk," he said.

I shrugged. "Very well, Joseph. You're a dybbuk. It's madness but I believe." I stared in astonishment at the Kunivar. Did I believe? Did I believe that I believed? How could I not believe? There was no other way for the voice of Joseph Avneri to be coming from the throat of a Kunivar. Sweat streamed down my body. I was face to face with the impossible, and all my philosophy was shattered. Anything was possible now. God might appear as a burning bush. The sun might stand still. No, I told myself. Believe only one irrational thing at a time, Shimon. Evidently there are dybbuks; well, then, there are dybbuks. But everything else pertaining to the Invisible World remains unreal until it manifests itself.

I said, "Why do you think this has happened to you?"

"It could only be as a punishment."

"For what, Joseph?"

"My experiments. You knew I was doing research into the Kunivaru metabolism, didn't you?"

"Yes, certainly. But—"

"Did you know I performed surgical experiments on live Kunivaru in our hospital? That I used patients, without informing them or anyone else, in studies of a forbidden kind? It was vivisection, Shimon."

"What?"

"There were things I needed to know, and there was only one way I could discover them. The hunger for knowledge led me into sin. I told myself that these creatures were ill, that they would shortly die anyway, and that it might benefit everyone if I opened them while they still lived, you see? Besides, they weren't human beings, Shimon, they were only animals—very intelligent animals, true, but still only—"

"No, Joseph. I can believe in dybbuks more readily than I can believe this. You, doing such a thing? My calm rational friend, my scientist, my wise one?" I shuddered and stepped a few paces back from him. "Auschwitz!" I cried. "Buchenwald! Dachau! Do those names mean anything to you? 'They weren't human beings,' the Nazi surgeon said. 'They were only Jews, and our need for scientific knowledge is such that—' That was only three hundred years ago, Joseph. And you, a Jew, a Jew of all people, to—"

"I know, Shimon, I know. Spare me the lecture. I sinned terribly, and for my sins I've been given

this grotesque body, this gross, hideous, heavy body, these four legs which I can hardly coordinate, this crooked spine, this foul, hot furry pelt. I still don't believe in a God, Shimon, but I think I believe in some sort of compensating force that balances accounts in this universe, and the account has been balanced for me, oh, yes, Shimon! I've had six hours of terror and loathing today such as I never dreamed could be experienced. To enter this body, to fry in this heat, to wander these hills trapped in such a mass of flesh, to feel myself being bombarded with the sensory perceptions of a being so alien—it's been hell, I tell you that without exaggeration. I would have died of shock in the first ten minutes if I didn't already happen to be dead. Only now, seeing you, talking to you, do I begin to get control of myself. Help me, Shimon."

"What do you want me to do?"

"Get me out of here. This is torment. I'm a dead man—I'm entitled to rest the way the other dead ones rest. Free me, Shimon."

"How?"

"How? How? Do I know? Am I an expert on dybbuks? Must I direct my own exorcism? If you knew what an effort it is simply to hold this body upright, to make its tongue form Hebrew words, to say things in a way you'll understand—" Suddenly the Kunivar sagged to his knees, a slow, complex folding process that reminded me of the manner in which the camels of Old Earth lowered themselves to the ground. The alien creature began to sputter and moan and wave his arms about; foam appeared on his wide rubbery lips. "God in Heaven, Shimon," Joseph cried, "set me free!"

✧

I called for my son Yigal and he came running swiftly from the far side of the fields, a lean healthy boy, only eleven years old but already long-legged, strong-bodied. Without going into details, I indicated the suffering Kunivar and told Yigal to get help from the kibbutz. A few minutes later he came back leading seven or eight men—Abrasha, Itzhak, Uri, Nahum, and some others. It took the full strength of all of us to lift the Kunivar into the hopper of a harvesting machine and transport him to our hospital. Two of the doctors—Moshe

Shiloah and someone else—began to examine the stricken alien, and I sent Yigal to the Kunivaru village to tell the chief that Seul had collapsed in our fields.

The doctors quickly diagnosed the problem as a case of heat prostration. They were discussing the sort of injection the Kunivar should receive when Joseph Avneri, breaking a silence that had lasted since Seul had fallen, announced his presence within the Kunivar's body. Uri and Nahum had remained in the hospital room with me; not wanting this craziness to become general knowledge in the kibbutz, I took them outside and told them to forget whatever ravings they had heard. When I returned, the doctors were busy with their preparations and Joseph was patiently explaining to them that he was a dybbuk who had involuntarily taken possession of the Kunivar. "The heat has driven the poor creature insane," Moshe Shiloah murmured, and rammed a huge needle into one of Seul's thighs.

"Make them listen to me," Joseph said.

"You know that voice," I told the doctors. "Something very unusual has happened here."

But they were no more willing to believe in dybbuks than they were in rivers that flow uphill. Joseph continued to protest, and the doctors continued methodically to fill Seul's body with sedatives and restoratives and other potions. Even when Joseph began to speak of last year's kibbutz gossip—who had been sleeping with whom behind whose back, who had illicitly been peddling goods from the community storehouse to the Kunivaru—they paid no attention. It was as though they had so much difficulty believing that a Kunivar could speak Hebrew that they were unable to make sense out of what he was saying and took Joseph's words to be Seul's delirium. Suddenly Joseph raised his voice for the first time, calling out in a loud, angry tone, "You, Moshe Shiloah! Aboard the Ark I found you in bed with the wife of Teviah Kohn, remember? Would a Kunivar have known such a thing?"

Moshe Shiloah gasped, reddened, and dropped his hypodermic. The other doctor was nearly as astonished.

"What is this?" Moshe Shiloah asked. "How can this be?"

"Deny me now!" Joseph roared. "Can you deny me?"

The doctors faced the same problems of acceptance that I had had, that Joseph himself had grappled with. We were all of us rational men in this kibbutz, and the supernatural had no place in our lives. But there was no arguing the phenomenon away. There was the voice of Joseph Avneri emerging from the throat of Seul the Kunivar, and the voice was saying things that only Joseph would have said, and Joseph had been dead more than a year. Call it a dybbuk, call it hallucination, call it anything: Joseph's presence could not be ignored.

Locking the door, Moshe Shiloah said to me, "We must deal with this somehow."

Tensely we discussed the situation. It was, we agreed, a delicate and difficult matter. Joseph, raging and tortured, demanded to be exorcised and allowed to sleep the sleep of the dead; unless we placated him he would make us all suffer. In his pain, in his fury, he might say anything, he might reveal everything he knew about our private lives; a dead man is beyond all of society's rules of common decency. We could not expose ourselves to that. But what could we do about him? Chain him in an outbuilding and hide him in solitary confinement? Hardly. Unhappy Joseph deserved better of us than that; and there was Seul to consider, poor supplanted Seul, the dybbuk's unwilling host. We could not keep a Kunivar in the kibbutz, imprisoned or free, even if his body did house the spirit of one of our own people, nor could we let the shell of Seul go back to the Kunivaru village with Joseph as a furious passenger trapped inside. What to do? Separate soul from body, somehow: restore Seul to wholeness and send Joseph to the limbo of the dead. But how? There was nothing in the standard pharmacopoeia about dybbuks. What to do?

I sent for Shmarya Asch and Yakov Ben-Zion, who headed the kibbutz council that month, and for Shlomo Feig, our rabbi, a shrewd and sturdy man, very unorthodox in his orthodoxy, almost as secular as the rest of us. They questioned Joseph Avneri extensively, and he told them the whole tale—his scandalous secret experiments, his post-mortem year as a wandering spirit, his sudden painful incarnation within Seul. At length Shmarya Asch turned to Moshe Shiloah and snapped, "There must be some therapy for such a case."

"I know of none."

"This is schizophrenia," said Shmarya Asch in his firm, dogmatic way. "There are cures for schizophrenia. There are drugs, there are electric shock treatments, there are—you know these things better than I, Moshe."

"This is not schizophrenia," Moshe Shiloah retorted. "This is a case of demonic possession. I have no training in treating such maladies."

"Demonic possession?" Shmarya bellowed. "Have you lost your mind?"

"Peace, peace, all of you," Shlomo Feig said, as everyone began to shout at once. The rabbi's voice cut sharply through the tumult and silenced us all. He was a man of great strength, physical as well as moral, to whom the entire kibbutz inevitably turned for guidance although there was virtually no one among us who observed the major rites of Judaism. He said, "I find this as hard to comprehend as any of you. But the evidence triumphs over my skepticism. How can we deny that Joseph Avneri has returned as a dybbuk? Moshe, you know no way of causing this intruder to leave the Kunivar's body?"

"None," said Moshe Shiloah.

"Maybe the Kunivaru themselves know a way," Yakov Ben-Zion suggested.

"Exactly," said the rabbi. "My next point. These Kunivaru are a primitive folk. They live closer to the world of magic and witchcraft, of demons and spirits, than we do whose minds are schooled in the habits of reason. Perhaps such cases of possession occur often among them. Perhaps they have techniques for driving out unwanted spirits. Let us turn to them, and let them cure their own."

✧

Before long Yigal arrived, bringing with him six Kunivaru, including Gyaymar, the village chief. They wholly filled the little hospital room, bustling around in it like a delegation of huge furry centaurs; I was oppressed by the acrid smell of so many of them in one small space, and although they had always been friendly to us, never raising an objection when we appeared as refugees to settle on their planet, I felt fear of them now as I had never felt before. Clustering about Seul, they asked questions of him in their own supple language, and when Joseph Avneri replied in Hebrew they whispered things to each other unintelligible to us. Then, unexpectedly, the voice of Seul broke through, speaking in halting spastic monosyllables that revealed the terrible shock his nervous system must have received; then the alien faded and Joseph Avneri spoke once more with the Kunivar's lips, begging forgiveness, asking for release.

Turning to Gyaymar, Shlomo Feig said, "Have such things happened on this world before?"

"Oh, yes, yes," the chief replied. "Many times. When one of us dies having a guilty soul, repose is denied, and the spirit may undergo strange migrations before forgiveness comes. What was the nature of this man's sin?"

"It would be difficult to explain to one who is not Jewish," said the rabbi hastily, glancing away. "The important question is whether you have a means of undoing what has befallen the unfortunate Seul, whose sufferings we all lament."

"We have a means, yes," said Gyaymar, the chief.

The six Kunivaru hoisted Seul to their shoulders and carried him from the kibbutz; we were told that we might accompany them if we cared to do so. I went along, and Moshe Shiloah, and Shmarya Asch, and Yakov Ben-Zion, and the rabbi, and perhaps some others. The Kunivaru took their comrade not to their village but to a meadow several kilometers to the east, down in the direction of the place where the Hasidim lived. Not long after the Landing, the Kunivaru had let us know that the meadow was sacred to them, and none of us had ever entered it.

It was a lovely place, green and moist, a gently sloping basin crisscrossed by a dozen cool little streams. Depositing Seul beside one of the streams, the Kunivaru went off into the woods bordering the meadow to gather firewood and herbs. We remained close by Seul. "This will do no good," Joseph Avneri muttered more than once. "A waste of time, a foolish expense of energy." Three of the Kunivaru started to build a bonfire. Two sat nearby, shredding the herbs, making heaps of leaves, stems, roots. Gradually more of their kind appeared until the meadow was filled with them; it seemed that the whole village, some four hundred Kunivaru, was turning out to watch or to participate in the rite. Many of them carried musical instruments, trumpets and drums, rattles and clappers, lyres, lutes, small harps, percussive boards, wooden flutes, everything intricate and fanciful of design; we had not suspected such cultural complexity. The priests—I assume they were priests, Kunivaru of stature and dignity—wore ornate ceremonial helmets and heavy golden mantles of sea-beast fur. The ordinary townsfolk carried ribbons and streamers, bits of bright fabric, polished mirrors of stone, and other ornamental devices. When he saw how elaborate a function it was going to be, Moshe Shiloah, an amateur anthropologist at heart, ran back to the kibbutz to fetch camera and recorder. He returned, breathless, just as the rite commenced.

And a glorious rite it was: incense, a grandly blazing bonfire, the pungent fragrance of freshly picked herbs, some heavy-footed quasi-orgiastic dancing, and a choir punching out harsh, sharp-edged arrhythmic melodies. Gyaymar and the high priest of the village performed an elegant antiphonal chant, uttering long curling intertwining melismas and sprinkling Seul with a sweet-smelling pink fluid out of a baroquely carved wooden censer. Never have I beheld such stirring pageantry. But Joseph's gloomy prediction was correct; it was all entirely useless. Two hours of intensive exorcism had no effect. When the ceremony ended—the ultimate punctuation marks were five terrible shouts from the high priest—the dybbuk remained firmly in possession of Seul. "You have not conquered me," Joseph declared in a bleak tone.

Gyaymar said, "It seems we have no power to command an earthborn soul."

"What will we do now?" demanded Yakov Ben-Zion of no one in particular. "Our science and their witchcraft both fail."

Joseph Avneri pointed toward the east, toward the village of the Hasidim, and murmured something indistinct.

"No!" cried Rabbi Shlomo Feig, who stood closest to the dybbuk at that moment.

"What did he say?" I asked.

"It was nothing," the rabbi said. "It was foolishness. The long ceremony has left him fatigued, and his mind wanders. Pay no attention."

I moved nearer to my old friend. "Tell me, Joseph."

"I said," the dybbuk replied slowly, "that perhaps we should send for the Baal Shem."

"Foolishness!" said Shlomo Feig, and spat.

"Why this anger?" Shmarya Asch wanted to know. "You, Rabbi Shlomo, you were one of the first to advocate employing Kunivaru sorcerers in this business. You gladly bring in alien witch doctors, Rabbi, and grow angry when someone suggests that your fellow Jew be given a chance to drive out the demon? Be consistent, Shlomo!"

Rabbi Shlomo's strong face grew mottled with rage. It was strange to see this calm, even-tempered man becoming so excited. "I will have nothing to do with Hasidim!" he exclaimed.

"I think this is a matter of professional rivalries," Moshe Shiloah commented.

The rabbi said, "To give recognition to all that is most superstitious in Judaism, to all that is most irrational and grotesque and outmoded and medieval? No! No!"

"But dybbuks *are* irrational and grotesque and outmoded and medieval," said Joseph Avneri. "Who better to exorcise one than a rabbi whose soul is still rooted in ancient beliefs?"

"I forbid this!" Shlomo Feig sputtered. "If the Baal Shem is summoned I will—I will—"

"Rabbi," Joseph said, shouting now, "this is a matter of my tortured soul against your offended spiritual pride. Give way! Give way! Get me the Baal Shem!"

"I refuse!"

"Look!" called Yakov Ben-Zion. The dispute had suddenly become academic. Uninvited, our Hasidic cousins were arriving at the sacred meadow, a long procession of them, eerie prehistoric-looking figures clad in their traditional long black robes, wide-brimmed hats, heavy beards, dangling side-locks; and at the head of the group marched their tzaddik, their holy man, their prophet, their leader, Reb Shmuel the Baal Shem.

It was certainly never our idea to bring Hasidim with us when we fled out of the smoldering ruins of the Land of Israel. Our intention was to leave Earth and all its sorrows far behind, to start anew on another world where we could at last build an enduring Jewish homeland, free for once of our eternal gentile enemies and free, also, of the religious fanatics among our own kind whose presence had long been a drain on our vitality. We needed no mystics, no ecstatics, no weepers, no moaners, no leapers, no chanters; we needed only workers, farmers, machinists, engineers, builders. But how could we refuse them a place on the Ark? It was their good fortune to come upon us just as we were making the final preparations for our flight. The nightmare that had darkened our sleep for three centuries had been made real: the Homeland lay in flames, our armies had been shattered out of ambush, Philistines wielding long knives strode through our devastated cities. Our ship was ready to leap to the stars. We were not cowards but simply realists, for it was folly to think we could do battle any longer, and if some fragment of our ancient nation were to survive, it could only survive far from the bitter world Earth. So we were going to go; and here were suppliants asking us for succor, Reb Shmuel and his thirty followers. How could we turn them away, knowing they would certainly perish? They were human beings, they were Jews. For all our misgivings, we let them come on board.

And then we wandered across the heavens year after year, and then we came to a star that had no name, only a number, and then we found its fourth planet to be sweet and fertile, a happier world than Earth, and we thanked the God in whom we did not believe for the good luck that He had granted us, and we cried out to each other in congratulation, Mazel tov! Mazel tov! Good luck, good luck, good luck! And someone looked in an old book and saw that mazel once had had an astrological connotation, that in the days of the Bible it had meant not only "luck" but a lucky star, and so we named our lucky star Mazel Tov, and we made our landfall on Mazel Tov IV, which was to be the New Israel. Here we found no enemies, no Egyptians, no Assyrians, no Romans, no Cossacks, no Nazis, no Arabs, only the Kunivaru, kindly people of a simple nature, who solemnly studied our pantomimed explanations and replied to us in gestures, saying, Be welcome, there is more land here than we will ever need. And we built our kibbutz.

But we had no desire to live close to those people of the past, the Hasidim, and they had scant love for us, for they saw us as pagans, godless Jews who were worse than gentiles, and they went off to build a muddy little village of their own. Sometimes on clear nights we heard their lusty singing, but otherwise there was scarcely any contact between us and them.

I could understand Rabbi Shlomo's hostility to the idea of intervention by the Baal Shem. These Hasidim represented the mystic side of Judaism, the dark uncontrollable Dionysiac side, the skeleton in the tribal closet; Shlomo Feig might be amused or charmed by a rite of exorcism performed by furry centaurs, but when Jews took part in the same sort of supernaturalism it was distressing to him. Then, too, there was the ugly fact that the sane, sensible Rabbi Shlomo had virtually no followers at all among the sane, sensible secularized Jews of our kibbutz, whereas Reb Shmuel's Hasidim looked upon him with awe, regarding him as a miracle worker, a seer, a saint. Still, Rabbi Shlomo's understandable jealousies and prejudices aside, Joseph Avneri was right: dybbuks were vapors out of the realm of the fantastic, and the fantastic was the Baal Shem's kingdom.

He was an improbably tall, angular figure, almost skeletal, with gaunt cheekbones, a soft, thickly curling beard, and gentle dreamy eyes. I suppose he was about fifty years old, though I would have believed it if they said he was thirty or seventy or ninety. His sense of the dramatic was unfailing; now—it was late afternoon—he took up a position with the setting sun at his back, so that his long shadow engulfed us all, and spread forth his arms and said, "We have heard reports of a dybbuk among you."

"There is no dybbuk!" Rabbi Shlomo retorted fiercely.

The Baal Shem smiled. "But there is a Kunivar who speaks with an Israeli voice?"

"There has been an odd transformation, yes," Rabbi Shlomo conceded. "But in this age, on this planet, no one can take dybbuks seriously."

"That is, *you* cannot take dybbuks seriously," said the Baal Shem.

"I do!" cried Joseph Avneri in exasperation. "I! I! I am the dybbuk! I, Joseph Avneri, dead a year ago last Elul, doomed for my sins to inhabit this Kunivar carcass. A Jew, Reb Shmuel, a dead Jew, a pitiful sinful miserable Yid. Who'll let me out? Who'll set me free?"

"There is no dybbuk?" the Baal Shem said amiably.

"This Kunivar has gone insane," said Shlomo Feig.

We coughed and shifted our feet. If anyone had gone insane it was our rabbi, denying in this fashion the phenomenon that he himself had acknowledged as genuine, however reluctantly, only a few hours before. Envy, wounded pride, and stubbornness had unbalanced his judgment. Joseph Avneri, enraged, began to bellow the Aleph Beth Gimel, the Shma Yisroel, anything that might prove his dybbukhood. The Baal Shem waited patiently, arms outspread, saying nothing. Rabbi Shlomo, confronting him, his powerful stocky figure dwarfed by the long-legged Hasid, maintained energetically that there had to be some rational explanation for the metamorphosis of Seul the Kunivar.

When Shlomo Feig at length fell silent, the Baal Shem said, "There is a dybbuk in this Kunivar. Do you think, Rabbi Shlomo, that dybbuks ceased their wanderings when the shtetls of Poland were destroyed? Nothing is lost in the sight of God, Rabbi. Jews go to the stars; the Torah and the Talmud and the Zohar have gone also to the stars; dybbuks too may be found in these strange worlds. Rabbi, may I bring peace to this troubled spirit and to this weary Kunivar?"

"Do whatever you want," Shlomo Feig muttered in disgust, and strode away, scowling.

Reb Shmuel at once commenced the exorcism. He called first for a minyan. Eight of his Hasidim stepped forward. I exchanged a glance with Shmarya Asch, and we shrugged and came forward too, but the Baal Shem, smiling, waved us away and beckoned two more of his followers into the circle. They began to sing; to my everlasting shame I have no idea what the singing was about, for the words were Yiddish of a Galitzianer sort, nearly as alien to me as the Kunivaru tongue. They sang for ten or fifteen minutes; the Hasidim grew more animated, clapping their hands, dancing about their Baal Shem; suddenly Reb Shmuel lowered his arms to his sides, silencing them, and quietly began to recite Hebrew phrases, which after a moment I recognized as those of the Ninety-first Psalm: The Lord is my refuge and my fortress, in him will I trust. The psalm rolled melodiously to its comforting conclusion, its promise of deliverance and salvation. For a long moment all was still. Then in a terrifying voice, not loud but immensely commanding, the Baal Shem ordered the spirit of Joseph Avneri to quit the body of Seul the Kunivar. "Out! Out! God's name out, and off to your eternal rest!" One of the Hasidim handed Reb Shmuel a shofar. The Baal Shem put the ram's horn to his lips and blew a single titanic blast.

Joseph Avneri whimpered. The Kunivar that housed him took three awkward, toppling steps. "Oy, mama, mama," Joseph cried. The Kunivar's head snapped back; his arms shot straight out at his sides; he tumbled clumsily to his four knees. An eon went by. Then Seul rose—smoothly, this time, with natural Kunivaru grace—and went to the Baal Shem, and knelt, and touched the tzaddik's black robe. So we knew the thing was done.

Instants later the tension broke. Two of the Kunivaru priests rushed toward the Baal Shem, and then Gyaymar, and then some of the musicians, and then it seemed the whole tribe was pressing close upon him, trying to touch the holy man. The Hasidim, looking worried, murmured their concern, but the Baal Shem, towering over the surging mob, calmly blessed the Kunivaru, stroking the dense fur of their backs. After some minutes of this the Kunivaru set up a rhythmic chant, and it was a while before I realized what they were saying. Moshe Shiloah and Yakov Ben-Zion caught the sense of it about the same time I did, and we began to laugh, and then our laughter died away.

"What do their words mean?" the Baal Shem called out.

"They are saying," I told him, "that they are convinced of the power of your god. They wish to become Jews."

For the first time Reb Shmuel's poise and serenity shattered. His eyes flashed ferociously and he pushed at the crowding Kunivaru, opening an avenue between them. Coming up to me, he snapped, "Such a thing is an absurdity!"

"Nevertheless, look at them. They worship you, Reb Shmuel."

"I refuse their worship."

"You worked a miracle. Can you blame them for adoring you and hungering after your faith?"

"Let them adore," said the Baal Shem. "But how can they become Jews? It would be a mockery."

I shook my head. "What was it you told Rabbi Shlomo? Nothing is lost in the sight of God. There have always been converts to Judaism—we never invite them, but we never turn them away if they're sincere, eh, Reb Shmuel? Even here in the stars, there is continuity of tradition, and tradition says we harden not our hearts to those who seek the truth of God. These are a good people—let them be received into Israel."

"No," the Baal Shem said. "A Jew must first of all be human."

"Show me that in the Torah."

"The Torah! You joke with me. A Jew must first of all be human. Were cats allowed to become Jews? Were horses?"

"These people are neither cats nor horses, Reb Shmuel. They are as human as we are."

"No! No!"

"If there can be a dybbuk on Mazel Tov IV," I said, "then there can also be Jews with six limbs and green fur."

"No. No. No. *No!*"

The Baal Shem had had enough of this debate. Shoving aside the clutching hands of the Kunivaru in a most unsaintly way, he gathered his followers and stalked off, a tower of offended dignity, bidding us no farewells.

✿

But how can true faith be denied? The Hasidim offered no encouragement, so the Kunivaru came to us; they learned Hebrew and we loaned them books, and Rabbi Shlomo gave them religious instruction, and in their own time and in their own way they entered into Judaism. All this was years ago, in the first generation after the Landing. Most of those who lived in those days are dead now—Rabbi Shlomo, Reb Shmuel the Baal Shem, Moshe Shiloah, Shmarya Asch. I was a young man then. I know a good deal more now, and if I am no closer to God than I ever was, perhaps He has grown closer to me. I eat meat and butter at the same meal, and I plow my land on the Sabbath, but those are old habits that have little to do with belief or the absence of belief.

We are much closer to the Kunivaru, too, than we were in those early days; they no longer seem like alien beings to us, but merely neighbors whose bodies have a different form. The younger ones of our kibbutz are especially drawn to them. The year before last Rabbi Lhaoyir the Kunivar suggested to some of our boys that they come for lessons to the Talmud Torah, the religious school, that he runs in the Kunivaru village; since the death of Shlomo Feig there has been no one in the kibbutz to give such instruction. When Reb Yossele, the son and successor of Reb Shmuel the Baal Shem heard this, he raised strong objections. If your boys will take instruction, he said, at least send them to us, and not to green monsters. My son Yigal threw him out of the kibbutz. We would rather let our boys learn the Torah from green monsters, Yigal told Reb Yossele, than have them raised to be Hasidim.

And so my son's son has had his lessons at the Talmud Torah of Rabbi Lhaoyir the Kunivar, and next spring he will have his bar mitzvah. Once I would have been appalled by such goings-on, but now I say only, How strange, how unexpected, how interesting! Truly the Lord, if He exists, must have a keen sense of humor. I like a god who can smile and wink, who doesn't take himself too seriously. The Kunivaru are Jews! Yes! They are preparing David for his bar mitzvah! Yes! Today is Yom Kippur, and I hear the sound of the shofar coming from their village! Yes! Yes. So be it. So be it, yes, and all praise be to Him.

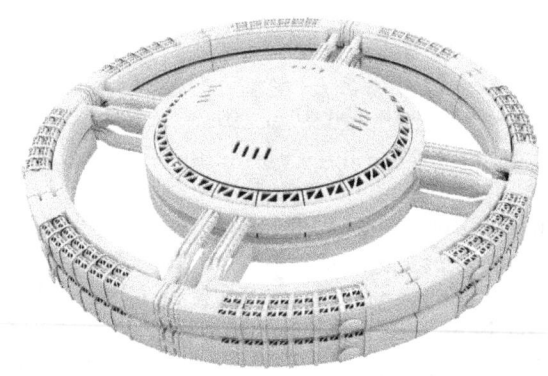

Jody Lynn Nye is the author of forty novels and more than one hundred stories, and has at various times collaborated with Anne McCaffrey and Robert Aspin. Her husband, Bill Fawcett, is a prolific author, editor and packager, and is also active in the gaming field.

RECOMMENDED BOOKS

by Jody Lynn Nye and Bill Fawcett

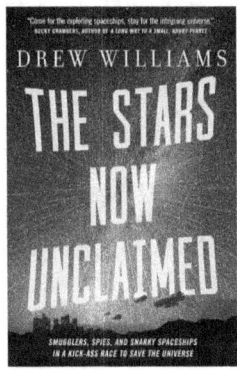

The Stars Now Unclaimed
by Drew Williams
TOR
August 2018
ISBN-13: 978-1250186119

To be honest, we were not sure at first we were going to recommend this book. The cover descriptions were rather generic. But then after getting a few chapters in, WOW. This book is a find. Not because of elegant prose, though it is competently written, but because Drew Williams can really tell a rip-roaring story that hardly lets the reader pause for breath.

The premise is that humans had settled on thousands of worlds, colonizing most of the galaxy over unknown millennia. At first, all had gone well, but gradually various sects with widely diverse and conflicting beliefs became dominant on many worlds. The once peaceful and high-tech galaxy began, at an accelerating rate, to tear itself apart. From minor conflicts, the battles had escalated until entire planets, or even solar systems, were being wiped out almost daily. Many felt humanity was on the verge of making itself extinct or nearly so.

One sect, Justified, was formed to solve the problem. They found a possible tech solution, a weapon that actively suppressed technology, and began to develop it. But before it could be tested, or even really finished, the Justified was attacked by a hostile space fleet. In desperation the Justified decided to try a prototype of their weapon. It worked, far too well. Instead of affecting one solar system, it spread undiminished across the Milky Way. Think of this weapon as a permanently active EMP blast that also continues to destroy new tech exposed to it and attaches itself to planets. The entire galaxy was swept over by "the Pulse" and thousands of civilizations collapsed. With that as the back story, we follow the adventures of a soldier and Justified agent who was born before the Pulse. Her job is to find and recruit mentally superpowered youths whose births were a side effect of the changes. Her main challenge is that a warlike sect known as the Pax has retained much of its tech and is determined to recruit and brainwash these youths themselves. She escapes with a young talent but receives an emergency call from another agent. In order to save her friend, the Justified agent finds herself up against a threat that is likely to wipe out Justified's hidden home world.

The book comes in short, action-filled chapters and moves intelligently from suspense to combat to battle. Far more than half the chapters portray some form of military or personal action. Williams does an excellent job of bringing both the large picture and the effects of the crisis on those directly involved. A sarcastic ship's AI and other deeply drawn characters add to your enjoyment. With something intriguing happening or building in every chapter, this is one of those books you will be reluctant to put down. Recommended for anyone who reads space opera, military science fiction, or just enjoys an action-filled, fast read.

Privateer
by Margaret Weis and Robert Krammes
Tor Books
August 2018
ISBN-13: 978-0765381095

Privateer is the second book in the *Dragon Corsairs* series. The world has no oceans; rather their oceans are simply thicker air which forms a boundary beneath which you cannot breathe. There is just enough surface tension that a ship supported by gas balloons and magic can sail on them as we do the seas. There is also magic, dragons, pirates, wars, and lots of intrigue.

In this novel, Prince Thomas Stanford continues to tour the islands of his father's realm and also those of his father's enemies. He discovers that his love, Kate, who just happens to also be a pirate captain made famous by a hack writer who never met her, has been captured and sentenced to be hung. First Tom has to free her from the middle of a fortress filled with enemy soldiers, then escape an alerted city on gryphons, then recover a ship hidden on a distant island in order to save Kate's trapped and suffocating crew. After that, the prince finds himself a pirate on his own seas.

The world is imaginative and unique. The characters well drawn and the swashbuckling action right out of a *Captain Blood*–era movie. But the real reason to read this series is that these books are just plain fun. These are set on the same fascinating world as the author's *Dragon Brigade* novels, so if you like the world and writing, there are more books out there for you, but you don't have to have read them to enjoy this new series.

Zion's Fiction: A Treasury of Israeli Speculative Literature
edited by Sheldon Teitelbaum and Emanuel Lottem
Mandel Vilar Press
September 2018
ISBN-13: 978-1942134527

Zion's Fiction is a collection of stories written and centering on Israel in the future. The quality of the stories ranges from quite good to really exciting. This is hardly a surprise as the editors had literally thousands of stories to pick from in a country that is a hotbed of science fiction writing and publishing. Most are science fiction and a number, if written here, are classic, hard science fiction that would have been at home in *Asimov's Science Fiction* magazine or John Campbell's *Analog*.

Beyond being good reading, perhaps the greatest appeal of this collection is the insight its stories give into the mind and attitudes of a place that is, in many ways, similar to the USA (a democracy, modern, and industrial) and yet very different, as a nation under virtual siege for two generations. The stories are generally optimistic and reflect a faith in both the future and in mankind. A good read that can also be a somewhat thoughtful one. Recommended for those who like short stories, hard science fiction, and those who wish to expand their world view.

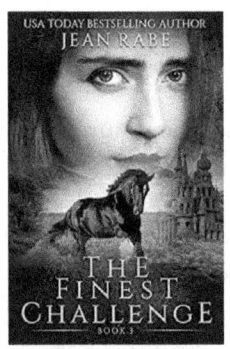

The Finest Challenge
by Jean Rabe
Boone Street Press
April 2018
ISBN-13: 978-1732003613

The Finest Challenge is book three of Jean Rabe's Finest trilogy. The creators of mankind saw we needed help, so they made their Finest Creations, which appear to humans to be elegant horses. But the Finest are intelligent, telepathic, can communicate with animals, and have a strong sense of morality. Each Finest, when trained and ready, forms a strong bond with one of those humans who has the greatest potential to do good or evil. But one young Finest has to rush into service before being fully trained. Set in a medieval world, these books are wonderfully different with unusual perspectives, good action, and characters you would like to meet. If you love horses or riding, they are a must. If you want to enjoy a different approach to a story full of nobles, villains, courts and combat then start with *The Finest Challenge* or look for all three books in the series.

Avatar Dreams
edited by Kevin Anderson, Mike Resnick and Dr. Harry Kloor
Wordfire Press
April 2018
ISBN-13: 978-1614755999

The amazing, or maybe frightening, fact is that we may not be that far from the everyday use of avatars today. Technology is weaving into our lives in new ways every day. Augmented Reality, where the pixelated universe interacts with the real world, has become a popular reality with the massive game of Pokemon GO. The military is using a wide range of drones. A drone firing a hellfire missile in Afghanistan is likely under the control of a soldier sitting at a control panel in the Midwest USA. Already psychologists are decrying younger generation's preference for sitting at their computer or preferring to use their phone to actually traveling or interacting. If things continue as they are today, then *Avatar Dreams* gives us a look at what could be the near future. The stories all focus on humans using their avatars in many different ways including entertainment, mountain climbing, rescues and sports. All are well written, as you might expect with short story guru Mike Resnick doing the editing. (Full disclosure here: the co-author of this review column, Jody Lynn Nye, has the wrap story in this volume, so this is Bill writing this review.) The technology is all plausible, thanks to Dr. Kloor, a leader in the field, and that adds to the stories' impact. You will easily be able to see yourself as part of the brave, new avatar-filled worlds. Thoughtful without taking away any of the fun, enjoyment, or even occasional humor.

The Boy from Tomorrow
by Camille DeAngelis
Amberjack Publishing
May 2018
ISBN-13: 978-1944995614

This charming young adult book brings the reader a pair of twelve-year-olds, Alec Frost and Josie Clifford, who live in the same house one hundred years apart. Josie's mother, Lavinia, is a noted oracle, who holds seances in the front room for a select clientele in 1915, and claims to speak to the spirits of the dead. Alec and his mother have just moved there in 2015 after his parents separated. Both children have difficult lives for very different reasons. Lavinia is selfish, secretive and abusive, cruelly isolating Josie and her younger sister, Cassie, from the rest of society. Alec is shy and introverted, finding it difficult to reach out to make friends in a new city.

They find one another, unexpectedly, through the use of a "speaking board" (i.e., Ouija board) that remains in the house. At first, Alec and Josie believe the other to be a spirit, but come to understand the truth, and become friends across the separation of a century. Alec is all too aware that he and his new acquaintance will almost certainly never meet in person, but he comes to enjoy the friendship, telling Josie all about the world of the future. Josie tells him about her life and the history of the house.

But all does not run smoothly. The secret, on both ends of history, comes out, threatening to ruin the bond between the children. Alec himself is betrayed by a jealous schoolmate, making him want to retreat from his new school. Lavinia, keen to keep her primacy as the foreteller of important events, discovers her daughter's conversation with a boy from the fu-

ture, and holds the board hostage, demanding facts about the future in exchange for letting Alec have access to his friend.

Both children are resourceful, though, and manage to maintain a relationship that will surprise and delight the reader. Alec is reluctant to find out the fate of his friends but picks up clue after clue that lead him to a marvelous, though realistic conclusion. Apart from the means of communication between the children, there are no miracles in this story, but it is a very good read. Recommended for young adults twelve and up (there is some discussion of death) and curious adults who wonder how they would handle a friendship with someone who lived a century away.

Low Chicago
edited by George R. R. Martin
Tor Books
June 2018
ISBN-13: 978-0765390561

The Wild Cards series are shared-world anthologies that have been published for literally three decades. They are noted for quality writing and fascinating characters. We have recommended another Wild Cards book in an earlier column and are not surprised to find ourselves doing it again. Most of the main characters in this long-running series of anthologies are "Aces." Just after World War II ended an alien virus spreads around the world. Most people are unaffected or die, but a few "draw the Ace" and are changed. For many this involves often painfully developing a single superpower.

In *Low Chicago*, a group of Aces and rich elites gather for a high stakes poker game at the Palmer

House hotel on the city's lakefront. Most are accompanied by their Ace bodyguards. Then an accident by a waitress escalates until one of the Ace's instinctively exercises his power to shift things into the past. In this case a room full of spoiled rich types and their Aces each find themselves alone and naked in 1929. Their problem is to survive and figure out a way to get home. However, having knowledge of the future, they immediately begin changing history.

Low Chicago follows each of those thrown back into time as they search for the time-shunting Ace and his partner to be returned to the future. The problem is that to return to the time stream they know, each discovers that they have to undo the changes they created, even if it means allowing the lives of those they have saved to be lost.

One Ace thrown back into the past is the bodyguard, Kahn. He is literally half cat (the left half) with feline strength, reflexes and instincts. Just to survive, Kahn takes a bodyguard job protecting the mobster Bugs Moran from Al Capone. To get the job, the Ace proves himself by preventing the St. Valentine's Day Massacre, but then finds himself fur-deep in a mob war. Another time refugee joins what was a very active silent movie studio movement in Chicago in the '30s. Using the successes of the future as a model for their own moving pictures, he becomes a real success. Based upon their nature and gifts, every Ace has to deal with the fact that they are in a time before the virus and no one understands what they are.

Time paradoxes, moral dilemmas and superpowered Aces all blend beautifully. As a resident of the city, I can even attest that the authors get the gritty and bloodthirsty feel of mob-driven old Chicago correct. *Low Chicago* is so much fun I can almost forgive Mr. Martin for not working on the next *Game of Thrones* novel instead of editing it. On a very positive note, while the details have not been released, it appears that a studio owned by NBC is working on a Wild Cards TV series. If you have not yet started the book series, you have a great treat and lot of reading to look forward to. Feel free to start with this collection. If you are already one of the many Wild Cards fans, this is another great book you will enjoy.

Gregory Benford is a Nebula winner and a former Worldcon Guest of Honor. He is the author of more than thirty novels, six books of non-fiction, and has edited ten anthologies.

A SCIENTIST'S NOTEBOOK

by Gregory Benford

COLLIDING CULTURES

This is a remembrance from 1997, when I first visited Arthur C. Clarke. It seems still relevant, though Arthur is not here any more.

Calcutta was a dry dust bowl simmering beneath a perpetual gray haze.

The drive from the airport recalled my last visit to India a decade before: endless shanties, rusting roofs, three-wheelers honking and milling in the chaotic roads, crowds stirring restlessly amid heaps of garbage and mysteriously common broken concrete.

The smells came out to greet me, classic third world tropical: spices, coal soot, cabbage, musty bare concrete, low-octane gasoline, dried sweat, urine, cheap perfume, unwashed frying pans, wood smoke. The aroma of history, and plenty of it.

Not an auspicious beginning for the International Conference on the Synthesis of Science and Religion, which was paying all my expenses. I began coughing within hours of my arrival on January 6, 1997. Every other day I had a massage and steam bath to feel clean again. I had thought myself seasoned by my three weeks in India in the mid-1980s, but this visit was different. A sense of a vast, brooding continent pervaded the streets.

It is easier to think like a scientist in the crisp West, with its air conditioning, ample lighting and orderly habits. The East seethes with age, musty atmospherics and a sense of how contingent anything is. Arrangements dissolve, distinctions blur. Western technology often seems an intrusion which will be digested while leaving the society unchanged. In the West, we often feel shaped by our technology, its pace driving us.

I tried to send an e-mail back to my secretary, going to the conference's sole computer. As I worked with the unfamiliar software I could look down into a courtyard where a cart pumped urine out of an underground vat. It collected there for harvesting; boiled, it yielded valuable chemical salts. The contrast between technologies was striking, and easy to smell.

Seeing a sleek Mercedes waiting at stoplights beside rickshaws drawn by men, and bullocks towing carts behind in the next lane, yields a sense of cultural vertigo. Technology inevitably gives birth to such dislocations when it collides with vast, distant cultures. In the West we tend to think of our technology as wedded to our time. That luxury the East cannot afford; centuries elbow each other for your attention.

Mature technology is discreet, simple, quiet, sinuously classical, even friendly. When it fits in, its use remains as obvious as a hammer, its effects as cheap as a floppy disk. Both it and its users have educated each other. New tech, though, strikes an oddly religious echo. The e-mail I used could only be accessed by one of the men who worked at the conference center, a devotee of the Hare Krishnas. Already he had become like a priest of the machine. The ordinary computer was central yet mysterious and the workers treated it with a hushed attention, like a sacred artifact of unknown powers.

Still, I had to remind myself that some of our Western abstractions are mere mannerisms, not essential. Why say 12:00 hours or 24:00 hours when *noon* and *midnight* work clearly?

☼

Calcutta seemed an unlikely venue to discuss science, a purely Western invention. We moved amid a world where religion seemed to shape the entire society. As with my 1980s visit, the longer I stayed the more alien the great subcontinent seemed. The veneer of the Raj, with its railroads and inventions bringing order, wore away. India has produced great scientists such as Bose and Chandrasekhar, but such names came from the tiny class at the top of a great population pyramid.

Coincidentally, English prime minister John Major was visiting Calcutta, and the anxious city managers cleared the streets of the homeless. Several hundred thousand live in downtown Calcutta;

from my hotel room I could see them bed down for the night on the sidewalks. I got caught up in the Hawker's Union demonstration against this temporary deportation to the suburbs; it was a fairly orderly march jamming the entire downtown, thickly patrolled by police. The hawkers demanded the right to sell in the streets and dwell there as well, at least during weekdays.

Meanwhile, the conference leaned heavily toward the more New Age brand of science; to me, New Age should be pronounced to rhyme with "sewage." There were plenty of references to cosmological issues and interpretations of quantum mechanics. Often, the subtle issues of distinguishing between observers in wave mechanics leads to a kind of verbal segue into consciousness-as-primary thinking.

This can easily slide into a view that intelligence is the most important property in physical theories, and so Mind truly holds sway over Matter. Eastern religions like Mind over Matter, so there were many talks about connecting modern physics to age-old doctrines from the major Asian faiths, especially those in the Vedantic tradition. The Hare Krishnas are the newest emergent group from those based on the ancient sacred texts of Hinduism.

I reflected, though, that the physical sciences also strived for a goal which was, if not The Truth—for such was impossible, in the common sense—then at least the most complex yet elegant, chimpanzee view of the world. And the gut feelings which guide scientists have an aesthetic base that does not differ fundamentally from the inchoate yearnings that emerged from many of the conference speeches.

Even in arcane ornamentation, there are similarities. The Krishnas have an elaborate cosmology with vast, long ages of humanity and "emerging essences," an arcane history.

Compare with one current quantum field theory, which begins in eighteen dimensions, and then "rolls up" all but four, so that fourteen are unobservably small—perhaps a billion billion billion times more tiny than an atom. Then the universe proceeds more or less as Einstein's gravitational theory dictates.

In this picture we are living in a universe only apparently three-dimensional in space; infinitesimal but real dimensions lurk all about. Without such an early rolling up, any resulting universe could not support life, for there could be no stable atoms. Further, only in odd-numbered dimensions can waves propagate sharply, so three dimensions are favored over two. So we live not only in the best of all possible worlds, but the only possible one.

Such surrealistically bizarre images came from considering the form and symmetries of abstruse equations. In such chilly realms, beauty was often the only guide. The embarrassment of dimensions arose from seeking a mathematical clarity in eighteen dimensions, then hiding the extra dimensions from actually acting in our physical world.

To physicists, "natural" has come to mean how equations should look, their beauty. Aesthetic considerations are in the end a mask for chimpanzee preferences. Religions are constrained in the same, basic way.

✿

A long day of listening to quantum queasiness demands some time off. One evening we speakers at the conference went to a posh estate tucked into the bleak cityscape. Through iron gates guarded by tough-looking men in suits, through a plush house festooned with tasteful art, into an ample yard where dozens of servants presented a wide-ranging Indian supper, some of it not recommended for the timid alimentary canal. Ancient dishes simmered in modern serving-table hardware, quite agreeably. No culture conflict here, I thought, digging in.

Our host was one of Bengal's leading industrialists, who said he supported the Communist ("Left Front") government that had been in power for more than two decades. I found his continuing support difficult to believe, since the regime had driven Bengal into poverty, but the host felt that, after so long, the communists at least knew how things worked. I asked, "You mean, who to deal with?"

The well-dressed jute baron smiled. "Economics here is not markets, but personalities." He saw economics not as the working out of laws, but of wills. Going back to our hotel, the bare sidewalks were covered with sleeping bodies, some in muddy rags. Some were erecting new shacks, which the police would eventually sweep away. Nobody thought

matters might someday be better. "India's path is different," I heard often. This seemed to mean that it had flatlined.

✿

One of the Ayatollahs of Iran spoke at the Conference, giving little away except platitudes about how Islam was more scientifically forward-looking than the Judeo-Christian faiths. His evidence proceeded rather obscurely from Genesis. That evening I pointed out to him at that in Genesis, God's first charge to Adam is to name the beasts—zoology, if not biology.

He blinked and said, "What would it take to make the United States friends with Iran again?"

The connection to Genesis was not obvious. Off the top of my head I said, "Remember that the U.S. doesn't forgive or forget enemies if it doesn't defeat them. Cuba, North Korea, North Vietnam…you're in that club." I wondered why he was asking me, a scientist.

"But there must be something we can do?"

"Cut out supporting terrorism and don't deploy weapons which can command the Persian Gulf, I'd say."

"The fundamentalists cause the terrorism."

Interesting, that he didn't try to deny Iran's role. "So?"

"The Jews are behind all the fundamentalists of Islam."

He seemed surprised when I laughed. It was an honest mistake; I had thought he was joking.

Despite modern communications, Iran lived not in the real world but in a culture of imagination. All the TV and email the West could inject could not dispel illusions held fast in hard minds. Later I realized that nearly all his thinking revolved around conspiracies of some form, that history was indeed the result not of blunt economic forces and individual invention, but of collusions large and small.

✿

After a week I began to see in a gut-deep way how much Indian society yearns to be free of the material world. Not surprising, considering how awful much of it is there, but the revulsion goes deeper, leading to a rejection of the body itself. Their myriad faiths all stress suppressing appetites; perhaps a shrewd move, in a place where satisfying them isn't on the menu. Here Marx seemed right, for once: religion keeps the swarming masses in the choked streets well laced with its opiate.

My instincts are utterly opposite. I grew up in a religious home, but early on learned a proper skepticism, the comfy doubt of frayed religiosity. The church has a polite glacial veneer that coats a flat disbelief in all things super-natural or super-human. Plainly this is not enough for the increasing numbers in the advanced nations who turn to fundamentalism. They dislike the squashing of all morality into a pale, thin social ethic. No God, no order.

☼

In the four-day conference we got yet more quantum mechanics, which seems to have become a passport for fuzzy thinking based on the hard results of physics. Describing the world mathematically, I realized, sometimes gives a misleading air of authority. Too many scientists and philosophers thought that numbers were sitting out there in nature, waiting to be found, sorted, totted up. With enough docile computers, they imagined, scientists could relax while the flood of number wrote their papers for them. The humanists' work was mostly matters of opinion. Poetry might be a perpetually moving target; science was not.

But "hard" facts can soften overnight, melt away under the pressure of newer hard facts. Interpretation shifts. Concepts once abandoned, like the corpuscular theory of light or the transmutability of the elements, have to be looked at again, centuries later. Science is far more provisional and tentative than many want to believe. It is really high adventure, precarious, the wildest of all explorations—not at all like cataloging or adding bricks to an already vast edifice.

Indeed, it was science's *strangeness* that drew me to it. Every era erects ornate explanations and trusts them enormously. But stiff science is harmful nonsense.

A speaker who had explicitly connected quantum effects and the religious experience came up to me at one of the coffee breaks. "Do you follow my line of argument?" He had a quick, ironic smile and pursed lips, a reserved gaze—the scholar's look.

"Too many leaps for me," I admitted.

"Perhaps in time these ideas will tunnel into your mind."

"Quantum tunneling?" I asked, but he did not think this was a joking matter.

☼

The conference took pains to be broad, admitting many points of view. I appeared on the program three times and quickly found that I was the Official Skeptic. I spoke on the moral/ethical problems soon to come from biotech, centering on the definition of what it means to be human, and found that the ethicists and religious figures there had done little thinking on these problems. Indeed, they were confounded by the present.

Males exceed females among the children of India by several million already, due to sex detection in the womb plus ready abortion: a classic collision of the modern liberal agenda, with its seemingly penalty-free menu. A true feminist dilemma.

What happens when urban China and the western U.S. cities produce a five percent differences between the sexes? And this sex difference arises from a decade-old technology; soon enough, parents will be able to edit out imbeciles or midgets, if they like. What boundary should society impose, or is all left to the parents?

Nobody had any answers. Nor did I, but I am not in that business. Scientists can sound the alarm; the big decisions should lie with those who lead society as a whole.

☼

The more I learned of one of the conference sponsors, the Hare Krishnas, the more odd they seemed. Only in a quarter of their lives could their devotees have sex, and then only once a month, strictly for reproduction. Otherwise, they were to avoid meat, alcohol, caffeine, TV, movies, even non-Krishna books; a mental claustrophobia. Of the four stages of life (Youth, Housekeeping, Retirement, Renunciation) the latter two were the most valued, for they withdrew more from the world.

These ideas emerged from the Indian culture itself, and were not mere tacked-on measures. The Krishnas are basically a chanting cult, recruiting those adept at auto-hypnosis. Their rules constrain their followers and fuel their expansion. Vedantic culture is inhospitable to our modern scientific worldview; followers regularly assured me that humans had been around for hundreds of millions of years, contrary to the "misleading" fossil evidence.

Indeed, their cosmology has a sense of futility about it. One must go through reincarnation, I was told, many thousands of times before reaching enlightenment. Nobody I met was going to get nirvana in the next life, by any means. With goals so far away, a listlessness sets in.

If the Hare Krishnas gain more power as India subsides into a lethargic wreck, they will become important. I decided to take a look at one of their major installations.

On the long four-hour journey from Calcutta to Mayapur, a religious retreat, our driver carefully explained that if he should strike any of the many bicyclists, he would have to drive speedily away, and would we please not shout at him for doing so.

The reason was simple. Villagers commonly dragged drivers from cars that hurt locals, no matter who might be a fault, and typically beat them to death. They also beat the passengers, robbed them and stole the car.

So we should understand and not criticize if this should befall us on this trip. This little speech focused my uneasy attention on the roadway, and three times we came very close to scattering a bicyclist from our path, but at the last instant the driver swerved away. I rode most of the way with held breath.

Along the way we stopped for a drink at a shack roofed in tin with no walls. A man stirred a soup over a fire and a few men sat at a table drinking Coke. Why was this a hotel? Then I saw the cane racks set out on the roadside, where lorry drivers could sleep within a few yards of the traffic. No walls, no rooms. The sense of a hotel setting a boundary between yourself and the world was gone, a fleeting Western concept.

Walking into the dusk, I found that beyond the road lay rice paddies as far as the eye could see, no stands of trees more than a few yards wide. Figures labored over them into the night. The natural world had vanished, replaced by incessant agriculture, a solely human landscape. Much of India is the same flattened spectacle, a stage for the endlessly cyclic Vedantic drama of birth and death and around again.

At the Hare Krishna compound I ate excellent vegetarian food, watched their pre-dawn dancing worship, and toured the temples and schools. The Vedantic reverence for all life extends famously to cows; here they had airy stables. Concrete chutes carry their dung into an underground dome, where it decays and methane collects above it. The concrete blister poked above the ground next to the school's kitchen. From the dome's pressure trap they pipe methane directly into the stoves and ovens upon which the cooks prepare lunch. The gas burns cleanly, blue and hot. A touch of Western engineering plus a plentiful resource.

How clean was it? I asked. Very, they said.

This is certainly a better solution than the traditional, which we saw along many plaster walls and the sides of houses: dung pancakes shaped by hand and stuck up to dry. When they are ripe they fall off, are collected and stacked in ricks to dry further. Eventually they are burned in the huts for heat and cooking fuel, the smoke inhaled by the whole family.

Among the neatly arranged, traditional, thatch-roofed classrooms I saw two women spreading a brown layer on the dusty paths. One mixed cow dung in a bucket of water and the other smoothed it everywhere with a broom.

Why? Ancient Vedantic lore holds that cow waste is medicinal. It sanitizes the area, my guide said; much cheaper than Western products.

Inside one of the classrooms they were using computers. The reputation of the Hare Krishna compound was exceptional, and indeed, it had a directed, orderly efficiency that reminded me of well run private (but not public) schools in the USA. Most of the compound is run by Americans, who have struck an odd and occasionally unsettling balance between cultures.

✿

Conferences never end with firm conclusions. This one had uncovered the expected oppositions between views, but without finding new pathways to reconcile them. No surprise. I was glad to escape Calcutta's claustrophobic atmosphere, winging off for an overnight in Bombay, speaking at the opening of a new Institute for the Study of Consciousness.

Bombay is the richest, biggest city in India, predicted to become the world's largest by 2020. The government has changed the city's name to Mumbai but it isn't sticking, and the inhabitants have no time to care; about half of them are homeless, and over a third of the houses do not have safe drinking water. From an air-cushion water bus, sipping drinks with umbrellas in them, you can watch swarms of the poor thronging the beaches. The trash service picks up bodies dead of starvation, hauling them away, past some of the city's 150 diet clinics.

Charles Townes, a retired but remarkably active University of California professor, had been at the meeting and the compound. In Bombay we sat together on the platform and wondered what one could say about trying to study the bewildering problem of consciousness by blending both scientific and Vedantic ideas. Townes invented the maser, whose central idea led quickly to the laser, and won a Nobel for it. He said that he had always had an interest in the interface of the scientific worldview and others. So far, he noted, not much had come of it in his lifetime. Science steamrollered on and other views seemed to have little impact on the world.

I made a few remarks on how the history of science, and my experience of it, shows that our most valuable instrument is a ready recognition of what we do not know, and our most valuable attitude is the willingness to question what we think we do. Certainly India had underlined that; I kept colliding with ideas quite foreign and unforgettable.

I duly showed up for my flight to Sri Lanka, only to find that it did not exist. How could the airline issue a ticket for a non-flight? Shrugs; "clerk error." But why did they then confirm the flight only three days before? "Another clerking error, sir." A mysterious smile; of Conradian darkness?

Waiting for the next day's flight, I watched Hare Krishna devotees in the temple next door as they ran their robot play, featuring their guru. With recordings of his voice, the guru-robot moved through little playlets, dispensing wisdom and even meeting a robot Lord Krishna.

The lifelike head and arm movements seemed unlikely to convince anyone of holy mysteries, but I found fascinating a parallel vision on the laptop at my elbow. In reasonable definition and color *Terminator 2*'s robots from the future slugged it out, running from the CD-ROM drive. The ritual faith of one set exactly countered the existentialist void of the other, leaving me suspended in a techno-oblivion amid the Third World miasma of Bombay.

☼

Arthur Clarke's driver found me readily at the airport. He simply held up the hardcover jacket of the book we did together, *Beyond the Fall of Night*, a language-independent signal.

When I reached Arthur's home in Colombo, Sri Lanka seemed a paradise compared with India. Arthur was as quick and merry as always, centered in his high-tech web, taking calls and e-mails and faxes from the whole linked globe. I took a photo of him playing the Rama game derived from his novel, on a laptop computer. The war of men and alien lifeforms was a useful distraction from the knowledge that a real civil war was raging right outside; I had to pass through several army checkpoints to get around the city.

When he had to rest in the afternoons he let me have his red Mercedes and driver to visit the Arthur Clarke University, allied with the larger university some miles away. Newly built, it concentrates on practical training in electronics appropriate for the region, particularly circuits that manage appliances during the nearly daily blackouts and brownouts of an infrastructure strained to supply adequate power.

Such hardnosed applications parallel Arthur's early technological career, when he worked on radar and then envisioned communications satellites linking the planet. Even so, his fiction has often been techno-mystical, with a touch of longing for the same release from the body. Arthur has lived in Colombo since the middle 1950s, yet has never lost his faith that in expanding humanity's knowledge and capabilities lies the secret to our destiny.

Dwelling in a culture which abhors the flesh, he none the less sings of extending the human reach to the stars. I remembered the night sky over a temple where I had stayed in Mayapur, sharp and clear, which one of the devotees described as "the gods watching."

This uncanny sense occurred many times, the sense that in India one meets both past and future. If we continue to swell our numbers and despoil our world, we could make all the Earth like this. Something in me rebelled at the thought.

The ancient consolations would emerge: the Krishnas reminded me of a chimpanzee troop, chanting and dancing as solace. To that devotee, the stars were unattainable entities, serenely passing judgment on our failings.

To Arthur, they are a goal. The fast-moving dots of light are planets, after all. Our robots—spindly spiders, not imitation gurus—have already been there, reconnoitering. In time we could climb to them and find ourselves in the realization of our own ever-expanding horizons. Yet beside this sense of opening would always run the strains of far antiquity, heartfelt longings and seething hates alike, the consolations of a species still finding its way.

We discussed the coming of Hale-Bopp, a promisingly bright comet. While writing this memoir, it has grown enormously. As well, thirty-nine cultists have killed themselves, hoping to be picked up by a spaceship following the comet. The dark side of religion haunts us still, wearing the trappings of pop-sf with its "sci-fi" simplicities.

Clarke's attitude, living immersed in a culture that struggles to embrace new and old, came as a breath of clean air in the tropical sun. Leaving Sri Lanka, I exhaled with pleasure. Out with the coal soot, cabbage, musty bare concrete. I banished the stinging dust and oily fumes of Calcutta from my lungs, like ancient, spoiled ideas.

Copyright © 2018 by Gregory Benford

Robert J. Sawyer is the Hugo, Nebula, Campbell Memorial, Heinlein, Hal Clement, Skylark, Aurora, and Seiun Award-winning author of twenty-three bestselling science-fiction novels, including the trilogy of Hominids, Humans, *and* Hybrids, *which won Canada's Aurora Award for the Best Work of the Decade. Rob holds two honorary doctorates and is a Member of the Order of Canada, the highest civilian honor bestowed by the Canadian government. Find him online at sfwriter.com.*

DECOHERENCE

by Robert J. Sawyer

MAY THE FORBES BE WITH YOU

My friend and fellow Torontonian Karl Schroeder, one of our best authors of hard science fiction, has just published his first new book in four years, *The Million*, with Tor. Pay attention to these words as we go along: *hard SF, four years, Tor.* Karl's book is dedicated to his daughter Paige (and yes, I enjoyed shocking him just after Paige was born by pointing out, "You're a writer, and you've named your daughter a homonym for *page*?"). The dedication reads, "Not everything's a dystopia," doubtless a reference to the fact that the kind of books Paige's father writes are thin on the ground these days.

And yet on June 19, 2018, no less an august bastion of business than *Forbes* magazine posted an article on its website entitled "Science Fiction and Fantasy Book Sales Have Doubled Since 2010." Hallelujah, right? Not so fast.

The source for the *Forbes* piece was a forty-five slide PowerPoint presentation by the pseudonymous "Data Guy" at the 2018 Nebula Awards conference hosted by the Science Fiction and Fantasy Writers of America; you can see the slides at authorearnings.com/sfwa2018/. The title of his presentation was *We're Going to Need a Bigger Ship: Uncloaking the Missing Half of the SF&F Market.* He claims "SF&F book sales by traditional publishers have become the minority."

True, but there's some photon decoupling: way down in his deck he suddenly starts talking about "Science Fiction E-book Unit Sales by Subgenre"— that is, fantasy has magically gone *poof* (as, well, only fantasy *can*).

In descending sales order, here are the subgenres (by retailer title categorization): Military; Adventure; Post-Apocalyptic; Dystopian (hi, Paige!); Space Opera; First Contact; Alien Invasion; Galactic Engineering; Galactic Empire; Hard Science Fiction; Colonization; Cyberpunk; Space Exploration; Time Travel; Exploration; TV, Movie, Video Game Adaptations; Metaphysical & Visionary; Steampunk; Alternative History; Classics; Anthologies & Short Stores; Alternate History; Anthologies; LGBT; Humorous; and Short Stories.

Set aside the fact that a lot of his smaller categories should have been consolidated—Alternative History and Alternate History are the same thing, for instance. But even if he'd cleaned up the data, they'd still be tiny.

But his first, second, and fifth categories—Military, Adventure, and Space Opera—are very similar, and his second two, Post-Apocalyptic and Dystopian, are likewise kin. Consolidate each of those already giant groups and they become behemoths, far, far outselling everything else (but still with the first combined category beating the second).

One could argue that some of the other categories might be rolled into hard science fiction too, but that's a tougher judgment call. Hard science fiction—at least as Karl Schroeder and I practice it—follows in the footsteps of Arthur C. Clarke, Isaac Asimov, Robert A. Heinlein, Larry Niven, and Gregory Benford. It's firmly grounded in real science, its predictions are reasonable extrapolations, and it requires lots and lots of research, conceptualization, and hard work to write. As I noted up front, Karl's *The Million* is his first new book in four years; this sort of book takes time.

Another Toronto resident, Peter Watts, also a hard-SF writer, just put out his first book in four years as well, a novella called *The Freeze-Frame Revolution* from small-press Tachyon (his novels are from—wait for it—Tor). And my own next novel, *The Oppenheimer Alternative*, won't be out until 2020, which will also be a gap of four years for me.

Robert Charles Wilson is yet another hard-SF writer who lives in Toronto (yes, it's something in the water). Bob's been doing a new novel every two or three years, always for Tor, making him seem positively bionic compared with the rest of us.

(For those who ignore the extra effort that goes into creating true hard SF and declare its practitioners should just write faster, I'm reminded of the time when an author known for his prolificacy declared, "I can understand writers who only do one book a year; what I can't understand is what they do with the other nine months." My wife had the perfect rejoinder: "Polish their awards.")

Actually, Data Guy does look at fantasy separately later in his slide deck. The top category there, Paranormal & Urban, clocks in at north of 11,000,000 unit sales in his data period of May 2017–April 2018. Even combining Military, Adventure, and Space Opera into one yields only around 9,500,000 units as I read his graphs, and hard SF is downright tiny at 1,500,000 or so.

Near the end of the deck there's a slide that lists "SF sub-genres where traditional publishers underperform" and, despite Baen's historical dominance in this space, lo and behold, his top over-all sales category, Military, is also number one here, with just eleven percent coming from traditional publishers.

So, yeah, there's a huge explosion in self-publishing (which was Data Guy's main point), but it's in precisely the kind of book that is *easiest* to write, a category dominated by fast-paced tales and endless series. The *only* categories in which traditional publishers account for more than half the sales are the exact one you'd guess: classics (because self-publishing of e-books, of course, hasn't been around long enough to have any acknowledged classics yet), and the tie-in category of "TV, Movie, Video Game Adaptations," because those have to be authorized, and traditional publishers preferentially get the licenses.

So, yeah, *rah, rah, rah* for the fact that independent entrepreneurial authors are doing so well. But not much *RAH, RAH, RAH* (an old Heinlein joke) for the hard-SF field. Among traditional publishers, only Tor seems to service that category with any great regularity, and although there's a sizable number of self-published books that the authors have chosen to categorize as "Hard SF," very little of it has struck me as any good, and most of it is nowhere near as ambitious as the works by Schroeder, Watts, or Wilson.

Still, if you'd like a recommendation of a good independently published hard-SF book, try *Pink Noise: A Posthuman Tale* by Leonid Korogodski. But note it's been eight years since this, Korogodski's most-recent book—I fully expect him to move to Toronto soon.

Copyright © 2018 by Robert J. Sawyer

Joy Ward is the author of one novel. She has several stories in print, in magazines and in anthologies, and has also conducted interviews, both written and video, for other publications.

Larry Niven, Hugo and Nebula-winning co-author of such science fiction classics as Lucifer's Hammer *and* The Mote in God's Eye *has seen and been part of more science fiction history than many people. Most people do not realize that he played an instrumental role in twentieth century real world politics—the SDI, commonly known as the Star Wars Initiative. But in this 2015 interview, Mr. Niven talked about his long-time collaborator, Jerry Pournelle. Since this interview, we have, sadly, lost the brilliant Pournelle. I hope that this interview gives a bit of a window into the depth and breadth of their decades of collaboration.*

THE *GALAXY'S EDGE* INTERVIEW

Joy Ward Interviews Larry Niven

Joy Ward: You are known for your epic collaborations.

Larry Niven: I depend quite a lot more on my collaborators.

Collaborating is less lonely. I've been collaborating for most of my career. My career is fifty years old come December in terms of being a selling author. The first check came in June of 1964. The first sale was the December issue of *World of Ptavvs*, which probably came out in October or November. So, fifty years.

Forty-odd years ago I collaborated on a novel with David Gerrold and that was fun. So when Jerry Pournelle suggested collaborating, I dove in. That was *The Mote in God's Eye*, which took three years to write. A pain in the ass, but lots of fun.

We sent it off to Lurton Blassingame, and to Robert Heinlein, who was a friend of Jerry's. Both of them suggested cutting off the first hundred pages and, uh, and various other suggestions too. We did that and had to re-write, of course, to embed the information in the first hundred pages that we wanted in.

JW: How did you get into writing science fiction to start with?

LN: This was where the ideas were coming from.

There was a book in Hawthorne School. Hawthorne was where I went to grade school, and they had a book in which Mars was inhabited by animated carrots and onions at war with each other. Quite a bad book. I could've been turned off by that, but then I discovered Heinlein. Heinlein's *Rocket Ship Galileo*. Nazis on the moon, but well written, much better written.

JW: How old were you when you discovered Heinlein's *Rocket Ship Galileo*?

LN: Make it ten years old; something like that.

JW: What told you that you wanted to write this?

LN: It just seemed an obvious thing to try. I didn't have an ambition, really, and I locked on to this one; forced myself. I eventually sold something for twenty-five bucks and never looked back.

JW: I think you said your first collaboration was with David Gerrold. How did that come to be?

LN: I invited him and a date for dinner with me and Marilyn Niven. So, this must've been in…in around 1968, four years into my career. We invited him. He showed up without a date. He and I got to talking puns and started writing.

The first character there was Quizzard from the stars, whom we named for Isaac Asimov. Asimov had a translator that wasn't perfect.

JW: How did you end up collaborating with Pournelle?

LN: From *The Flying Sorcerers* it went to a script for *Land of the Lost*. Eventually, three scripts for *Land of the Lost* while he was story editor there. And the ideas were all his.

You always get paid in the TV industry. Getting paid is not the problem.

JW: What would you tell people about your time working with television?

LN: What you do may not appear. Fools may interfere with your precious prose. Also bright people, but they'll look like fools 'cause they're interfering with your precious prose.

When you write a book, it's all yours. When you write a script for TV, it's many people's. You get collaborators and you don't choose them.

JW: How does that work out?

LN: You can get pissed off and go away, or you can make a career out of it and make a lot of money. And not as much fame as you think. The fame belongs to the people who write the books.

JW: So which do you like writing?

LN: There is nothing comparable to the feeling of… of writing a story when it's really got its grip on your imagination.

JW: Tell me about that.

LN: Okay. I'll tell you a story. Jerry Pournelle and I were at work on *Lucifer's Hammer*. It's getting on toward Christmas season and I remember telling him that *Lucifer's Hammer* had cost me my Christmas season one year. I get a call from Jerry about 10, 10:38 p.m., and he's at work on *Lucifer's Hammer*. He says, "I got a problem here. I want to show how awful things are in the valley outside The Stronghold. I've got the spacemen characters now, Deke Wilson and their men. I wanna show how terrible it all is, but they're not noticing anymore. None of the characters are noticing. What are they gonna see that I can describe? Think about it." And he hangs up.

I thought about it for an hour or two or three. I called him around two in the morning. I said, "I've got it. They're gonna notice a dead kangaroo." Then the astronaut is gonna freak out 'cause he's new to this and he's seeing nothing but corpses.

He loved it, of course, and did not complain about being awakened at two in the morning.

I don't do that a lot, mind you. I've never done that a lot, but it was too good to rest.

You're collaborating in order to get a better story than either of you could write alone. The bad news is you each have to do about eighty percent of the work.

JW: What do you look for in a collaborator?

LN: I don't go looking for collaborators so much as collaborators track me down. Steven Barnes did that. Jerry Pournelle did that. I was at the first Boucher-Con. Sunday afternoon a bunch of us were in the restaurant and Jerry suggested writing together. I'd done it with David Gerrold; it must be fun.

And Steven Barnes went a little further than that. He was looking for a career and he figured getting a collaborator who knew something was vital. He started reading my stuff with intent to keep reading until he could say he admired me. Really, the guy is organized.

JW: When somebody comes to you to collaborate, what are you looking for with them? What tells you this is someone you can work with or someone you can't work with?

LN: Each one has been different. Each collaboration has been different; each collaborative book has been different.

I don't write with an amateur. And I don't need to write with somebody who thinks exactly like me. They're contributing something I don't have. Jerry and I worked it out pretty quickly. Jerry knows military. Jerry knows politics. Jerry does these. Jerry's a better scientist too. Aliens are mine and madness is mine.

A character slo...slogging his way through a sea of troubles, w-with some success and some background to work with, that's Jerry's. Character gets hysterical, that's mine.

JW: How did you get the hysterical characters?

LN: I've got a little more madness than he does and it appeared quite quickly.

JW: What is it that Pournelle provides to the collaboration?

LN: Really structure. Uh, he-he's, uh, much better at plotting than I am. He does more of the text. He doesn't do it all, by any means, but he does more of the text. And then he complains that everything people remember about a novel in detail is m— is mine.

JW: What else have, other than a number of best-selling and Hugo winning novels, what has your collaboration with Dr. Pournelle provided you?

LN: We're good friends and he's a little more ambitious in researching a novel. So there have been some trips. I took him to the River Valley Ranch, which the movie industry calls the Murder Ranch. River Valley Ranch became the foundation for The Stronghold.

JW: Let me kind of backtrack a little bit. You've been in science fiction a long time. What trends are you seeing in science fiction?

LN: First off, fantasy is easier to write. It's become far more popular than it used to be. I was there when the del Reys decided to start a science fiction line and there wasn't any up to then. There's a lot more fantasy being published, because science fiction has become a lot harder in both of two senses. First off, too many readers really understand the sciences, so there's less that you can get away with. It's become less likely that a writer will choose to go with faster than light travel.

JW: What has been one of the high points in your very distinguished career? One that you'd say, "That's got to be the best, or close to the best"?

LN: I met Marilyn a couple of nights before the Hugo awards ceremony at which I won my first Hugo.

I was a new writer. It was 1967. I was just getting to be known but they knew me at MIT. I'd followed a friend into a party thrown by the MIT fans and started having a wonderful time. Then I met Marilyn and we talked a lot. It was crowded. We were lying with our backs against the footrest of a bed. That was that night.

That was also the New York Worldcon at which the elevator operators were throwing a strike. A slow-down strike was going on elsewhere, so you couldn't get anything done at this hotel.

I didn't notice anything. We had dinner in the hotel restaurant and I didn't notice how bad things were because we were having fun together.

I didn't notice Lester del Rey throwing a salad at a waiter because he couldn't stand being treated like a serf anymore.

JW: How long before you asked her to marry you?

LN: We married September 6, 1969. I may have asked her in April '69.

JW: What effect has she had on your writing? How has she affected your writing as your wife?

LN: Keeps me sane. Marilyn keeps me sane. I'm not sure how organized I would be without her. You're not seeing the piles of paper in this house. We're both being swamped by paper, but it would have been a lot worse without Marilyn's help.

And I made her the heroine of a short story called "Inconstant Moon." That won a Hugo award.

Copyright © 2018 by Joy Ward

Starting with this issue, we're serializing this fine novel by the late Charles Sheffield. Charles was a Hugo and Nebula winner, as well as a Campbell Memorial Winner. He served as President of the Science Fiction Writers of America, and also put in time as Chief Scientist of the Earth Satellite Corporation.

TOMORROW AND TOMORROW

Charles Sheffield

PART ONE: LOVE AND DEATH

1

The Edge of Doom

Time: The Great Healer, the Universal Solvent

And if time cannot be granted?

When Drake finally received a clear medical diagnosis after months of secret terrors and false hopes and specialist hedging, Ana had less than five weeks to live. She was already in a final decline. Suddenly, after twelve marvelous years together and a future that seemed to spread out before them for fifty more, they saw the world collapse to a handful of days.

It had begun simply—more than simply. It had begun with nothing, a red car in the driveway when he did not expect one. Ana's car.

He had been passing the house almost by accident, on his way from a teeth-cleaning appointment to a meeting at the new concert hall. Like everyone else, Drake had complained about the acoustics, and the hall managers had called him in to be more specific. The grace period for construction changes without extra charge would end in less than thirty days, and they were worried.

Well, he could be specific, very specific, about bass absorption and soggy midrange sound and resonant high frequencies. But Ana should not be home. She had a rehearsal in the afternoon. She had told him when she left that she planned an early lunch with the pianist and clarinet player, and she would not be home until about six o'clock.

Car problems? The Camry had been balky for the past week.

He parked in the drive and went inside, noticing the puddle of water on the blacktop and vowing for the hundredth time to have it resurfaced. Ana was not in the kitchen. Not in the dining room or den or living room.

He felt the first twinge of anxiety as he ran upstairs. His relief when he saw her, fully clothed in blue jeans and a tartan shirt and peacefully sleeping on their bed, was surprisingly strong.

He went across and shook her. She opened her eyes, blinked, and smiled up at him.

He bent forward and kissed her lightly on the lips. "Are you all right?"

"I'm fine, love. Except I feel so *tired.*"

"Did you stay up late?" Drake had been downtown to hear a performance of one of his own recent works, and glad-handing his public afterward had kept him out until after midnight.

Ana shook her head. "I was in bed by ten. I've been feeling this way a lot recently. Weak and feeble. But never as bad as this."

"It's not like you. Why don't we give Tom a call?"

He had expected her to say it wasn't necessary, that all she needed was a little more relaxation—Ana, between singing engagements and teaching, drove herself hard.

To his surprise, she nodded. "Would you call him for me?" She lay back and closed her eyes. "I just want to lie here for a little longer."

Drake had worried from that moment on, even if at first no one else seemed to. Tom Lambert was a close friend as well as their family doctor. He came over the same evening, grumbling about what other patients would say if they thought he made house calls.

He examined Ana for a long time. He seemed more puzzled and curious than concerned.

"It could be simple fatigue," he said when he was done. He accepted a small Scotch in a large glass and added lots of ice. The three of them were sitting in the den. Tom raised his glass to Ana before he took a sip. He sighed. "All I can say is, if it is anything, then it's something that I've never seen before."

"Do you think we should just forget about it?" Ana asked. She was sitting on the couch with her feet tucked under her. Drake, studying her now rather than simply accepting her presence, decided that she seemed thinner. "You know, take two aspirin and wait for tomorrow."

"Forget about it?" Tom sounded shocked. "Of course not. What sort of doctor do you think I am? I want to send you to a specialist."

"Of course." Ana's tone was teasing. She and Tom had had the argument before. "Today's typical physician: can't possibly tell you what's wrong with you unless you see at least four other doctors—who of course all get their fees. If you people were musicians, nothing would be written for anything less than a quintet."

"Sure. And if you people were doctors, you'd only perform with hundreds of people watching. Anyway, don't change the subject. I want you to see a specialist. I'm going to make an appointment for you to see Dr. Kevin Williams."

"But if you don't know what it is," Drake protested, "how do you know what sort of specialist she needs?"

Tom Lambert seemed slightly embarrassed. "I said I'd never *seen* anything like this, in my own practice. But it doesn't mean I don't have ideas. Kevin Williams specializes in diseases of the blood and lymph systems. He's head of a group at NIH. He's a friend of mine, and he's damned good. Don't worry, Ana."

"I wasn't going to. I don't believe in it. Drake's the worrier in the family."

"Then don't you worry, either, Drake. We'll get to the bottom of this." Tom nodded, and when he spoke again it was as though he was talking to himself. "Yes, we will. And we'll do it quickly."

Tom did his best. Drake never doubted that for a moment. Ana saw Dr. Williams the next day, then there came a bewildering succession of other doctors and tests in the following two weeks. Ana's teasing remark to Tom was an understatement. Drake counted twelve different physicians, not counting the individuals, many of them also MDs, who administered the MRIs, IVPs, myelograms, and multiple blood workups.

Tom said little, but Drake knew in his heart that there was a big problem. Ana's lassitude continued.

She was definitely losing more weight. She had been forced to cancel her teaching and her near-term concert engagements. One morning she was sitting at the kitchen table, pale winter sunlight slanting through onto her fair hair. Drake noticed the translucent, waxen sheen to her forehead and the pattern of fine blue veins on her temples. He was filled with such dread that he could not speak.

The grim biopsy result, when it finally came, was no surprise. Tom delivered the news himself, one drizzly evening in early March.

"An operation?" Ana, as always, was calm and rational.

Tom shook his head.

"How about chemotherapy?"

"We'll try that, naturally." Tom hesitated. "But I have to tell you, Ana, the prognosis is not too good. We can certainly treat you, but we can't cure you."

"I guess that's it, then." Ana stood up, already a little unsteady on her feet because of muscle loss in her legs. "I'm going to bring coffee for all of us. It ought to have perked by now. Cream and sugar, Tom?"

"Uh…yes." Tom looked up at her unhappily. "No, I mean, cream, no sugar. Whatever. Anything is fine."

As soon as Ana was out of the room he turned to Drake. "She's in denial. That's natural, and it's not surprising. It will take a while for her to adjust."

"No." Drake stood up and went across to the window. The last heavy snow of the winter was melting, and fresh green shoots of spring growth were poking through. A few more days would bring bloom to the snowdrops and crocuses.

"You don't know Ana," he went on. "She's the ultimate realist. Not like me. Ana's not in denial. I'm the one that's in denial."

"I'm going to prescribe painkillers for her," Tom continued, as though he had not been listening. "All the painkillers she wants. There's no virtue in pain. In a case like this I don't worry about addiction. And I'm going to prescribe tranquilizers, too… for both of you." Tom looked toward the kitchen, making sure that Ana was out of earshot. "You might as well know the truth, Drake. There's not one damned thing we can do for her. Forget the chemotherapy. If it buys more than a few weeks for Anastasia, I'd be surprised. I feel that medical science is still in the dark ages about this disease.

As a doctor I have to worry about you, too, Drake. Don't neglect your own health. And remember I can be here, night or day, whenever either one of you needs me."

Ana was coming back. She paused on the threshold, holding a tray of cups, coffeepot, cream and sugar. She smiled and arched an eyebrow. "You two all done? Safe for me to come back in now?"

Drake looked at her. She was thin and fragile, but she had never been more beautiful. Beautiful and brave and loving. At the idea of living without her his chest tightened. He felt as though he could not breathe.

Ana was his life, without her there was nothing. How could he ever bear to lose her?

2

"O! Call Back Yesterday, Bid Time Return."

Tom was gone before ten o'clock. He could tell that Ana, who had been putting on her best front just for him, was exhausted.

Ana went off to bed as soon as Tom had left. Drake followed, half an hour later. She was already asleep. He lay down beside her without undressing, convinced that would be a waste of time. His mind was too active for any form of rest.

He closed his eyes. He imagined Ana, as she had been when they'd first met.

He always told people that he had loved her before he even saw her. The occasion of their first meeting was an end-of-term examination. Drake, as Doctor Bonvissuto's star pupil in musical composition, had been taking a test alone, in a small room next to Bonvissuto's austere office.

It was not the ideal setting for concentration, but Drake had been through the routine several times before. While he was setting down the parts of a fugal theme provided by his teacher, Bonvissuto was interviewing would-be choral scholars and students in the next room.

The test material was not inspiring work, and Drake could do it almost automatically, using sheets of lined score paper and a pencil. Bonvissuto scorned computers and all other aids to the rapid writing out of music.

"You think you need computer to write fast, eh?" He had scowled at Drake on their very first session together. "Handel, he write *Messiah*, every note, in twenty-four day. You do as good in two-three month, I don't grumble. You want computer to help? Fine. Provided you write more and *better*. Better than Bach. Better than Monteverdi, better than Mozart. They had no computer."

From Bonvissuto, that counted as mild comment. But he meant what he said. Drake slaved away at the test, without benefit of centuries of technological development, while in the next room a succession of young men and women came and went.

Most of them, Drake knew, arrived prepared to sing as Brünnhilde or Tristan or the Queen of the Night. Bonvissuto would have none of it.

"Something simple. Not the grand opera. The simple song, the folk song. You sing that real good, a cappella, *then* maybe we think about Verdi an' Mozart an' Wagner."

They would sing unaccompanied, often off-key and loud. And Bonvissuto would comment, equally loudly.

"What key did you think you were in at the end there? And what *language*? Did you ever hear about diction? This song is in *English*, for Christ's sake. Listening to you it could have been in Polish or Chinese or anything."

Bonvissuto reversed the traditional pattern. When he was angry and excited, the Italian accent disappeared. In its place came perfect English and a Kansas twang. The same thing happened during his lessons with Drake, who had once been unwise enough to mention that fact. The teacher had winked at him and said, "Whoever heard of an Italian from Kansas? Whoever heard of a *composer* from Kansas?"

Drake finished writing out the fugue, turned the page, and went on to the final question. "Provide a suitable melody to go with the given accompaniment."

He looked at what followed and realized that the question was going to be a snap. He knew the original piece. He was looking at the piano part of "Erstarrung," the fourth song from the Winterreise song cycle. All he had to do was write out the vocal part. The accompaniment happened to be given in A-minor, up a tone from the version that he was most familiar with, so he would have to transpose; but that was trivial.

He read the question again to be sure. *"Provide a suitable melody."* It didn't say, *"Compose a suitable melody of your own."* And he certainly could not improve on Schubert.

As he wrote in the vocal line he heard the door open again in the next room. There was a mutter of conversation, then a single chord, E major, on Bonvissuto's piano.

A woman's contralto voice began to sing, "Blow the wind southerly." It was a strong, true voice, slightly husky in the lower register and with just a touch of an attractive vibrato on the high notes. Drake paused to listen. After the final note there was a pause, then again a single chord on the piano. It confirmed what Drake already knew. The woman had finished exactly on E natural, in the key where she had started. She had been right on pitch all the way through.

Drake heard another muttered sentence or two spoken in the next room, then the door opened and closed again. He waited, writing in the last few bars of the exercise. Surely Bonvissuto hadn't sent her away, just like that, without talking to her some more. Drake wanted to hear her sing again.

On an impulse he collected his answer sheets, stacked them neatly, and walked across to the connecting door. He turned the doorknob and went through without knocking.

He braced himself. Anyone who entered Bonvissuto's office uninvited could expect a hot welcome.

The expected blast did not come. Professor Bonvissuto was not there. Alone in the room, standing by the piano and staring at him uncertainly, was a slim, blond-haired girl.

He stared back. Her hair was cut a little lopsided. She wasn't very tall, maybe five four, and her pale blue dress didn't look quite right on her. Drake, no connoisseur of clothing, did not realize that it had been intended for someone a couple of inches taller. But the most striking thing about her, far more significant than clothes, was her age. She looked about fifteen. It was hard to believe that the mature contralto voice he had heard came from her.

"Are you next?" she said finally. "I thought I was the last one. He won't be long."

He realized that he had been staring, but so had she. She must assume he was there for a vocal audition. He thrust his sheaf of papers out toward her. "I'm not here to sing. I was taking an exam. I'm one of Professor Bonvissuto's students. Was that you?"

"What me?"

"Singing. 'Blow the wind southerly.'"

"Yes. Why?"

"It was good." He wanted to add that it was wonderful, heart-stopping, soul-searing. Instead he said, "Where is he?"

"The professor? He went to register me. I didn't think I'd be accepted, and it's the last day to sign up. He said he could push it through."

"He can. He knows how." Drake, not knowing what to do next but reluctant to leave, sat down on the piano stool.

She asked from behind him, "Do you play?"

"Yes. Not very well." He was convinced that he could feel her critical stare burning into the back of his head. Music was full of prodigies: tiny infants picking out chord sequences, concert performers under ten years old, composers who wrote great works in their teens. And here he was, over eighteen and still a student. He wanted to blurt out that he had started late, that his family had been too poor to think of music lessons, that he had come to music only when he found that, almost against his will, melodies arose in his head to go with poetry that he was reading.

He couldn't say any of that. Instead, to hide his self-consciousness, and with "Erstarrung" still in his head, he began to play the restless, uneasy triplets of the song's introduction.

"I've heard that a couple of times," said the voice behind him. "But it's a man's song. Do you know 'Gretchen am Spinnrade'?"

" 'Margaret at the spinning-wheel'?" Drake was much more comfortable with the English translation. He paused for a moment, then began to play a steady, pulsing figure.

"That's it," the girl said at once. "Did you know that Schubert wrote it when he was only seventeen?"

"I know." It was a possible criticism, making the point that Drake was a lot older than seventeen and had done nothing. But before he could say more she went on: "It's a little bit high for me. But I can handle it. Start over."

After the four brief figures of the introduction she began to sing, *"Mein Ruh is hin, mein Herz ist schwer."* "My peace is gone, my heart is heavy." Drake, understanding the German words only vaguely but feeling the strong musical rapport between them, put all his mind into his playing, sensing and adapting to her vocal line.

They performed the whole song. After the final slowing chords on the piano there was total silence. He turned and found a smile on her face that matched his own delight. Before they could speak, a sound came from the doorway: four steady hand claps.

"You know, don't you, the penalty for playing my Steinway without my permission?" Bonvissuto walked toward them. "What are you doing in here, Merlin?"

Drake picked up his exam papers and held them out. "I finished."

"Yeah?" Bonvissuto skimmed the sheets for a couple of seconds. He snorted. "I told Leila Nielsen, using 'Erstarrung' was one dumb idea, you were sure to know it. No matter. Plenty of stuff you *don't* know for next time." He smiled sadistically. "How's your Webern?" And then, before Drake could reply, "Go on, go on. Out of here, both of you." He waved his hands at them. "Merlin, we'll discuss your test tomorrow morning. Werlich, I registered you. You're legal. You come in at one tomorrow, we'll work on your middle register. Now, go. What you waiting for?" And then, when they were almost out the door, "Since you two are going to be performing in public together, you'd better practice. You need polish."

Drake knew her name, or at least part of it. *Werlich.* And she knew his. They stood in the corridor, staring at each other.

"Did you hear that?" she said at last. "Performing together. Do you think he meant it?"

"I don't know." Drake had played before small groups only. The idea of a public concert froze his blood. "But he usually means what he says when it's about music."

She held out her hand. "I'm Anastasia Werlich. Ana for short."

"I'm Drake Merlin." He took her hand and felt an odd compulsion to admit his secret. "It's actually *Walter* Drake Merlin, but I really hate *Walter.*"

"So don't use it. You didn't pick it. I'm not too fond of *Werlich."* She frowned. "How much money do you have?"

The question threw him. Did she mean in the world, or in his pocket? Either way, it was an unsatisfactory answer.

"I have four dollars."

She nodded. "All right. And I have nine. So I'm the rich one. I buy you a Coke."

"I don't drink Coke. Caffeine doesn't agree with me. It gives me the jitters." Drake wondered why he was saying something so terminally stupid. Here he was, keener to continue a conversation with Ana than he had ever been with anyone, and he sounded like he was freezing her off.

But all she said was, "Sprite, then, or 7UP," and she steered them off toward the cafeteria at the end of the building.

They talked through the rest of the afternoon and all evening, so absorbed in each other that the presence of others in the cafeteria was totally irrelevant.

It had pleased Drake at first to learn that she was as badly off as he was. Her fluent German and knowledge of the world came not from an expensive private-school education in Europe, but because Ana was an army brat, whose tough childhood had dragged her from school to school all over Europe and most of the rest of the world. Like him, Ana was poor, too poor to attend a university without a scholarship.

And then, after just a few hours together, money or the lack of it didn't matter.

What did matter was that they were so keen to talk and listen to each other that Ana came close to missing her last bus home. What mattered was that when they were at the bus stop she said, with the directness that she would never lose, "I've been waiting to meet you since I was five years old."

What mattered was her face, gray eyes closed, upturned for a brief good-night kiss. When the bus drove away Drake felt the deepest loss of his eighteen years. He knew, even then, that he had found the girl he would love forever.

That first day set the pattern for all their time together. They were with each other every moment that they could manage. When Ana had an out-of-town performance she would return home on the earliest possible flight. When commissions or premiere performances took Drake away to New York or Miami or Los Angeles, he chafed at the obligatory dinners and cocktail parties that were part of the deal. He didn't want free dinner and drinks or extravagant praise of his talents. He wanted to be with Ana. Even in the early days, when they were desperately poor, he would go without dinner so he could take a taxi rather than a bus, and be home an hour sooner.

Drake recalled one day when Ana was involved in a major traffic accident on the Beltway. He was in bed with a fever of 102 when a telephone call came in from a total stranger, telling him about the accident but assuring him that Ana was all right.

He did not remember getting out of bed or dressing or driving to the scene. He recalled only the terrible feeling of possible loss, of doom hanging over him until he had his arms around her. Her car was totaled, and he didn't notice or care. He had been consumed with the fear of losing her.

And now....

Drake looked at the illuminated face of the bedside clock. It was past midnight, almost one o'clock. He rose, went through to the bathroom, and flushed the prescription for tranquilizers that Tom had given him down the drain.

There would be opportunity for sorrow later. Now he had work to do, and little time to do it. He needed all his faculties, unblurred by drugs. For twelve years he and Ana had done their thinking and planning together. It couldn't be like that this time. She needed all her strength to fight her disease. He didn't know what he would do, or how he would do it. He only knew he would do *something*.

Ana was his life; without her there was nothing.

He could not bear to lose her.

He would not lose her.

Ever.

3

Second Chance

Three and a half weeks of his efforts proved futile. After the first half-dozen tries Drake learned how to dispose ruthlessly of false leads. Unfortunately, before each one could be rejected it had to be explored. And there were so many: homeopathy, acupuncture, bipolarized interferon, amygdalin, ion rebalance, meditation, chelation, Kirlian aura manipulation, biofeedback, quantum energy....

The list seemed endless, and hopeless. Whatever else they might do, they would not cure Ana.

By the fourth week it was obvious that Drake had to do *something*. Ana, though she never complained, was failing fast. He was approaching the end of his endurance. He had been sleeping only a couple of hours a night, making his data-bank searches and long-distance telephone calls when Ana lay in drugged sleep. He had canceled or postponed all commitments, except for one short television piece that could not wait. He disposed of that in a desperate seventeen-hour session, hearing as he worked at his computer the far-off voice of Professor Bonvissuto: "You think you write fast and good, Merlin? Maybe. Mozart, he write the overture for *Don Giovanni*, full score, in one sitting."

When Ana was awake they spent their time in an opiate dream world, touching, smiling, savoring each other, drifting. Except that Drake had taken no drugs and he could not afford to drift. Or wait.

At last it crowded down to a single desperate option. He would have liked to discuss it with Ana, but he could not do so. If she knew what he had in mind, she would veto it. She would make him promise, on her dying body, that he would abandon the idea.

So. She must not know, must never even suspect.

When he had done all that he could and was ready for the final step, he called Tom Lambert and asked him to come over to the house.

Tom arrived after dinner. It was fantastic weather for early April, with daffodils, tulips, and hyacinths bursting into blossom after a cool spring. Life and energy seemed everywhere except inside the darkened house. Ana was sleeping in the front bedroom. Tom gave her a brief examination and led Drake into the living room. He shook his head.

"It's going faster than I thought. At this rate Anastasia will pass into a final coma in the next three or four days. You ought to let me take her to a hospital now. There's nothing you can do for her, and you need the rest. You look as though you've had no sleep for the past month."

"There'll be time enough for sleep. I want her to stay here with me. In fact, it will be necessary." Drake placed Tom in the window seat and sat himself down opposite, knee to knee. He explained what he had been doing for the past week, and what he wanted Tom to do in the next few days.

Lambert heard him out without a word. Then he shrugged his shoulders.

"If that's what the two of you want to do, Drake, it's your call." There was a pitying look in his eyes. "I'll help you, of course I will. And I agree, Anastasia has nothing at all to lose. But you realize, don't you, that they've never done a successful freeze and thaw?"

"On fish, and amphibians—"

"Don't kid yourselves, Drake. Fish and amphibians mean next to nothing. We're talking *humans* here. I have to tell you, in my opinion you are wasting your time and money. Just making the whole thing harder for yourself, too. What does Ana have to say about it?"

"Not much." It was a direct lie. The idea had never been discussed with her. But how could he make a decision, this one above all, without telling Ana? Drake forced himself away from that thought and went on. "She's willing. Maybe more for my sake than hers. She thinks it won't work, but she agrees that she has nothing to lose. Look, I'd rather you don't mention this to her. It's like—like assuming she's already dead. I'll prepare the papers. And I'll get Ana's signature."

"Better not wait too long." Tom's face was grim. "If you're going to do this, she has to be able to hold a pen."

"I know. I told you, I'll get her signature."

After Tom left, Drake wandered out into the backyard. It was still warm outside, with the promise of summer. But spring was a mockery, an unkind and cruel joke. He roamed from one flowering border to the next. They had created this garden with their own hands. When they moved into the house, seven years ago, the yard had been badly neglected. It had been nothing but weeds and bare earth. He had done most of the work, but it had been according to Ana's design and under her direction. These were *her* walkways and flower beds, not his. How could he bear to look at them, if she was gone?

After five minutes he went inside. He had to check all the legal procedures one more time.

Three days later Drake called Tom Lambert again to the house. The doctor went to the bedroom, felt Ana's pulse, and took blood pressure and brain-wave readings.

He emerged stone-faced. "I'm afraid this is it, Drake. I'll be very surprised if she regains consciousness. If you are still set on this thing, it has to be done while she has some normal body functions. Another three days…it will be a waste of time."

The two men went together into the bedroom. Drake took a last look at Ana's calm, ravaged face. He told himself that this was not a last farewell. At last he nodded to Tom.

"Go ahead." He could not tear his gaze away from her face. "Any time."

Time, time. A waste of time. To the end of time. Time heals all wounds. O! call back yesterday, bid time return.

"Drake? Drake? Are you all right?"

"Sorry. I'm all right." Again he nodded. "Go on, Tom. There's no point in waiting."

The physician made the injection. Working together, they lifted Ana from the bed and removed her clothes. Drake wheeled in the prepared thermal tank. He laid her gently into it. She was so light, it was as though part of her was already lost to him.

While Tom filled out the death certificate, Drake placed the call to Second Chance. He told them to come at once to the house. He set the tank at three degrees above freezing, as instructed. Tom inserted the catheters and the IVs. The next stages were automatic, controlled by the tank's own programs. Blood was withdrawn through a large hollow needle in the main external iliac artery, cooled a precise amount, and returned to the femoral vein.

In ten minutes Ana's body temperature had dropped thirty degrees. All life signs had vanished. Ana was now legally dead. To an earlier generation, Drake Merlin and Tom Lambert would have been judged murderers. It was hard not to feel that way as they sat in the silence of the bedroom, awaiting the arrival of the Second Chance team. Tom was filled with pity—for Drake. Ana was now beyond pity.

Drake's thoughts and plans were fortunately beyond his friend's imaginings.

He had a hard time with Tom Lambert and the three women who arrived from Second Chance. Not one of them could see a reason for Drake to go over to the Second Chance preparation facility with Ana's body.

Tom thought that Drake couldn't face the idea that it was all over. He urged his friend to come home with him and have a drink. Drake refused. The preparation team didn't know what to make of it as he hovered close by them. He seemed like a ghoul or some sort of necrophiliac, yet the look on his face showed he was clearly suffering. They carefully explained that the procedures were very unpleasant to watch, especially for someone so personally involved. They agreed with Dr. Lambert. Drake would be much better off leaving everything in their experienced hands and going home with his friend. They would make sure that everything was all right. If he was worried, they would be sure to call him as soon as the work was finished.

Drake couldn't tell them the real reason he wanted to see the whole preparation procedure, down to the last grisly detail. But by simply refusing to take no for an answer, he at last had his way.

The head of the team then decided that Drake wanted to come along because he was afraid that some element of the job would be botched. She explained the whole procedure to him, kindly and carefully, on the one-hour drive to the facility. They were sitting together in the rear of the van, next to the temperature-controlled casket.

"Most of the revivables—we much prefer that term to cryocorpses—are stored at liquid nitrogen temperatures. That's about minus two hundred degrees Celsius. It's almost certainly cold enough. But it's still about seventy-five degrees above absolute zero. All measurable biological processes become imperceptible long before that. However, there are still some chemical reactions going on. The laws of statistics guarantee that a few atoms will have enough energy to induce biological changes. And mind and memory are very delicate things. So for people who are worried about that, we make available a deluxe version. That's what you bought. Your wife will be stored at liquid helium temperatures, just a few degrees above absolute zero. That's super safe. When it's so cold, the chance of change—physical or mental—goes way down."

And the cost, although she did not mention the fact, went way up. But cost was not even a variable to be considered from Drake's perspective. When they arrived at the Second Chance facility he hung around the preparation room, ignoring all hints that he should wait outside; and he watched closely.

The team members became more sympathetic. They were now convinced that he was simply terrified that a mistake would be made. They allowed him to see everything and answered all his questions. He was careful not to ask anything that sounded too clinical and dispassionate. The main thing he wanted was to *see*, to know at absolute firsthand what had been done, and in what sequence.

After the first few minutes there was in any case not much to see. He knew that all the air cavities within Ana's body had been filled with neutral solution, and her blood replaced with anticrystalloids. But then she went into the seamless pressure chamber. The body was held there at three degrees above freezing, while the pressure was raised slowly to five thousand atmospheres. After that was done, the temperature drop started.

"Back in the eighties and nineties, they had no idea of this technique." The team leader was still talking to Drake, perhaps with the idea that she might make him feel more relaxed. "They used to do the freezing at atmospheric pressure. There was a formation of ice crystals within the cells as the temperature dropped, and it was a mess when the thaw was done. No return to consciousness was possible."

She smiled reassuringly at Drake, who was not reassured at all. So they didn't know what they were doing in the eighties and nineties. Would they claim in twenty more years that people didn't know what they were doing *now*? But he had no alternative. He couldn't wait for twenty years, or even twenty hours.

"The modern method is quite different," she went on. "We make use of the fact that ice can exist in many different solid forms. Ice is complicated stuff, much more than most people realize. If you raise the pressure to three thousand atmospheres, then drop the temperature, water will remain liquid to about minus twenty degrees Celsius. And when it finally changes to a solid, it isn't the familiar form of ice—what is usually called phase 1. Instead it turns to something called phase 3. Drop the temperature from there, holding the pressure constant, and at about minus twenty-five degrees it changes to another form, phase 2. And it stays that way as you drop the temperature still farther. If you go to five thousand atmospheres pressure—that's what we are doing here—before you drop the temperature, water freezes at about minus five degrees and adopts still another form, phase 5. The trick to avoiding cell rupture problems at freezing point is to inject anti-crystalloids, which help to inhibit crystal formation, then by the right combination of temperatures and pressures work all the way down toward absolute zero, passing into and through phases 5, 3, and 2.

"That's what we are doing now. But don't expect to see much except dial readings. For obvious reasons, the pressure chamber is made without seams and without observation ports. You don't get pressures of five thousand atmospheres, not even in the deepest ocean gulfs. Fortunately, once you have the temperature down below a hundred absolute, you can reduce the pressure to one atmosphere, otherwise the storage of revivables would be quite impracticable. As it is, we have many thousands stacked away in the Second Chance wombs. Every one of them is neatly labeled and waiting for the resurrection. That will come as soon as someone figures out a way to do the thaw."

She glanced at Drake, aware that her last comment might have been the wrong thing to say. The official position at Second Chance was that *everyone* was revivable, and that the organization had full control of all the necessary technology. In due course everyone would be revived.

Drake nodded without expression. He had researched the whole subject in detail, and nothing that she had said so far was news. In his opinion it would be as hard to revive the early cryocorpses as it would be to get Tutankhamen's mummy up and moving again. They had been frozen with the wrong procedure, and they were being stored at too high a temperature.

But who was he to make that decision? They had paid their deposits, and they had the right to sit there in the wombs until their rentals ran out. He had started Ana with a forty-year contract, but he thought of that as just the beginning.

He had brought with him a copy of Ana's medical records. He added to it a full description of everything he had seen in the past hour or two, copied the whole document, and made sure that a complete set was included with the file records on Ana. When Ana's body was finally taken away for storage he went back to the house, fell into bed, and slept like a cryocorpse himself for sixteen hours.

It was time for the next step. And it was not going to be easy.

When Drake was fully awake again, fed and bathed, he called Tom Lambert and asked to see him—at Tom's home, rather than his office. He accepted the hefty drink that Tom prepared, after one look at him, for "medicinal purposes," and laid out his plans.

After he was finished Tom walked over to Drake, poked the muscles in his shoulders and the back of his neck, pulled down his lower eyelid and stared at the exposed skin, and finally went to sit opposite him.

"You've been under a monstrous strain for the past few months," he said quietly.

"Very true. I have." Drake kept his voice just as calm.

"And it would be quite unnatural for your behavior or your feelings to be completely normal. In fact, if you seem normal now, it's only because you have completely walled in your emotions. You certainly don't understand the implications of what you are proposing to me."

Drake shook his head. "This isn't new. It's only new to you. I've been thinking of this since the day I gave up on all other options."

"Then that was the day you put the lid on your feelings." Tom Lambert leaned forward. "Look, Drake, Ana was a wonderful woman, a unique woman. I won't say I know what you have been through, because obviously I don't. I do have some idea of your sense of loss. But you have to ask yourself what Ana would want you to do now. You can't let the past become your obsession. She would tell you that you still have a life of your own. Even without her, you have to live it. She would *want* you to live it, because she loved you." He paused. "Let me make a suggestion...."

While Tom was talking, Drake found it harder and harder to listen. The room felt dull and airless and he had trouble breathing. Tom Lambert's words came from far off. They didn't seem to say anything. He forced himself to concentrate, to listen harder.

"...of your work. You are still a young man. Forty to fifty good years ahead of you. And already you have a reputation. You are one of this country's most promising composers, and your best works still lie ahead. Ana may have performed your work better than anyone else, but there will be others. They will learn. With your talent you owe it to the rest of us not to cut your career off before it reaches its peak."

"I have no intention of doing so. I will compose again. Later."

"You mean, later after *that?*" Tom was frowning and shaking his head. "Suppose there is no later? Drake, take my advice as both your doctor and your friend. You desperately need to get out of your house, and you need to take a vacation. Go off on a cruise somewhere, take a trip around the world. Expose yourself to some new influences. I know how you must feel now, but you should give it a year and see how you feel *then*. I guarantee you, everything will seem different. You'll want to live again. You'll give up this crazy idea."

The breathless feeling was fading. Drake again had control of himself. He waited patiently until Tom was finished, then nodded agreement.

"I'll do as you say. I'll get away from here for a while. But if it turns out that you are wrong—if I come back to you, in, say, eight or ten years, and I ask you again, will you do it? Will you help me? I want you to give me an honest answer, and I want your word on it."

The tension drained visibly from Tom Lambert. He snorted in relief. "Ten years from now? Drake, if you come back to me in eight or ten years and ask me again, I'll admit I was completely wrong. And I promise you, I'll help you to do what you've asked."

"An absolute promise? I don't want to hear some day that you changed your mind, or didn't mean what you said."

"An absolute promise. Sure, I'll give you that." Tom laughed. "But I'm not worried that I'll ever be called on it. I'll bet you everything I own that after a year or two have gone by, you'll never mention that promise again. Hard as it seems to believe today, you'll be living a new life, and you'll be enjoying it." He walked over to the sideboard and poured himself a drink. "I'd like to propose a toast, Drake. Or actually, three toasts. To us. To your future. And to your next—and greatest—composition."

Drake raised his glass in return. "To us, and the future. I'll drink to those. But I can't drink to my next work, because I don't know when I'll create it. I have lots of other things to do—for one thing, you told me to get out of town. I'm going to do that, right away. But don't worry, Tom. I'll be in touch when the time is right."

4

Into the Abyss

There were two problems. The first was easy to define but hard to solve: money.

In the early days, Drake and Ana had been very poor. As a result they talked about money quite a lot. She would glance through their joint checking account book, with its zero balance, and groan. He would laugh, with more worry than humor, and once he quoted something he had just read by Somerset Maugham: "Money is the sixth sense that enables us to enjoy the other five." He added: "I guess that leaves us six senses short."

Unfortunately, neither groans nor quotations produced income. Money, or the lack of it, seemed important, as important as anything in the world except music and each other.

Career success brought a change of attitude. Ana had her teaching and her concert appearances,

Drake had pupils and occasional commissions. Their needs were modest. They bought a house, a big old-fashioned brick Colonial with four bedrooms and half an acre of fenced yard, expecting that someday they would need all the space for an expanded family. Neither of them wanted to travel or be wealthy. Wordsworth was quoted rather than Maugham: "Getting and spending, we lay waste our powers."

Now all that was past. Drake needed money, lots of it. He had to make sure that Ana could remain safe within her icy womb for the indefinite future, until she could be safely thawed and her disease cured. Then her life would begin again. There were a few things he couldn't guard against, such as a total collapse of the world to barbarism, or the rejection of all present forms of currencies and commodities. Those were risks that Ana—and he—would have to accept.

The other problem was more subtle. According to Tom it might be a long time before a cure was found for Ana's rare and highly malignant disease. As he pointed out, something that killed only a few people a year did not get the attention of common cancers and heart diseases, which ended the lives of hundreds of millions.

Suppose that a cure was not discovered for a century, or even for two centuries. What knowledge of present-day society would interest people in the year 2200? What must a man know or a woman be, for the inhabitants of that future Earth to think it worthwhile to revive them? Drake was convinced that even when a foolproof way of resuscitating the revivables was discovered, most bodies in the cryowombs would stay exactly where they were. The contracts with Second Chance provided only for maintenance in a cryonic condition. They did not, and could not, offer a guarantee that an individual would be thawed.

Why thaw anyone at all? Why add another person to a crowded world, unless he or she had something special to offer?

Drake imagined himself back in the early nineteenth century. What could he have placed into his brain, then, that would be considered valuable today, two hundred years later? Not politics, nor art. Knowledge of them was quite adequate. Certainly not science or any technology—progress in the past two centuries had been phenomenal.

What would the people of the future want to *know* about the past?

He decided that he had lots of time to ponder his own question; time, which had been denied to Ana. It would be foolish to hurry, when he could plan and calculate at his leisure. He set a goal of ten years. That would still allow forty of the shared fifty that he had looked for and longed for. But he was quite willing to stretch ten to fifteen if he had to.

If it did take more time, it would not be because he allowed himself to be distracted by other activities. His only diversion was to estimate the probabilities that everything would work out as he hoped. Always, the odds came out depressingly low.

While he was trying to decide what he needed to learn, he still had to solve that difficult first problem: making money.

He decided to visit his old teacher. His relationship with Bonvissuto had passed through three distinct phases. At first there had been absolute awe of the professor's musical skill and encyclopedic knowledge. Bonvissuto seemed to know, and be able to play by heart at his cherished Steinway, his own piano transcription of any work by any composer. After three years of study, Drake's attitude changed. He still respected and admired his mentor's learning, but in matters other than music he came to think Bonvissuto a bit of a comic figure. He could not ignore the elevator heels, red carnation buttonholes, dyed-brown shoulder-length tresses, unreliable Italian accent, and relentless romantic activity.

It was Ana, in Drake's final year as Bonvissuto's student, who revealed to Drake another side of their teacher.

"Can't you see how much he envies you?" she said, as they sat one afternoon poring over a marked-up score of *Carmina Burana*.

"Who?"

"Bony. Who else?"

"Me?" Drake put down the score. "Why on earth do you think he would envy me? He knows ten times as much about music as I'll ever know."

"He does. But just the same he envies you—for the same reason as *I* envy you. He teaches music. I perform music. But you *create* music. Neither of us is able to do that. Can't you see the look in his eyes, whenever you bring him a beautiful original melody? He's delighted, yet sad. It must kill him inside, to be so gifted and yet be missing that one essential spark."

Ana's insight led Drake to a final opinion of his teacher. The professor could be sarcastic and short-tempered. He was certainly vain, and a dedicated womanizer. But he loved music, with a passion and a strength and a devotion far beyond anything else in life.

And again it was Ana who stated it best. When a discussion of Haydn's "English" songs was interrupted by a telephone call from Bonvissuto's current flame, she said to Drake, quietly and with real affection for their teacher, "Listen to him. He tells Rita—and Charlene and Mary and Leah and Judy—that he loves them, and I think he really does. But he'd trade the lot in for one new Haydn symphony."

Or one new original work by Drake Merlin? Drake wasn't sure, then or ever. But two months after Ana had been placed in the cryowomb, he appeared in Bonvissuto's office one morning without warning. The teacher gave him one startled look, then turned his eyes away. "I know, I know," he said. "I'm terribly sorry."

It had been three years since the two last met, but Bonvissuto had followed the careers of all his former students. He took vast pride in them. Naturally, he knew about Ana.

"I didn't come here to talk about her," Drake said, "unless you want to, I mean. I came to ask your advice."

"Anything that I can do, I will. For you and little Ana, I will be happy...." Bonvissuto paused, swallowed, and turned away. The volatile Italian persona was not all fake.

"I have to make money." Drake spoke dispassionately to the other man's back. He needed advice, not emotional support. "A lot of money. I wondered if you could suggest a way."

"You! The least commercial of all my students. Oh!" Bonvissuto turned again, and Drake saw in his eyes a sudden understanding. "I know. I went through some of it myself, two years ago. The damned hospitals—the tests, and all the drugs, and prices you wouldn't believe —five dollars for an aspirin, two hundred dollars a day for a room, fifty

dollars for a doctor who drops in on you for two minutes and doesn't even look at you—they bleed you dry."

Drake nodded. It was a mistaken assumption, but letting it stand saved lots of explanation. "I need to make as much money as I can. As quickly as I can. I don't know how."

"But I do." Bonvissuto went across to his piano. "Provided you are willing to lower your standards. Are you?"

"I don't know. What do you mean?"

"Don't worry. I am not about to suggest that you form a rock group. You compose well, and you compose fast. But your music is too difficult to be popular. This is what Drake Merlin is writing." Bonvissuto played a sequence of spare chords with no clear tonal center, and above them on the right hand a wandering angular melody.

"That's from my *Suite for Charon*!"

"It is indeed. I took the liberty of making a piano transcription." Bonvissuto sounded not at all apologetic. "It is very beautiful—to you, and me, and maybe a few thousand others. But if you want to appeal to a few *million*, you must be simpler, more accessible. Like this." Bonvissuto played a jaunty bass theme, accompanied by dazzling prestissimo downward runs on the right hand.

Drake frowned. "That's by Danny Elfman. It's film music."

"It is. Are you saying you are above such things?"

"Not at all. It's first-rate. But I can't walk into a film studio and say, let me score a movie. They'd throw me straight out."

"Of course." Bonvissuto shrugged. "It is obvious that you don't start there. Or rather, if you choose to start there, I can't help you. But a dozen paths can lead in that direction." He stood up, went to his old oak desk, and picked up a cheap black notebook with a spiral binder. "All the time, I hear of musical markets. I write them down. They are open to you, provided that you don't insist on writing compositions that break new ground. People are most comfortable with the familiar. They say they know what they like, but really they like what they know. See here."

He opened the book and ran down the list of entries with his long, thin index finger. "I include concerts and recitals on this list, but for you I strongly recommend composition. Are you willing to write a commemorative overture for the hundredth anniversary of the first heavier-than-air flight? That offers four thousand dollars, for eleven minutes. The time requirement is precise, no more, no less. The work will be played after the national anthem, after a *Star Wars* selection and before 'The Stars and Stripes Forever.' I would not recommend march tempo. Or how about this one, which came to me through private channels: a commission to ghost-write a violin concerto for a Cabinet member with musical delusions of grandeur."

"What would I do?"

"You would write the music, after listening for half an hour to Lamar Malory's vague and off-key humming of themes. Your name will not, of course, go on the finished work. His name will. The fee offered, for your music and your silence, is four hundred dollars per composed minute. It is not much, but the music does not have to be very good. In fact, it would be suspicious if it were."

Drake bit back the urge to ask why Bonvissuto did not take the commissions himself. "What are the deadlines?"

"How soon can you produce?"

"Faster than anyone else they can find. I'll take both of them. As many as I can get, in fact. I'll write around the clock if I have to."

"I'll see what I can do. I can't guarantee these or any other commissions, but I can make sure that you are on the short list. After that it's up to you. I warn you, you will be dealing with people who have no more music in them than a dog who howls at the moon." Bonvissuto shrugged. "I am sorry, but that is the price. Never mind. When you have the money that you need, you can return to normal life."

A normal life was not what Drake had in mind—not for a long time yet. But he could not discuss his plans. He thanked Bonvissuto and left.

It was the beginning of a long period of incessant work. Drake took commissions, wrote commemorative pieces, gave concerts, and made recordings. As his reputation for good, fast, and reliable work grew, he produced reams of music for good, bad, and indifferent shows and movies. If anyone compared his recent work with his earlier work, and thought that he was debasing his art, they were too polite to comment. His own attitude was simple: if it was lucrative, it was acceptable.

Once a month he visited Ana's cryowomb facility. He could not see her, but he could sit outside the room where she was housed. Knowledge of her presence produced in him a strange tranquility. After a couple of hours with her, he could again face his work.

Sometimes that work was unpleasant, grinding toil. Since he agreed to tight deadlines, he was often forced to compose late at night when he was close to exhaustion. But sometimes the odd commercial challenges brought out the best in him. The finest melody of his life came to him as the theme music to a successful television show. And after four years he had an even bigger stroke of luck.

He had written a set of short pieces a couple of years after he and Ana first met, a kind of musical joke designed especially to appeal to her. They were baroque forms, with period harmonies, but he had added occasional modern harmonic twists, piquancy inserted where it would be most surprising and most appealing.

They had been quite successful, although only among a limited audience. Now, given a commission to provide the incidental music for a series of television dramas on life in eighteenth-century France, and facing another impossible delivery date, Drake returned to cannibalize, adapt, and simplify his own earlier work. The dramas turned out to be the hit of the decade. His music was credited as a big part of the reason for their success. Suddenly his minuets, bourrées, gavottes, sarabands, and rondeaux were everywhere. And as they flooded from the audio outlets, the royalties flooded in from every country around the globe.

Drake went on working as hard as ever. He established a foundation and trust fund. It guaranteed continued care for Ana's cryocorpse for many centuries, no matter what happened to Drake himself.

Freed from a need for money, his work changed direction. Instead of endless composition he became feverishly busy soaking up all that he could learn of the private and personal lives of his musical contemporaries. He interviewed, entertained, courted, and analyzed them, and he wrote about them extensively. But never quite in full. In every piece he was careful to leave a hanging tail, a hint that said, "There is much more to say and I know what it is; but for the moment I am deliberately leaving it unsaid."

What would the people of the future most want to know about their ancestors? Drake had his own answer. Their fascination would not be with the formal works, the official biographies, the text-book knowledge. They would have more than enough of those. What they would want would be the personal details, the chat, the gossip. They would want the equivalent of Boswell's journals and of Samuel Pepys' diaries. And if there was a way that they could have not only the written legacy, but the recorder himself, to talk to him and ask more questions....

It was not work that could be hurried. But finally, after nine long years, Drake was as ready as he would ever be. There was always the temptation to add one more interview, write one more article.

He resisted, and briefly worried a different question. How would he earn a living in the future? It might be only thirty years, but it might be eighty, two hundred, or a thousand. Could Beethoven, suddenly transported from 1810 to the year 2010, have earned a living as a musician?

More realistically, how would Spohr, or Hummel, or some other of Beethoven's less famous contemporaries have fared? Drake was betting that they, and he, could manage very well as soon as they had picked up the tricks of the time. Better, probably, than the far greater genius, the titan of Bonn. The others were more facile, more flexible, more politically astute.

And if he was wrong, and there was no way that he could make a living from music? Then he would do the twenty-third-century equivalent of washing dishes for a living. That was the least of his worries.

One day he stopped everything, put his affairs in order, and returned home. Without notice he headed for Tom Lambert's house. They had kept in touch, and he knew that Tom had married and was busy raising a family in the same house he had lived in all his life. But it was still a surprise to walk along that quiet tree-lined street, look over the same untidy privet hedge, and see Tom in the front yard playing baseball with a stranger, an eight-year-old boy who wore a flaming new version of Tom's graying red mop.

"Drake! My God, why didn't you call and tell me you were in town? How do you do it? You're as thin as ever." Tom had lost some of his hair but added a paunch to make up for it. He ushered Drake into the house and fussed over him like the Prodigal Son, leading the way into the familiar study. While his wife went into the kitchen to kill the fatted calf, he stood and beamed at Drake with pride and pleasure.

"We hear your music everywhere, you know," he said. "It's absolutely wonderful to know that your career is going so well."

Judged by Drake's own standards, it was not. He felt that he had done little first-rate composition in years. But Bonvissuto had been right: Tom, like most people, was comfortable musically with what he found familiar. From that point of view, and in terms of commercial success, Drake was riding high.

He itched to get down to business right away, but Tom's three young boys hovered around the study and the living room, curious to see the famous visitor. Then came a family dinner, and liqueurs after it watching the sunset. Drake sat in the guest-of-honor seat, with Tom and his wife, Mary-Jane, doing most of the talking.

At ten o'clock Mary-Jane disappeared to put the boys to bed. Drake was alone with Tom. *At last.* He took a deep breath, pulled out the application, and handed it to his friend without a word.

As Tom looked at it and realized what it was, the happiness faded from his face. He shook his head in disbelief.

"I thought you put all this behind you years ago. What started it going again?"

Drake stared at him without speaking, as though he had not understood the question.

"Or maybe it never stopped," Tom went on. "I should have guessed it hours ago. You used to be so full of life, so full of *fun.* Tonight I don't think I saw you smile once. When did you last take a vacation?"

"You gave me your word, Tom. Your promise."

Lambert studied the other man's thin face. "Never mind a vacation, when did you last take *any* sort of break from work? How long since you relaxed for an evening, or for an hour? Not tonight, that's for sure."

"I go out all the time. I go to concerts and to dinner parties."

"You do. And what do you do there? I bet you don't relax. You interview people, and you take notes, and you produce a stream of articles. You *work*. And you've been working, incessantly, year after year. How long since you've been with a woman?"

Drake shook his head but did not speak.

Tom sighed. "I'm sorry. Forget that I asked that. It was a dumb and insensitive thing to say. But you need to face a fact, Drake, and you shouldn't try to hide from it: She's dead. Do you hear me? *Ana is dead.* Work won't change that. Wishing won't change it. Nothing can bring her back to you. And you can't go on forever with your own emotions chained and harnessed."

"You promised me, Tom. You gave me your solemn word that you would help me."

"Drake!"

"Do you ever make promises to your children?"

"Of course I do."

"Do you keep them?"

"Drake, you can't use that argument, the situations are totally different. You act as though I made you some sort of solemn vow, but it wasn't like that at all."

"Then how was it? Don't bother to answer." Drake took the little recorder from his inside jacket pocket. "Listen. Listen to yourself."

The words were thin in tone but quite clear.

…if I come back to you, in, say, eight or ten years, and I ask you again, will you do it? Will you help me? I want you to give me an honest answer, and I want your word on it.

Ten years from now? Drake, if you come back to me in eight or ten years and ask me again, I'll admit I was completely wrong. And I promise you, I'll help you to do what you've asked.

An absolute promise? I don't want to hear some day that you changed your mind, or didn't mean what you said.

An absolute promise. Sure, I'll give you that…. There was the sound of Tom's relieved laugh.

Drake turned off the recorder. "I said, eight to ten years. It has been nine."

"You recorded us, back then when Ana had just died? I can't believe you would do that."

"I had to, Tom. Even then, I was convinced that you would change your mind. But I knew that I wouldn't. You have to live up to your agreement. You promised."

"I promised to *help* you, to stop you from doing something crazy to yourself." Tom's face went ruddy with intolerable frustration. "For God's sake, Drake, I'm a *doctor*. You can't ask me to help you kill yourself."

"I'm not asking that."

"You might as well be. No one has ever been revived. Maybe no one ever will be. If they do learn how, Anastasia will be a candidate. She is in the best Second Chance womb, she had the best preparation money could buy. But you, you're different. You're not sick! Ana was dying before she was frozen, she had nothing to lose. You have *everything* to lose. You're healthy, you're productive, you're at the height of your career. And you are asking me to throw all that away, to help you take the chance that someday, God knows when, you might—just might—be revived. Don't you see, Drake, I can't help you."

"You gave me your promise."

"Stop saying that! I also have my oath as a physician: to do no harm. You want me to take you from perfect health to a high odds of final death."

"I have to do it, Tom. If you won't help me, I'll find someone who will. Probably someone less competent and reliable than you."

"*Why* do you have to do it? Give me one good reason."

"You know why, if you think about it." Drake spoke slowly, coaxingly. "For Ana's sake. Unless I go on ahead, they may never choose to wake her. She could be one of the last on their list. You and I know her for what she really is, a unique and marvelous woman. But what will the records show? A singer, still not as famous as she would have been, who died young of a devastating disease. I've had time to prepare, I'm sure that they will wake me. And it's an advantage that I'm in good health, because there will be no reason to delay my revival on medical grounds. As soon as I am sure that they have a cure for what killed Ana, I can wake her. We'll start over, the two of us."

Tom Lambert's cheeks had gone from fiery red to pale. "We have to talk about this some more, Drake. The whole idea is crazy. Did you really mean what you said, that if I won't help you will go to someone else?"

"Look at me, Tom. Tell me if you think that I mean it."

Lambert looked. He did not speak again; but his hands slowly came up to cover his eyes.

It took six days of solid argument, another seven to make final preparations. Drake Merlin and Tom Lambert drove together to Second Chance.

Drake took a long last look out of the window at the wind-blown trees and the cloudy sky, then climbed slowly into the thermal tank.

Tom injected the Asfanil.

Drake decided that the easy part was ending. That the hard part, if there was another part, was about to begin.

A few seconds later the long fall began, dropping him steadily down the longest descent that a human can ever make.

Down, down, down.

All the way down, to two degrees absolute; colder than the coldest hell ever conceived by Dante.

5

Awakening

*T*he great gamble had paid off more successfully than he had dared to hope. Ana was alive, she was reanimated, she was healthy. But the technology of the future went far beyond health. It had made her, always beautiful, much more vigorous and desirable than she had ever been.

She was dancing, and as she danced she sang; not a serious work by her usual favorites, Mahler or Hugo Wolf or Brahms, but a frothy and light-hearted confection by Gilbert and Sullivan. "My object all sublime, I shall achieve in time," she caroled.

And then she was fading. Her body became as transparent as glass, her rich contralto a vanishing thread of sound. "To let the punishment fit the crime, The punishment fit the cri-i-i-me...."

She was gone.

Afterward, Drake could never be sure. Had he dreamed some superconducting dream, as he lay in the cryowomb twelve degrees colder than a block of solid hydrogen? Or had he only *dreamed* that he dreamed, as he came slowly back through the long thaw?

It made little difference. After the vision of Ana, all feelings of peace and certainty bled away. In their place came an eternity of twisted images, a procession of pale and terrifying lights moving against a pitch-dark background. They arrived ahead of consciousness, and they went on forever. He fought his way through them, through torment that went on and on with no promise that it would ever end.

It was daunting to learn later that he had been one of the lucky ones. In his case the freezing process had gone very smoothly. Some revivables awoke armless and legless, some shed their whole epidermis and had to be kept cocooned and motionless until it could re-grow. He lost nothing during the thaw but an insignificant few square centimeters of skin.

But the pain of waking...that was something else. The final stages, from three degrees Celsius to normal body temperature, could not be rushed. They occupied a full thirty-six hours. For all that time Drake was pierced with an agony of waking tissues and returning circulation, unable to move or cry out. In the last stages, before full consciousness, hearing came before sight. He could hear speech around him. It was not in any tongue that he could recognize.

How long? How far had he traveled in time? Even before the pain faded, that question filled his mind.

The answer did not come at once. While he was still half-conscious he felt the sting of an injector spray. He blanked out again at once. After another infinite hiatus he came up all the way, opening his eyes to a quiet sunlit room not too different from the Second Chance facility where he had begun the descent.

A man and a woman in yellow uniforms were watching him, talking softly together. As soon as they saw that he was awake the man pressed a point on a segmented wall panel. The two went on with their work, lining up two complex and incomprehensible pieces of equipment. One sight of that told Drake that he had succeeded in at least one way. Nothing that he saw was familiar. He was in the future—but how far in the future?

The person who came in presently through the white sliding door was dark haired and oddly androgynous, with a face both clean shaven and also smooth and womanly. The clothing was equally uninformative, a loose-fitting suit of pale gray that concealed body shape. The newcomer stepped to the side of the bed and stood staring down at Drake with a pleased and proprietary air.

"How are you feeling?"

Drake knew then that it was a man. The language was English, oddly pronounced. That was reassuring. Drake had suffered two other worries as he slipped under. What if he were revived in just a few years' time, when nothing at all could be done to cure Ana? Or what if he surfaced after fifty thousand years, a living fossil, quite unable to communicate his needs to the men and women of the future?

"I feel all right." He had trouble speaking. His tongue felt swollen, and his mind was slow to produce the words that he needed. "But I feel very weak and confused." Drake thought of trying to sit up, and knew at once that he could not do it. "I can barely move."

"Naturally. But are you Drake Merlin?"

"I am."

The man had an open eager face, with furry eyebrows and a high forehead. He laughed aloud in delight and rubbed his hands together. "Excellent! My name is Par Leon. Can you understand me easily?"

"Perfectly easily." Drake's second worry returned. "Why do you ask that question? *When* am I?"

"I ask it because the old languages are not easy, even with augments and much study. For your second question, in your measure we are now in the year 2512 of the prophet Christ."

Five centuries! It was longer than Drake had expected and hoped. But better long than short. Before he was frozen he had entertained awful visions of diving down to the bottom of the Pit and clawing his agonized way back up to thawed life, not once but over and over.

"I have waited here through the whole warming and first treatment," Par Leon continued. "Soon I will leave you so you can have rest, more treatment, and first education. But I desired to speak with you at once when you became conscious. It is not rational, but I feared that there might have been a mistake in identity—that it might not be Drake Merlin, the Drake Merlin of my curiosity, who was awakened." Par Leon glanced at the equipment standing at the bedside and shook his head. "You are a strong man, Drake Merlin. Uniquely strong. The record shows that you did not once cry out or complain during all the thawing."

There had been more important things on Drake's mind. Could Ana be cured? Where was she now? Had she been kept safe, for however much time had passed? Was it possible that she had been awakened before him, even long before him? That would be a disaster.

He glanced across at the other two workers, who were still chatting together in an alien tongue. "Language must have changed completely. I can understand you easily, but I cannot understand them at all."

"You mean, understand the doctors?" The stranger Leon replied with a surprised expression on his lean face. "Of course you cannot. Neither can I. They are doctors. To each other they are naturally speaking Medicine."

Drake raised his eyebrows. The look must have survived with its meaning intact across the centuries, because Par Leon went on, "That is right, Medicine. I cannot help you. I myself am fluent in Music and History—and, of course, Universal. And I learned Old Anglic to be able to study your times and to speak with you. But I know little or no Medicine."

"Medicine is a *language*?" Drake felt that his mind had been slowed by the long sleep and thawing treatment.

"Of course. Like Music or Chemistry or Computing. But surely this was already true in your own time. Did you not have languages specific to each—what is the word you use?—discipline?"

"I suppose that we did; but we didn't realize it." Par Leon's question explained a great deal. No wonder that Drake had found psychologists, professional educators, social scientists, and physicists—to name but a few—incomprehensible. Even in his original time, the special jargon and odd acronyms had been signaling the arrival of new protolanguages, emerging forms as alien as Sanskrit or classical Greek. "How do you speak to the doctors?"

"For ordinary things? We employ Universal, which all understand. I do not attempt to speak actual Medicine. If I am in that subject-matter area, we keep a computer in the circuit to provide exact concept equivalents between language pairs."

It occurred to Drake that multidisciplinary programs must be hell. But not as bad as they had once been. Here at least there was an understanding that the problem *existed*. And what were computers like, after five more centuries of development? In his day they had been in their infancy. They ought to be able to do anything now, anything at all—like curing Ana. It was almost a surprise to see that there was still a place in the world for humans.

He was beginning to feel oddly and irrationally euphoric, a combination of drugs and the idea that he might succeed more easily than he had dreamed.

He made a more determined effort to sit up. His head lifted maybe five centimeters from the pillow, then fell back despite everything he could do to hold it up.

"Slowly. Rome—was not built—in a day." Par Leon glowed, clearly delighted at coming up with such a prize example of genuine Old Anglic. "It will be moons before you are fully strong. Two more things I will tell you, then I will allow your treatment to continue.

"First, it was I who arranged for you to be brought here and revived. I am a musicologist, interested in the twentieth and twenty-first centuries, and in particular your own time."

Drake's five-hundred-year-old bet had paid off. He wondered what modern music sounded like. Would he be able to listen to it with pleasure? To compose it?

"Under our laws," Par Leon went on, "you owe me for the cost of your revival and treatment. This amounts to six years of work from you. You are most fortunate that you were healthy and correctly frozen and maintained, or the time of service would have been much longer. However, I also believe that you will find your indenture with me both pleasant and interesting. I am proposing that you and I, together, write the definitive history of your own musical period."

So the question of earning a living was postponed for at least a few years. Par Leon would presumably have to feed Drake Merlin while he was paying off his debt.

"Second, I have good news for you." Par Leon was gazing at Drake expectantly. "When we examined you, our doctors found certain problems—*defects* is the word that you would use?—with your body

and its glandular balance. They hope that they have cured the simpler body malfunctions, and they have provided standard stabilization of your chromosomal telomeres. You will still age, but slowly. You should live between two and three hundred years.

"However, the glandular imbalance represented a more subtle problem. It was likely to manifest itself as some form of madness, some uncontrollable compulsion. The doctors observed this as soon as you were thawed enough to respond to psychoprobes. They made small chemical changes and have, we hope, corrected the difficulty." Par Leon was watching Drake closely. "Please tell me now of your feelings toward your former wife, Anastasia Werlich."

Drake felt his heart racing. He could hear the blood pounding in his ears, and in his weakened condition it was as hard to breathe as if heavy weights had been dropped onto his chest. He closed his eyes for a long moment and thought about Ana. Gradually, he became calm again.

It was obvious what the other wanted to hear; and Ana was worth a million lies. Drake looked up at Par Leon and shook his head feebly. "I feel very little for her. No more than a faint sense that something was once there. I know that she was once very dear to me, but I am not sure how. It is like the scar of an old wound."

"Excellent!" The smile had kept its meaning. "That is most satisfying. The disease that killed the woman was eliminated from the human stock long ago, by careful mating choice—*eugenics*, as your language put it. We could certainly reanimate her, but according to our doctors it is still not clear that we would be able to cure her. However, we can see no reason to awaken her at all. Like most in the cryowombs, she is of little or no value to us. Most important of all, an involvement with her might interfere with your work for me."

"So her body is still stored?"

"Of course. We keep all the cryocorpses. Although most are of no present value, who knows what our future needs might be? The cryowombs are like a library of the past, to open whenever it will serve a purpose. Two hundred years from now someone may find a use for her, and her disease perhaps easily cured. Then she, too, may live and work again."

"Is Anastasia stored near here?"

"Of course not!" For the first time, Par Leon appeared to be shocked. "What a waste of space and energy that would imply. The cryowombs are maintained on Pluto, where space is cheap, cooling needs are small, and escape velocity is low."

That sentence, more than any other that Par Leon had spoken, wrenched Drake forward in time. What technology was it that could casually ship millions of bodies to the edge of the solar system rather than keep them in cold storage on Earth? If, that is, Pluto *was* the edge of the solar system. How many planets were known now? Even in his day, there was talk of many more bodies out in a region known as the Kuiper Belt. *Five centuries.* It was the time from Monteverdi to Shostakovich, from Copernicus to Einstein, from the Columbus discovery of America to the first landing on the Moon. He had come a long, long way.

Par Leon was still gazing at him, now a little suspiciously. "Again you ask about the woman, Anastasia Werlich. Why? Are you sure that you are in fact fully cured? If not, another course of treatment is easy to arrange."

Drake cursed his own stupidity and did his best to smile reassuringly. "I feel sure that will not be needed. Already her memory fades. As soon as I am strong enough, I am eager to begin my work with you."

"Wonderful." The smile was back, but Par Leon was wagging his finger in warning. "We will certainly work together, but only *after you* are fully recovered and have had some essential training. First, you must learn to speak Universal and Music and you must have enough background knowledge to live comfortably in this time. It will also be my responsibility to see that you are able to find suitable activity when your work with me is done, and for that you will need skills that today you lack.

"Rest now, Drake Merlin. I will return tomorrow, or the next day. By that time you will already find yourself stronger. And you will be far more knowledgeable."

As Par Leon left, the medical technicians carried forward a transparent helmet with silvered lines inscribed on its upper part. They lowered it carefully onto Drake's head.

He lost consciousness at once, too quickly to be aware of its cool touch.

6

Brave New World

He awoke to the sound of two voices. One was an unfamiliar wordless chatter, a high-pitched and irritating tingle more in his brain than in his ear. The other voice he already knew. It was Par Leon, asking what seemed like an odd question after their previous conversation.

"Do you understand me, Drake Merlin?" There was a pause, then, more loudly: "Can you hear me? Do you understand me?"

"Of course I can. Of course I do." But Drake was having trouble controlling his own speech. He had to seek out each word. He opened his eyes. "We already…established that we can…understand each other."

Leon was standing in front of him, nodding in satisfaction. "We proved yesterday that we could communicate *in English*. But listen again to me… and listen to yourself."

The words were perfectly understandable—but they had been spoken in an alien tongue.

"What happened?" Drake asked. The sense of what he said was clear, but it sounded peculiar. With a deliberate effort, he repeated it in English, and the words came more easily. *"What happened?"*

"You learned, exactly as I hoped and expected." Leon replied in the same language. "But now"— Drake felt no decrease in his level of comprehension, yet he heard the change in the sounds—"now it is better if we both speak Universal."

"You said *yesterday*." Drake's shift from one language to the other was labored and sluggish. "You taught me Universal…in a single day? How were you able to do that?"

"I am the wrong person to ask." Leon shrugged. "If I were to attempt an explanation, beyond saying that the helmet taught you, it would surely be inadequate. A suitable reply would be provided in Electronics or Medicine, possibly using dialects of the latter such as Neurology. I was taught something of those languages, long ago, but I found them uncongenial. If they are to your taste, you will have opportunity to learn them later. For the moment, relax. Go slowly. In two or three weeks, Universal will come easily to you. But now we have other priorities. Can you stand up?"

Rather than replying, Drake made the experiment. He pushed the helmet away from his head and rose to his feet. As he came upright there was one moment of unsteadiness, then he felt balanced and alert. Yesterday's weakness was gone completely.

"I feel fine," he said, and meant it.

"Splendid. Are you hungry?"

Drake had to pause and consider that question. The prospect of food produced no physical reaction. It was as though during five centuries of sleep his body had forgotten the need for sustenance.

Finally he shook his head. "I'm sorry. I just don't know."

Leon nodded sympathetically. "Let us then make the experiment. We will eat a meal at a restaurant. The world has changed much since your time, and there will be much that is different. But the need for nourishment has not changed. It will be reassuring for you to learn that some things are still the same."

Par Leon meant what he said; but to Drake, following him along a short corridor into a deserted white-walled room containing an array of cubicles, each equipped with a single chair and some kind of computer terminal, it seemed that nothing could be less familiar.

This was a restaurant? There were no waiters, no menus, no signs of food or drink. Each cubicle would hold only one person.

His bewilderment showed.

"Ah," Leon said. He seemed uncomfortable for the first time. "I am forgetting the customs of your era. Food today is normally taken alone. Only close associates and family eat in each other's presence." He pointed to a cubicle. "Sit down. The arrangement permits us to talk freely, even though we will be out of sight of each other."

Drake did as he was told, wondering what to do next. Was he supposed to indicate his preferences to the computer? Or would he somehow be fed automatically and ethereally, without the appearance of material foodstuffs? That was inconsistent with Par Leon's claim that food was a constant of the world, but five hundred years was a long time. Interpretations would surely have changed, even when the same words were used.

He looked more closely at the device before him. There was no screen or keyboard, only a flat rectangular box, and in front of that a level featureless surface like a small table.

Par Leon had vanished into a neighboring cubicle.

Drake waited through a long silence. Finally he said, not sure he would be heard, "I have a problem."

"Nothing is to your taste?" Leon's voice was clear, though no other sound had come through from the next room.

"I don't know. I haven't been offered any food."

"That is strange. What did you order?"

"Nothing. I don't know how."

"One moment." Then, after another and shorter silence, "This is my fault entirely. I assumed that general information had been provided to you along with your knowledge of Universal, but that is not so. It is scheduled for your next indoctrination period. The chef in front of you is simple enough to use, and tomorrow you will have no difficulty with it. This evening, however, with your permission I will order the meal for you."

"That's fine." It was Drake's first indication as to the time of day. The room where he had awakened lacked windows, and so did this place. Physically, he had no sense of night, morning, or any diurnal rhythm.

He waited and watched, until in a couple of minutes the box in front of him slid open where he had seen no seam, and delivered a steaming square container of food, a combined knife and fork utensil, and a transparent cylinder filled with red liquid.

The vegetables were colorful but unfamiliar. The meat—if it was meat—could have been flesh, fish, or fowl. But Drake had not been widely traveled in his own time. For all he knew the whole meal could have existed then, as part of the little-known cuisine of some foreign country. He leaned over and sniffed the sauce. A satisfying combination of odors filled his nostrils: cumin, sage, fennel, tarragon. He lifted the tall cylinder and tasted.

At last—thank God—something he recognized. He should have known. Wine had endured through five millennia before his time; it should be no surprise that it continued to cheer humans now, five hundred years later.

He raised his glass in a silent toast—*To us, Ana; we made it this far*—and took a first, deep draft.

Drake had no urge to talk while they were eating, but Par Leon was in a chatty mood. After promising that the world would be explained later while Drake slept, far better than he could do it during dinner and in much greater detail, Leon went ahead and explained anyhow.

It became clear in the next hour where his own interests lay. He had a good but superficial knowledge of Earth civilization and society, but he knew and cared little about the rest of the solar system.

The population of Earth, he said, was half a billion, less than one-tenth of what it had been in Drake's era. It was holding steady now. In the next two centuries it would undergo a planned rise to almost one billion, then decrease again to about its present level. He did not know the reason for the change. That sort of thing was in the hands of the resource management specialists.

And the population of other planets and moons? It was one of Drake's few questions. Par Leon replied with a verbal shrug. There were people living out there, certainly, but who cared how many? Other planets and moons had no long history, in particular no long musical history. Therefore, they were without interest. If Drake wanted to know such strange things, he could do so without taking the valuable time of a human. The machines and data banks were available. Even if Drake had to learn a new language, that also would be no problem. Vocabulary and grammatical rules could be instilled almost instantly using the feedback helmets. Use of language, particularly spoken language, came a little more slowly, because it required physical coordination and practice. A week, maybe, rather than a day.

"But now"—Leon had clearly spent as much time as he wanted to on such dull matters—"let's talk about music."

He did. Happily, and incomprehensibly. Drake did not tell him that he could not understand. He would do his duty and learn about modern music when the time came. For tonight, he was content to sit back, eat and drink, and build his resolve for whatever lay ahead.

A civilization consists of far more than facts, rules, and languages. After a couple of weeks of induced-knowledge nights, Drake began to wonder if some aspects of his new world would be forever beyond him, no matter how long he lived there.

Science was one of them. Twenty-sixth-century science, particularly the basic assumptions that lay beneath it, totally eluded him. It was no surprise that he would find the subject difficult. That had always been the case. In his own time his teachers had accused him of having talent but no interest, and of dreaming his days away with words and music.

Even so, the general ideas of science ought to be accessible. They were supposed to be no more than common sense, elevated to become a discipline. But he found himself struggling hopelessly—and he *was* struggling, hard, working to understand more than he had ever done as a young man. Ana's salvation, when it finally came, would derive from science, not from music.

Finally he sought help—not from Par Leon, who was itching for Drake's indoctrination to end so they could get to work, and who neither knew nor cared about science. Instead Drake dived into the data net, developed beyond anything dreamed of in his own time. He asked for someone who would be willing to translate for him from Science, which he could not speak or write, to Universal. In return he offered knowledge of his own times.

The woman who contacted him had no apparent interest in the early twenty-first century, or at least in the things that Drake might have to say about it. That confirmed the wisdom of his long-ago decision to provoke the curiosity of musical specialists. Cass Leemu was a specialist also, but her own field was one that Drake was unable to comprehend, even in general terms and even after hours of conversation and study. She said it was a form of physics. It seemed to be no more than pictures, that somehow yielded quantitative results.

Cass was a black woman whose age, like Par Leon's, was difficult to determine. She was a tall brunette with a slightly large and blocky head, no eyelashes or eyebrows, and a sumptuous body. Drake suspected minor genetic modifications. Her motive in meeting was either pure curiosity in a specimen of primitive humanity—Drake—or it was for a reason beyond his comprehension.

Her explanations were as clear as they could be, given Universal's limits for scientific explanation.

"It is the typical problem of a major paradigm shift." They were in her private quarters. Cass Leemu was almost naked, lolling back on a couch and scratching her bare belly thoughtfully as she spoke. In an earlier time, Drake reflected, her exposed body would have been a major obstacle to simple information transfer. It would also have been considered a clear invitation.

She went on, "Is the name of Isaac Newton familiar to you?"

"Of course. Gravity, and the laws of motion."

"Right. Familiar, and easy to comprehend. We agree on that. But did you know that most of his contemporaries found his work quite beyond them? He introduced notions of absolute space and time, which they found implausible. They argued, with justice, that only the *separation* between objects could have physical meaning. The idea of absolute coordinates, as opposed to relative distances, made no sense to them. Also, his work was most easily derived and understood employing the calculus, which to the scientists of the seventeenth century was shrouded in the paradoxes of infinitely small quantities. It took three generations to resolve the paradoxes, absorb the new world view, and work with it comfortably. The same thing happened two centuries later, when Maxwell elevated the concept of a *field* to central importance. Many of his contemporaries, to the end of their lives, tried to devise mechanical analogies that dispensed with the need for an electromagnetic field. And in the twentieth century, when uncertainty and undecidability assumed a dominant position in the prevailing world view, even the greatest scientist of his time—Einstein—had trouble accepting them."

"Are you telling me that the same thing happened again, after I entered the cryowomb?"

"Indeed it did." Cass Leemu smiled and stroked her right nipple. It was clear that she considered her action quite empty of erotic content. *Paradigm shift.* Drake was tempted to ask her to have a private meal with him, and see if and where she blushed.

"It has happened not once," she went on, "but three times. There have been three major viewpoint shifts. Our understanding of Nature differs more from the perspectives of your time, than yours differed from the Romans."

"So I am going to be like Newton's colleagues, unable to comprehend a new foundation."

"I am afraid so. Unless you can master the concept of…." She paused, then smiled again at Drake, this time apologetically. "I am sorry. The word for the idea that now underpins science lacks any adequate useful paraphrase in Universal. Even the general data banks are silent. But if you really wish to study science, and learn the Science language beginning with the absolute basics, I would be willing to help you."

"I can't do that. Not yet." Drake had already given up any notion of learning science for himself, but he was reluctant to say an outright no to Cass Leemu—he might need her later. "You see, Cass, I owe the next six years to Par Leon. He revived me."

"Of course. Six years only? He is being generous. A sponsor like Par Leon, who chooses an individual in whom no one else has an interest, can set his own terms with the Resurrect."

And there again was the paradigm shift. Cass was pointing out to Drake that the brave new world he now lived in contained other elements at least as hard to grasp as science.

After he had returned to his own spartan living quarters, he worried over the problem. Slavery did not exist. On the other hand, six years of absolute service to Par Leon was taken for granted. It was a form of slavery, but its ethical basis was never questioned. Drake could not understand that basis. He comforted himself with the thought that Henry VIII would have been appalled at wars that killed civilians, while accepting as natural a public hanging, drawing, and quartering.

As he placed his helmet over his head, he wondered what induced lesson he would receive tonight. He felt beyond surprise. Before he lost consciousness, it occurred to him that humanity was able to manage with very few absolutes. Why? Because people could live within—and apparently justify—any imaginable variation of ethics and morality.

Maybe that was why humans had survived.

Gradually, Drake became resigned to his own situation. He did not need to hurry. He had survived. Ana was safe in the Pluto cryowombs. Before he could do anything to change her status he would first have to earn his own freedom. He resolved to give Par Leon six good, solid years of effort toward the other man's great lifetime project: the analysis of musical trends in the late twentieth and early twenty-first centuries. In any case, as a Resurrect what other option did he have?

After the first few months, the shrewdness of Leon's act in reviving Drake was apparent. More important than any facts that he might provide were the perspectives that he could offer into the lifestyles of the late twentieth century. It was far more than just science and ethics that had changed.

Often, his information had Leon shaking his head. "It is truly astonishing. An insanity. Did man-woman relationships really play so large a part in *everything* in your society?"

"You know they did." Drake was learning his way around the data banks, with no help from Leon. "Your own records show it, the ones that we were examining just two days ago."

"Yes. They do show it, but believing it is difficult. Men and women actually appeared to hate each other in your era. Yet at the same time there was much random mating, mating on *impulse*. I do not mean mere sexual acts that I can comprehend. But random mating that produced *offspring*, without benefit of genome maps or the most rudimentary genetic information on parents and grandparents...."

Drake started to explain, and quickly realized that it was hopeless. Here was another five-hundred-year gulf that could not be crossed. To Par Leon, mating was always dictated by the selection of desirable gene combinations. As he said, there was no other way to make sure that the children would be healthy. How could any other approach be justified? He reacted to the idea of reproduction between comparative strangers as Drake regarded public burning at the stake.

In any case, Drake was beginning to have problems of his own. There really was no case to be made for the production of children, without thought for their future or for their physical and mental well-being. It was, as Par Leon said, "the blind mating urge of the primeval slime, deified to become religious principle and blind dogma."

Drake listened to those words and decided that he was beginning to view his own epoch with a new perspective. He must control that tendency, or his main value to Par Leon would disappear. For that reason, and one other, he had to remain an outsider in this century.

After six months, Drake realized that he was earning his keep and more. Leon might be the century's foremost expert on the music of Drake's period, but of some events and forces he knew nothing. He was endlessly fascinated by the smallest details.

"You say you *knew* him?" Par Leon leaned forward, eyebrows raised on his high forehead. "You met Renselm in person?"

"A score of times. I was present at the first performance of Morani's *Concerto concertante,* written especially for Renselm, and I went backstage afterward. Then we went to dinner, just the three of us. I thought you already read about all this in one of my articles."

"Oh, yes." Par Leon made a dismissive gesture. "I certainly *read* it. But this is different. Tell me about his fingering, his posture at the keyboard, his strange reaction to applause. Tell me what he said to you about Adele Winterberg—she was his mistress at the time, you know." He laughed in delight. "Tell me, if you can remember it, what you all ate for dinner."

Only once or twice did Par Leon express dissatisfaction. And then it was because Drake had been frozen just before some event that especially interested him. "If you had only waited another three years..." he would say; but he spoke philosophically and with good humor.

It was by no means a one-way transfer of information. From his vantage point five centuries ahead, Par Leon had insights into the musical life of an earlier era that left Drake gasping. For the first time he understood where certain contemporary musical currents had been heading in his own time. Krubak, in his much-ridiculed late works, had been feeling his way toward forms that would not mature until thirty years after Drake had been frozen.

The work went on, ten to twelve hours a day. If Leon ever wondered why Drake showed no curiosity at seeing firsthand the world as it had become in the twenty-sixth century, or in making other friends, or even in learning the twists and turns of human progress over the past five centuries, he never mentioned it.

For his part, Drake had no desire to be absorbed by or become part of the current society. Yet he had to know certain subjects in great detail, far more than Par Leon could tell him. Fortunately, the general data banks permitted near-infinite cross-checking and depth of inquiry.

Drake began to satisfy his own unique information needs.

The whole solar system had been explored and mapped in detail. Venus was in the first stages of terraforming, the acid witch's brew of its atmosphere creeping down in temperature and pressure. Mars had been colonized, not on the surface but within the extensive natural caverns beneath. There were permanent active stations—many of them "manned" by self-replicating computers and repair devices—on all the satellites of the major planets.

It was progress; yet to Drake it was less than expected. The projections made in his own time had seen the whole solar system crawling with humans and their intelligent machines. Sometime in the past five centuries, priorities had changed.

But what about Pluto?

Drake gave that little world his special attention. A small crew of scientists had a research station on Charon, the outsized satellite that made the Pluto-Charon system into a small planetary doublet. Pluto itself was uninhabited, unless one counted the dreaming serried ranks of the cryocorpses. The cryowombs were too cold for the comfortable permanent presence of animate humans. They hovered down at liquid helium temperature (Drake's earlier suspicion of liquid nitrogen storage had proved well founded). The vaults were tended, to the extent that they needed any sort of attention, by machines especially designed for extreme cold.

With the idea of money subsumed into some incomprehensible system of electronic credit, it was not clear to Drake when he would be able to afford to make the long trip out to Pluto. He forced himself to be patient, putting the question to one side until his time of service was closer to its end.

The work went on, hard but certainly not unrewarding. The text that they were producing grew steadily. By the beginning of the fourth year, Drake shared Par Leon's conviction that they were producing a classic. He listened to the suggestion that in fairness the two of them should be given equal credit, and shook his head.

"It was all your idea, Leon, not mine. You could have found someone else to do what I have done. But without you to revive me I could have done nothing...."

...and if you shared credit with me, I would not be here long enough to take it. As soon as possible, I will be gone.

That was the secret goal, thought about constantly but never mentioned.

And then, at the end of the fourth year, an event took place that changed all Drake's plans.

continued in issue 35...

TOMORROW AND TOMORROW

A LOVE STORY TO THE EDGE OF TIME

CHARLES SHEFFIELD

"One of the most imaginative, exciting talents to appear on the SF scene."—*Publishers Weekly*